Roman Senchin

MINUS

a novel

Translated by Arch Tait

GLAS PUBLISHERS
tel./fax: +7(495)441-9157
perova@glas.msk.su
www.russianpress.com/glas

DISTRIBUTION

in North America
NORTHWESTERN UNIVERSITY PRESS
Chicago Distribution Center
tel: 1-800-621-2736 or (773) 702-7000
fax: 1-800-621-8476 or (773) 702-7212
pubnet@202-5280
www.nupress.northwestern.edu

in the UK
INPRESS LIMITED
tel: 020 8832 7464; fax: 020 8832 7465
mail1@inpressbooks.co.uk
www.inpressbooks.co.uk

Within Russia
JUPITER-IMPEX
www.jupiters.ru
shop@jupiters.ru

Edited by Natasha Perova and Joanne Turnbull
Camera-ready copy by Tatiana Shaposhnikova

ISBN 978-5-7172-0083-7

ABOUT THE AUTHOR

Roman Senchin, born in 1971, grew up in Siberia. His family had to flee his native Tuva and move to Minusinsk in the wake of the post-Soviet nationalist strife that flared up there. He now lives in Moscow. Senchin is one of the most talented and expressive spokesmen for his generation and a leader of the so-called "New Realism", which tends towards narrative nonfiction. He has five novels and many short stories to his name and has won several prestigious literary prizes. His work has been translated into German, French and other languages. Minus was published in Germany by DuMont to very good reviews.

■ ■ ■ ■ ■ ■ ■ ■

1

She is sitting on the windowsill again, posing. Kind of sideways, with those legs of hers, watching whatever is going on outside. The trainer on her right foot is jiggling. She is plugged into the ear-buds of her personal stereo. I hear its percussive hissing.

I was on my way to the WC but stopped when I saw her. Just like yesterday evening, she is sitting with her legs tucked up, wearing tight black jeans, facing the window. She has long, straight hair, sort of golden auburn, and she wears it in a ponytail with an elasticated green velvet band. They sell them in the market at ten roubles for five.

She is alone in the tiled, empty box of what used to be a communal kitchen.

What can she see through the window? That's easy: the other wing of our lousy hostel; puffy, stultified faces in square yellow windows; and down in the yard by the canteen a mountain of rotting crates, boiled bones in the container, and forty-litre tanks for waste. The dozy labourer in his greasy blue workcoat is probably having a fag. Actually, that's a load of crap, she can't be seeing anything. It's dark out there, night fell long ago. The canteen is shut and the lights are out in practically all the windows. People are asleep ahead of another working day.

It's obvious she isn't actually looking at anything, just not looking at the corridor. Her eyes are hooded by her eyelids. She is just listening to music.

She's quite something. She sits there every evening plugged into the music, and I stare at her like a total creep, goggling at her hair, her little sweater, her jeans, and that trainer on her foot.

What's she doing? She wasn't here a week ago. Perhaps they're refugees from Kazakhstan or, like me, from Tuva, or the north. Every other room in this hostel is occupied by people like us who've come flooding in to a small Russian town from every direction.

That cassette must finish eventually, and when it does she'll turn and look over here. I really want to see her face. If she's nice, I've got a couple of chat-up lines prepared. We might get on. If that wretched hissing and thumping ever stops.

I waited here like this yesterday, shifting from one foot to the other. I kept thinking she was about to move, press the button on her stereo and turn round, but it didn't happen. I gave up in the end. When I was going back to my room she was in exactly the same position. The only way you could tell she wasn't a big, lifeless doll was because she was jiggling her foot.

I don't hang around so long this evening. Sod it. I go on. I'll just play cards with Lyokha. Who knows, maybe tomorrow.

"That dolly's there again," I report back.

Lyokha is lying on the bed staring at the ceiling as usual.

"I've found a new flower," he says, raising a hand. "See, there, it's a bit like a tulip. Can you see it?" The ceiling is covered in tiny cracks and in the evenings Lyokha finds flowers, faces, and patterns in them.

"You dick!" I retort. "That dolly bird is out there again, sitting on the windowsill. Let's go and say hello."

"Too young." Lyokha pulls a face.

"Who cares!"

No reply. Lyokha frowns, concentrating on studying the ceiling. I lie down on my bed. After a while, I take my shoes off and look up at the cracks. I don't see any patterns. The girl on the windowsill has unsettled me.

"Lyokha, let's chat her up. At least we'll find out what she looks like. How about it?"

"Wash your socks first. I can't breathe!"

"O-oh..." I turn to the wall.

For a time we say nothing. I am thinking that tomorrow is only an evening performance so we have nothing to do until four. Also, that I could use a drink. Very much so. I start feeling really fed up. The boredom pokes and prods me with cold, scratchy fingers.

"We've got to get the cassette player mended," I say. "Without it, life is just..."

"Gimme the cash and I'll get it repaired," my roommate replies laconically.

"O-oh..."

I turn from my side on to my back, and a bit later on to my stomach. I bury my face in the pillow.

Our room is like all the others: five not very large paces long and two and a half wide. Two metal bedsteads that squeak, a table, two bedside lockers, two chairs.

There are nails in the walls for hanging clothes and towels from. Some people manage better. They have furniture, a telly and stuff, but it doesn't make much difference what you put in it: a room in a hostel is still a room in a hostel.

The theatre rents it for us from the furniture factory quite cheap. There's all sorts living here, apart, it would seem, from factory workers: refugees, young couples with small children who have moved to get away from their parents, Chinese, Vietnamese, Asiatics, Caucasians and what have you. Also old alkies who've run away from their families. From the theatre, other than Lyokha and me, there are Ksyukha, an obese, mannish woman with thick hairs on her chin who is our hair stylist, and an actor, Waliszewski, a burnt-out alky who hasn't acted for years. For its more valued employees the theatre rises to an apartment, not to buy, of course, only to rent, but still. Actually, Lyokha and I haven't got much to complain about: he left his wife and two-year-old daughter, so he's deliberately made himself homeless; and heaven knows what category I fall into. I lived with my mum and dad in Kyzyl, the capital of what in Soviet times was the Autonomous Republic of Tuva and has now become independent. The natives turned nationalistic and tensions turned to nasty incidents. Several Russians were stabbed to death, and a lot more were just stabbed, including my father. When he recovered he moved us here, back to Russian territory.

We found a little, half-ruined log cabin in a village, bought it for next to nothing, made it more or less habitable, and moved in. It was only fifty kilometres or so from the regional capital, Minusinsk, which is where I live now. I used to come here to look for a job and struck it lucky. They took me on as a stagehand at the theatre and even gave me a roof over my head. We thought it was a miracle.

We hadn't been poor in Kyzyl. My father worked in the Republic's Ministry of Culture and was considered irreplaceable, until one day he was replaced. We had a three-room apartment in the town centre, on the banks of the Yenisei. We had a cosy dacha in the country, a solid garage, and a Moskvich-412. We sold the lot except for the Moskvich, but all the money went on the move and refurbishing the log cabin. Our only major acquisition was a truck, written off by a transport enterprise because of its old age. It has turned out very useful in the countryside and brings in quite a bit on the side. We can use it for transporting logs or firewood for people, or to shift a stiff to the cemetery. In Minusinsk apartment prices have gone through the roof, although my parents are hoping that some day they may be able to afford at least a one-room apartment. They've been trying to raise the money, for over four years, by selling vegetables. They grow them in their vegetable garden and bring them here to the market, but have barely managed to put two or three thousand roubles aside. The rest goes on necessities.

Money seems to be a problem everywhere. Our neighbours in Khakassia have issued their own currency, the Katanov, which is worth five roubles. I've seen one. It is green, black, and white like a dollar, only instead of an American President they have Khakassia's celebrated educationalist, Nikolai Katanov, in what looks like the uniform of a state prosecutor, or maybe a railway worker. As for us, the theatre pays part of our salary in food coupons. One coupon is worth a hundred roubles, and you can exchange them in shops, which have an agreement with the theatre. Actual money you get paid rarely, and not much then. I remember the first time they issued the coupons. Oh, dear! They dished out a full month's ration in one go and the whole theatre went on a spree. Several performances had to be cancelled because everyone was pigging themselves, only to complain later in the month that they were starving. They had to survive on credit from the theatre canteen, on frankfurters, sandwiches and coffee, till the end of the month. Since then the cashier's office issues vouchers one week at a time. The actors and other staff have more or less learnt to make them last and everything has settled down. We can make ends meet. A lot of people are much worse off, I imagine.

"Lyokha, let's play Durak."

"Good idea."

I get up, put a chair next to Lyokha's bed, and pick the cards off my locker. I sit down and start shuffling.

"Shit, we need new cards," I grumble. "These are really past it."

"Buy some," Lyokha suggests sarcastically.

We hear heavy footsteps in the corridor, then somebody

kicking the wall a few times, which usually signals the return of our neighbour on the right.

"Sanya's back!" Lyokha reads the signs and grins. "Wait for it!"

Sanya is off to the army soon, because of his wife. They have one child, an eighteen-month-old boy, and were expecting another but something happened and she had a miscarriage with only a couple of months left to go. Perhaps Sanya overdid it one time he was drunk. They get drunk a lot. Anyway, the upshot is that he's off to the army now.

I throw down six of the battered, dog-eared cards. Spades are trumps.

"Oh, oh, oh." Lyokha looks at his hand grimly. "What have you dealt me, you ass! Go on, then."

I toss down a couple of sevens for starters.

Through the wall our neighbours are beginning their evening performance. "You're all such whores, you're such bitches!" Sanya yells. "You godforsaken bastard!" his wife shrieks in response.

"They're off," Lyokha commentates.

"I'll kill the lot of you! It's no odds to me now! What fucking difference can it make?!" We hear the sound of plates being smashed and the frantic squealing of their small son.

"I can't believe how much crockery they've got," I say in genuine amazement. "They break more every evening."

"It's just families," Lyokha shrugs. "Me and the wife went at it worse than that."

"Why get married then?"

"Libido."

We throw down cards, parry, try to beat each other. A real row is blazing next door. It sounds like they're hitting each other.

"Do you think we ought to take a look?" I suggest. "We wouldn't want anyone getting killed."

"Leave them to it. It's what they deserve. Everything's fine."

"His wife's not too bad looking, though, is she."

"Lena? No. That's why he's so furious. He's being sent to join the armada, which leaves her behind here with us."

"I wouldn't kick her out of bed," I sigh.

"Come off it. Once they've given birth they aren't worth a toss. A nineteen-year-old bit of crumpet, now, that's more like it!"

"You have such high standards! Of course, I don't mean... I mean, obviously a young girl is better." My imagination gets going again on the girl from the windowsill. "Let's take a look. She might still be there!"

"Who?"

"You know, the one in the kitchen."

"Well, go and look, if you're going to. What a bullshitter."

"How can I on my own? I can't just walk up to her, can I?"

We play a dozen games until we're fed up. There's nothing much to eat, just bread and potatoes. Potatoes may indeed be a staple of the Russian diet, but right now I don't fancy them.

"I'll go back to the village on Monday," I say, picturing it, "and bring back some meat, and cucumbers..."

"Good idea! We'll stuff our faces."

Lyokha, unlike me, has no safety net. His wife is off-limits, already with a new man, while his parents in Prokopievsk aren't much help. His father is an ex-miner, disabled now. There's something wrong with his mother too. If anything, he should be helping them, not expecting them to send him money or goodies.

"We need to get pissed," Lyokha opines, stretching out on the bed.

"Let's go round to Pavlik and Ksyukha."

"Just so you know, the very sight of her face makes me want to puke!"

"I'm not asking you to screw her. We'll just ask Pavlik if he's got anything to smoke."

"A joint? Well, great! And what do we do afterwards when we get the munchies? Where's the grub coming from?"

He has a point there. Smoking is fine, but when you come down you want to pig yourself. All those Uzbeks know what they're doing when they puff away in teashops. They have a smoke, yak on about matters philosophical, and the next moment they're stuffing plov in their mouths, and shashlyk, and shaurma.

"Well, then, let's go and see Waliszewski," I persevere. "He might have some booze."

"Come on! When did he ever have any booze?!" Lyokha's head falls back on to the pillow despondently. "He's always trying to cadge it himself."

He relapses into scrutinising the cracks on the ceiling and I wander round the room. The alarm clock is showing half-past eleven and we usually fall asleep around two in the morning. How is the time to be filled?

"Well, what do you suggest?" I start getting tetchy. "You don't want this, you don't want that. If at least we could get our hands on some skirt."

"Oh, you dumbo," Lyokha groans in reply. "Skirt is all you've got on your brain. Big problem. Just go downstairs. They are queueing up at the hostel entrance, just waiting for someone to pick them up, get them drunk and shag them."

"That's just the problem. What good am I to them without a bottle?"

Lyokha narrows his eyes and looks me up and down.

"You're right. No one's likely to take you without a bottle."

"Idiot!" I collapse on to my bed.

Silence. On the other side of the wall Sanya seems to have crashed out. He's living out his last few days in civvy street and it's getting to him. I remember the feeling. You think it's the end. You're about to be put on a train, your head shaven, weak and scared witless, and carted off to the slaughter, yet all around life goes on. Free people are walking about not even noticing that you're taking leave of them. They don't give a shit about you. They're happy while, for you, it's the end of everything.

I turn to the wall and scratch at the faded, half rotten wallpaper.

"Tell me though, Roman," Lyokha begins with unwonted civility and evident irony, "how old are you?"

"Twenty-five, all but. Why do you ask?"

"Oh, just... to listen to you, you'd think you were fifteen. Have you really..." – he's about to burst out laughing, "never done it?"

"Dickhead," I say. "You should understand, I need to get to know them. It's a slow, gradual... For me a woman is not just some... you know... She's a miracle, can't you see? I believe, okay, there should be love, sweet words, gentle caresses before... But for you it's just, grab a bottle and go fuck 'em."

"Don't you believe it. I can just as well empty my own bottle, no problem," Lyokha interrupts, "without needing any bitches. Three years of marriage and I'd had it up to here. And still have, incidentally!"

"Well fine. Go back to sleep." I don't want to continue. Those fine, romantic phrases I'd meant as little more than a joke have stirred something inside me and now I feel completely wretched.

I sit down on the bed and start putting my shoes on.

"Where are you going?" Lyokha asks anxiously.

"I'm going to take a walk down the corridor."

"I'll come with you."

It's a long corridor, extending the length of the building. We live in the left wing of the hostel, and it's a good three hundred metres to the end of the right wing. Doors follow in quick succession to left and right of us. The corridor is narrow and dimly lit because half the daylight lamps have burnt out. The other half fizz and flicker feebly. The walls are painted dark blue and the doors are a kind of swampy colour.

We walk past the abandoned kitchens, the stinking caverns of the washrooms and toilets, and the locked laundry rooms which have replaced the showers. The girl on the windowsill is not there, which is a pity because now I'm in just the mood to go in, start a conversation, and really get to know her. Whatever. Lyokha, if he was only a couple of steps away, would have to come and help things along.

"Why don't we look in on Pavlik anyway," I suggest when we come to a dead end in the right wing and turn back. "You never know, eh?"

"Fuck you, OK."

Some of the rooms have elegant metal plates with their numbers. Others have the numbers painted, or even just chalked, on the door. Some have nothing at all. Pavlik and Ksyukha live at No. 457. They have a large plaque, with twiddles round the number, as if theirs was a very grand apartment.

Pavlik is pushing thirty. He's a short, scrawny guy, already balding, with an ashen face and small, bad teeth. He doesn't have a job, naturally. He's got hitched to a big, fat, truly hideous woman who, for just that reason, has an indulgent attitude towards men. Her room wasn't too bad, so Pavlik climbed into her bed. He calls Ksyukha "Mom", and she proudly calls him "my man". Pavlik occasionally makes forays outside the city to gather hemp in the steppe. He also visits the library and loves reading adventure stories and undemanding detective novels.

I knock.

"It's open!" a not particularly inviting woman's voice calls from inside.

We go in. The room seems cramped because of a wardrobe, a large bed, two tables and all the junk, which makes a room into a home.

Ksyukha is busy cooking something on the hob and Pavlik, needless to say, is lying reading a book.

"What're you doing here, then?" our hair stylist enquires.

"Oh, erm..." I mumble. Lyokha maintains a dour silence, propping himself against the door. "We just looked in. Er, Pavlik..."

No reaction. Pavlik makes it a rule to read to the end of his paragraph, bookmark the page with an out-of-date twenty-five rouble note, and only then acknowledge guests.

He finally finishes, gets up, and shakes hands.

"How is everything?" he asks.

"Mm, so-so. Hey, Pavlik, I don't suppose you might happen to have..." I flick the side of my neck to indicate a need to imbibe. "We're on our last legs. Any chance?"

"Come on, guys! Mom and I have forgotten what that stuff tastes like."

"Oh, bad news. Got any weed, then?"

Pavlik doesn't look pleased. He's obviously just smoked a small joint, has had enough, and doesn't particularly like scroungers anyway.

"You need to give yourselves a shake, lads. All the uncultivated ground around here is overgrown with it. Get out there and help yourselves to as much as you want."

"Yes, of course, Pavlik, you're absolutely right," I nod remorsefully. "We keep meaning to do that, but somehow... and now we really need some, we're desperate." I give a deep sigh and try to sound totally piteous: "Perhaps just a tumbler full, on credit? To make Kuzmich."

Ksyukha is looking daggers, ready at any sign of uppitiness on my part to drive us out into the corridor, but Pavlik, bless him, relents: "I can shake you out some stems, no sweat. I thought you wanted leaf or flower tops."

"Goodness me, no, of course not! Just a little ditchweed to fry."

Ksyukha turns her back on us and gets on with stirring whatever's in the saucepan. Pavlik dives under the bed and produces first a small, rough bag, which he kneads and puts to one side. After that comes a second, a bit larger. He unfastens the tapes.

"Mom, pass me a tumbler, would you?"

"I bet they don't give it back," Ksyukha mutters in her low, bear-like voice, but nevertheless hands over the tumbler.

"By the way, lads, have you read James Chase's *The World in My Pocket*?" Pavlik asks, cramming into his receptacle a mixture of withered blades of grass and leaves which he breaks and grinds.

I reply perkily, "It's the only really good thing he wrote!" But then, to be on the safe side, I amend that to, "What I mean is, it's really brilliant."

"Absolutely!" Pavlik smiles. His pinched little face looks like a thoroughly desiccated skull covered with a thin layer of skin. "It's a really good read. Those guys just overdid it. They so nearly got away. Shame, and then it all fell through. Too bad."

I shake my head and also smile, empathetically registering sorrow as soon as Pavlik starts grieving for his dead heroes. I haven't read the book but I did once see a Soviet screen adaptation called *The Mirage*, and I've heard people say this novel is Chase's best.

"If only their leader hadn't been done in," Pavlik muses. "Everything would have turned out fine. He would have known how to..."

"Well, there you are," I sigh, taking the tumbler. "Life's like that every step of the way. Something always goes wrong. Anyway, thanks, Pavlik, thanks a lot! We owe you one. Goodbye. Goodnight!"

Ksyukha responds by muttering something about giving the tumbler back. Lyokha and I retreat, and Pavlik follows us into the corridor, fingering a cigarette.

"Give me that armoured vehicle with the bucks, and that oxy-acetylene torch..." He sounds completely zonked. "I wouldn't have got caught out. I'd have ripped it open with my teeth."

"What the fuck do you want that hay for?" Lyokha looks down scornfully at the tumbler.

"We'll have it nicely fried up in no time."

"I want vodka."

"You think I can piss vodka? If this isn't good enough for you I'll chew it on my own."

"That much would blow your head off."

"Well, at least I'd have done something with my life."

Kuzmich doesn't taste too good. You end up with a kind of oily, bittersweet, crunchy straw, but if getting it down is fairly disgusting, what follows makes it all worthwhile. Actually, I like Kuzmich and Managa a whole lot better than taking a joint. Kuzmich is when you fry the straw in vegetable oil, and Managa is when you steam it in milk for an hour, strain it through a sieve, and drink it. It tastes a bit like a coffee drink, like our Kolos. You can put it in pancakes too. They're light green, a bit bitter, and you get an unusual rush that comes in waves. You make them like any other pancakes, only you add hemp to the dough along with the other ingredients.

I only learned these recipes quite recently, after I came to live here. Of course, I tried grass in Kyzyl – there it would have been a disgrace not to – but I preferred fortified "port wine". I was quite a well-brought-up young man, enjoyed reading, tried to write poetry. Now that's all gone overboard. I've been knocked out of orbit, lost my bearings. Mostly now, when I'm not on a high, I just feel bored. Evenings like this, in a shitty room with only shitty Lyokha for company, drive me up the wall. You want to get stoned just to break the monotony. And that other natural wish...

2

Behind the scenes it's the usual pre-performance slanging match. Wardrobe have overlooked a sizeable stain on the ample pleats of a frock. Tanya Tarosheva, one of the actresses, must have brushed against the scenery, and the paint they use smears like soot off a stove.

"This is your job, for heaven's sake! It's your job and yours alone to ensure that all the costumes are clean, pressed, and ready on time!" Wardrobe are getting it in the neck from Victor Arkadievich, the theatre manager. He looks fearfully cultured, but really he's just a hysterical, jumped-up ex-actor. "This is not the first time either, is it? I remember shirts going missing, and in Bulgakov's *Last Days* a top hat was dented!"

Valya, one of the wardrobe girls, is scrubbing at the stain with bleach, while the other, Olga, just stands in front of the manager, nodding, abjectly acknowledging the justice of his every word.

Dubravin, the play's director, is twisted up in an armchair, smoking distractedly and looking hurt. The actors are keeping out of it, killing time in a tight space, already wearing their costumes. The women have been transformed into ladies in bright fancy dresses, their real-life faces painted over with a thick layer of slap. The men have been transfigured too: the slim ones into ardent coxcombs, and the podgier ones into dignified penguins. They look a right sight in their frock coats and all their other bits and pieces, but also a good more attractive – it's a definite improvement on the sweaters, tattered jeans and bobble hats they wear the rest of the time.

We five stagehands are sitting in a row on a long leather sofa, listening without the slightest interest to the manager's ranting, which at one moment is deafening, the next quiet and insinuating, and at all events never-ending. We are smoking, relaxed after getting everything in place for the coming performance.

"So what do you suggest?" Victor Arkadievich asks icily. "Given that the curtain goes up in ten minutes?"

Olga looks round hopefully to where Valya is scrubbing at the dress. The stain isn't so dark now, but has spread over half the skirt.

"Well?" The manager again raises his voice. "Should I cancel the performance? My God, I'll, I'll..." More hysterics: "I'll sack the whole fucking lot of you!"

At this point Pashnina emerges from make-up, our leading lady, our prima donna. She is capricious, ageing, unvarying but, as all the directors are used to her, irreplaceable. She has acted her way through the entire repertoire of female leads in world theatre and now, in a husky, martyred voice, she cries to high heaven:

"How long, how long is this going to continue? Victor Arkadievich, I beseech you! One needs to focus, to concentrate. What on earth is the matter?" She stands, dramatic, beseeching, at the door of the greenroom. Her dress classically understated, her head modishly bewigged, her wrinkled face so caked with foundation as to be unrecognisable, she is at this moment the acme of hideous perfection.

"Get her a shawl. She can pretend she's got a cold or something and has to wrap up warmly," the prima donna proposes testily. "Oh, this is impossible, I've forgotten my lines. I've quite forgotten my lines!" She clutches her head. "I've forgotten my lines! Oh, whatever next?" Pashnina teeters on the brink of a nervous breakdown.

Saved by the long ringing of the third bell. Anya, our stage manager, appears instantly. She's out of breath, clutching her invariable sheaf of papers and, as always, looking terrified, as if every show is like a visit to the dentist.

"B-beginners on stage now. P-p-please!" she stutters in a panicky voice.

Pashnina straightens her lithe, reptilian body. Ksyukha hastily straightens her wig, which has shifted slightly. Valya rushes off in search of a shawl to hide the problem stain.

The actors file through a narrow entrance on to the stage. Dubravin throws his head back in the armchair and eyes the chandelier with neurotic intensity. Victor Arkadievich retires to his office with the air of a policeman who has re-imposed public order.

"What do you reckon, guys?" asks Vadim, our team leader. He's the senior stagehand, having stuck the job for seven years.

"Well, why not?" Andrei, a massive giant, decodes his question. "By luck I've got twenty-five on me."

"And I've got ten," Dima, another of our number, chimes in.

"A good start," Vadim nods. "We have lift-off. How about you, Rom?"

"Well, I do have eighteen," I admit reluctantly, "but I need it for the bus. I really have to go and see my parents on Monday."

"Forget it! Let's get jolted instead."

I say nothing. I can hardly refuse. Vadim is meanwhile extracting such small change as Lyokha still possesses. I have to accept that my trip home this week is off. Following the others, I put my hand in my pocket. We pass the coins and notes over to Vadim and he carefully sorts them.

"Very good," he says at last. "One hundred and twelve roubles. Enough for a respectable piss-up. Who's going for it?"

"I'll go."

The money comes my way.

"Right, then, a litre and a half of the usual," our leader instructs me, "something to eat..."

"Sausage, definitely sausage! Tomatoes!" The orders rain down as if what I hold in my hands is not a pathetic hundred roubles but a good five hundred.

I slip cautiously across the stage, behind the backdrop, to our bolthole. Two steps away, on the other side of the canvas, the actors are cavorting in their brightly lit habitat. At this precise moment they are representing the gentry having a picnic.

On stage their little imaginary plywood world lives out its

allotted two-hour span, but these are the moments when the actors are really alive, expressively proceeding down routes plotted for them by the director, articulating with deep emotion lines they have memorised and assimilated to a point where they believe these are their own, heartfelt words. They want to get the audience carried away, so it can be brought back to earth with a bump at the end of the performance when they let them see it was all just a trick. This is something you need to hear our scene-painter, Sergei Petrachenko, going on about.

I often feel like wrecking that little world of theirs. I could just borrow a sheepskin tunic from wardrobe right now, glue on a beard, and march out under the lights. "Arr, you swine, you masters, you... All having a fine time together, is it? Tee-hee," I would croak. "Well, soon, but very soon now it's curtains for you. You'll get a poker up the arse, the lot of you!" I would shake my fist at them and hobble back off into the darkness. I'd like to see them get out of that! How would they put their carefully directed plywood acting back on the rails after my unscripted appearance? That would have them in a cold sweat, not least the goddess-like Pashnina!

Anya is hiding in the wings following the action, wide-eyed with fear as usual. She puts a warning finger to her lips to silently shush me. I nod in complicity and soundlessly descend the metal ladder to the space beneath the stage. We have a cramped, stuffy little room down there which we hardly ever use, but which is good as a bolthole, a place to sleep, even, at a pinch, a place to live for a time. With a little forethought, you could take a girl down there.

I retrieve a one-and-a-half litre plastic bottle from beneath the camp bed and put it in a bag, pull on a jacket and slip the bag inside it. I feel bad about the money and letting my parents down. Of course I do. Digging the potatoes can't really wait, but then neither can my need to get hammered, or, as Vadim puts it, "jolted".

Mid-October. By seven o'clock it's completely dark and the streets are deserted, but the performance will only end at around ten. The theatre's hundred and sixteenth season has just begun and I have nearly ten months of drudgery to look forward to most evenings, except Mondays.

It's an old theatre, with its traditions and history, like everything else in this city. The foyer has several stands with cracked, faded photographs, ancient posters (some going back a hundred years), and yellowing reviews from local newspapers. Along with much else, the theatre is proud of its dogged will to survive. Old Natalia Yurievna, our literary director, likes to talk about the battle to save it in the 1960s. There were plans to close the theatre on the grounds that one palace of culture was as much as any regional centre needed, but the local people rose in its defence. How many Tsarist exiles walked on these boards! How many revolutionaries received spiritual sustenance from the theatre's performances! The famous writer Yan worked here, as did Amfiteatrov, a friend of Gorky's! It was more than likely, indeed, that Lenin himself attended a play, given that he only had to walk a hundred metres from the library, where he studied! The theatre was reprieved, and here it is today. What is truly amazing, though, is that in Minusinsk, a town with a population of less than a hundred thousand, the theatre is full nearly every evening, and some nights tickets even sell out completely.

It stands in the middle of the old city, on the bank of an almost stagnant tributary of the Yenisei and has hydro-electric dams in several places. The theatre is surrounded by one- and two-storey stone houses from the nineteenth century, and blackened huts built from massive logs and with cramped little vegetable plots. The largest buildings are the local history museum, founded about 130 years ago, and the Cathedral of the Redeemer consecrated in 1815, I think. The Cathedral animates the central square and gives unity to the adjacent buildings. It reminds you that Minusinsk is a real old Russian town, an outpost of the

Russian empire in the south of Siberia on the frontier with Turkic Asia. At one time that frontier was pushed back a bit, to Mongolia, but today Asia is right back on our doorstep. To the south, beyond the passes of the Sayan Mountains, is Tuva; twenty kilometres to the west is Khakassia; to the east are the Buryats.

I remember my half-childish impressions of Minusinsk, from when I came to visit my grandmother here. It was only 400 kilometres from where we lived in Kyzyl (no distance to a Siberian), but everything was completely different – the scenery, the houses, the air, the language, the way of life. I used to wander through the quiet, town, which seemed half-asleep, over the flagstones of its pavements. I would gaze dreamily at buildings that seemed to exude the attitudes and smell of the distant past, and half expected to find myself among people in homespun kaftans, old-fashioned peaked caps, and concertina boots. Then there was the Cathedral in the main square, the ancient graveyard with its massive monuments, granite crosses, vaults, inscriptions in the old pre-reform characters, semi-mythical dates like "1854" and "1871", and a ruined chapel there that looked a dead ringer for the one in Savrasov's painting "The Rooks Return". At the time I felt this was living history, and that, without all these crosses, avenues of apple trees, rusting wrought-iron gates, without the ramshackle houses with the crumbling stucco on their facades, I could never fully understand Chekhov and Bunin, or appreciate the full import of the word "Russia". All sorts of fancy ideas a place like Minusinsk can put in the head of a 14-year-old steeped in the "classics" of Russian literature!

When crunch-time came and we had to decide whether to leave Kyzyl, I was all in favour. What was there to Kyzyl? Okay, so it was the place I was born. Sure, I had my friends, the clear, swift waters of the Yenisei, the hot dry sun, the steppe, the encircling mountains on the horizon. But when I came back from the army after more than two years, I saw that all rather differently. Kyzyl just seemed like a tight sack I was going to have to live in. Those nearby mountains seemed threatening and scary, like walls you couldn't rely on. My friends had changed and no longer attracted me. I just wanted to get out and move away to the world my mind had painted from those brief, happy childhood memories.

Now I actually live in Minusinsk, I find it depressing and annoying. I feel like just demolishing all those pathetic, dusty old houses and uprooting the twisted, maggoty apple trees. Now I want to get away from here too.

I notice every city goes at its own pace, and that it's difficult for an outsider or a newcomer to fall in with it. In Minusinsk the rhythm is laboured and sluggish, like blood in old veins, whereas in Kyzyl, as in most newish capitals, it is rapid, effortless and free. Minusinsk people seem to have more inertia to overcome. Everything costs them an effort. Now I miss the closeness of a fast-flowing river, the hot, dry sun of summer, and real frosts, which made sure there were no unexpected thaws in winter. I miss the tireless young people who until old age are going to have their minds full of amazing, grandiose plans for literary anthologies and rock groups and who, while knocking back the vodka, recite their poetry with a droll and affecting gravitas, as if it's the greatest poetry ever written. We have none of that in Minusinsk. The summer is hot, but within bounds, winter is not too severe, and the people themselves are just as middling, with the exception of a few greying bohemians. These drink in Victory Park for days at a time and kid themselves that some day they will finally buy that electric guitar, write some mind-blowing songs, and get themselves discovered. Oh, and a few alky artists. It's puzzling how so many people can be drawn here from all directions: Central Asia, Kyzyl, Norilsk. You would think they were bound to stir this backwater out of its age-old stagnation, but instead they seem to dissolve in it like some useless powder in marsh water, without affecting its colour or taste.

I know I can't go back. We were forced out of Kyzyl and are practically refugees. I need to find something to make up for the life I lived and the world I inhabited before the move to Minusinsk. The nearest town is Abakan, which is the capital of Khakassia and about twenty-five kilometres away. It reminds me a lot of Kyzyl; in fact many of the buildings, the theatre, the town hall, the department store, are practically identical. They probably built both towns to a blueprint for republican capitals. The people are much the same too.

I go there whenever I get the chance. There are people there I can regard as friends. I like it there. I almost feel at home. It's odd, but I feel in my element in a town in the barren steppe where the oldest buildings date from the 1950s, Asia is everywhere, and you can feel that underlying unrest you get wherever different peoples and cultures are thrown together.

Given half a chance, I would move to Abakan like a shot; but in dozy, insipid Minusinsk I at least have a job of sorts, somewhere to stay, and my parents nearby in the countryside.

Thoroughly preoccupied, I have arrived on autopilot at the familiar log cabin on Red Partisan Street (formerly Alexander II Street, as a sign on the first house still proclaims). I bash the metal ring of the latch against the gate. A dog starts barking and bounding round the courtyard, rattling its chain. It is a large, vicious dog because it is guarding treasure: five or more barrels of the spirit, which goes into the making of Gypsy Girl, a home-made hooch renowned throughout the city. It costs just twenty-five roubles a half litre, which is unbelievably cheap, and seems to be harmless. At least, I haven't heard of anyone being seriously poisoned, and the hangover is no worse than you get from ordinary vodka.

"Who is it?" someone growls from the porch.

"I need some fuel," I give the customary reply. "Got any for sale?"

The dog had been quietening down but, at the sound of my voice, starts barking frenziedly again and hurling itself against the gate.

"Quieten down. Hey, quieten down, boy," its master commands amicably enough as he comes to the gate. "Oy! Pack it in!"

The gate opens slightly and two piercing eyes rapidly and professionally size me up. I hold out the bottle.

"How much d'you need?"

"Oh, fill her up."

While the proprietor is filling my container I count out seventy-five roubles, mostly in change.

I swap the handful of coins for a weighty one-and-a-half litre bottle of Gypsy Girl, full to the brim. Things could be worse. After the show, once we've cleared the stage and waited for the theatre to empty, we'll down it at our leisure, accompanied by unexciting food and equally unexciting conversation. What more can we expect or hope for from the evening when this is all we can afford, and, to tell the truth, all we have the energy and imagination to come up with?

I get back just in time for the interval, slip the bottle under the bed in our bolthole, throw off my jacket, and head for the stage.

I grab a light cheval mirror and move it to a different position, side on. I help Andrei and Vadim to shift a plywood grand piano off-stage, and get my hands smeared with soot.

"Did you get it?" lowered, anxious voices ask from all sides.

"I got it, I got it," I nod. "Everything's okay."

Vadim cheers up and drags a plywood fountain shaped like a vase to centre-stage.

An animated buzz comes from the auditorium, from which we unglamorous scene-shifters are hidden by a heavy curtain. The audience will be busily studying their programs, queuing in the bar, eating chocolates, and at last able to have a smoke, languidly readying themselves for the second act. They have no interest in what we do on stage during the interval, and see only the dazzling, ethereal result of our long, grimy labours: the appetising dish brought to table from a greasy, fume-filled kitchen covered in husks and peelings and the diminutive, squashed corpses of cockroaches. Nobody wants to know where the morsels they are nibbling come from.

When everything is in place we take ourselves off-stage to the greenroom. The curtain swishes, the countless light bulbs in the chandelier above the audience are smoothly dimmed, and once again those high, unnaturally articulate voices ring out. The show goes on, with its boring women temporarily transformed into slim, seductive ladies, and scrawny geezers who have become distinguished gentlemen, and who elegantly promenade with them arm in arm. They laugh, they love, they languish.

Out of the lot of them, only one actor, Semukhin, looks more or less realistic: small, shabbily dressed, crestfallen; and that is only because of the role he is acting. Today's production is Kuprin's *The Garnet Bracelet* and Semukhin plays that romantic idiot, Zheltkov; but tomorrow is *The Seagull*, and he will be the supercilious, established writer Trigorin, burdened by his own popularity. Today he is a short little balding fellow, but tomorrow he will have a modish coiffure, hold himself erect, and appear to have grown a good fifteen centimetres in height.

So, here we are again, side by side on our sofa, smoking and waiting for the show to be over. All five of us would like a drink right now but it's too risky, even though we shouldn't have much more work to do. In theory, we only have to clear the stage at the end of the performance, but things can go wrong, sometimes disastrously. I remember, last year a cable snapped which was holding up a flower-entwined crystal (actually, perspex) dome in the moronic tale of *Snow White*. We had to shin up into the rigging and hang on to it manually, dangling above the stage among the hot lights until the fairy tale ended.

The sodding actors, dressed as fairies and dwarfs, came out again and again to take their bows! They really seemed to want to spite us as they smiled at the little brats, bowing from the waist (they're great benders) and accepting posies of flowers. We felt like dropping the sodding dome on top of them. It did finally come crashing down, after the stage had emptied. To this day I can feel how my stretched arms hurt. The upshot is, we can't relax just yet. Shit could still happen.

3

Uncle Gena, though, our bus driver, there's someone I do feel sorry for. If the performance drags for us, it's a complete pain in the bum for him. He just endures it, looking like he wants to howl. He comes in twenty times or more, looks at the wall clock, checks it against his watch, sits down and slowly smokes a cigarette, wanders off again, checks his bus is ready, comes back, dozes in a corner or sandpapers some spark plugs. His pockets are always full of them.

At the first sign that the show is ending, Uncle Gena is out there in his bus, ready and raring to go. He does two runs an evening, one for the actors and a second one for the technical staff (wardrobe, hair, riggers, props). His working day usually ends around midnight.

We're making things marginally easier for him today by finding our own way home. We've told him already, he winked conspiratorially and murmured, "Great, go ahead then," peering anxiously at Dubravin who has been looking petrified for over two hours now.

Of course, getting stirred up and excited can be a good thing, especially if you're directing a play, but dear old Dubravin really overdoes it. He completely cuts out. He's prostrate with anxiety during any of his productions. Whether it's the first or the thirtieth time it's playing, he sits there ashen-faced, staring into space. Only when the applause at the end comes from the auditorium and the actors run back in here with flowers, flushed and smiling, is Dubravin restored to life, pulling out a handkerchief, dabbing at his face at great length, and starting to breathe again. People tug him this way and that, congratulate him, kiss him. They finally get through and he breaks out in smiles, admittedly rather wan, as if he has dragged a heavy sack all the way to where it had to go and, having finally dumped it off his shoulders, can feel relief now, straighten his back and mop his brow.

The actors quite like just hanging around the theatre. They get here three hours or so before rehearsals or a performance and sit around aimlessly, smoking, rattling on about nothing in particular. They often drop in over the summer, when there are no performances, and on Mondays, which is their day off. Something draws them back. They can't seem to do without this building for long, pining for it like smackheads in need of a fix. After a show, though, they're off like scalded cats, can't wait to pile into the old bus which is wheezing and gasping by the stage door. They're still in their greasepaint, half-dressed, men with a lacquered quiff, women rubbing doll-like faces with vaseline-laden cotton wool on the run. They've done the business, taken the drug, and now they just want to get away.

There they go, stampeding down the stairs. Down, down! The door crashes open as they burst out into the fresh air. Half an hour from now they'll be good mothers and fathers, a bit weary, perhaps, but immensely happy, satisfied and rejuvenated; but tomorrow when they wake they'll hurry back here for another fix. You can tell how much the audience appreciates the actors' hallucinations from the look in their eyes, the silence in the theatre, and the applause, as they try to get off on it too.

Our job as stagehands, however, is to set up the stage with fake objects that look real or, on the contrary, to strengthen an illusion of fairy-tale pageantry. Without our scenery and stage props all those actively or passively involved in the performance would find it far harder to get into the throes of ecstasy.

The show is over, the theatre is empty, the actors in that old bone-shaker are revelling in a sense of lightness and short-lived freedom as they head for home, and we get on with clearing the stage, hauling back to the store the walls of plywood houses, the fake grand piano, and dry birch trees with green paper leaves. It's a different play tomorrow with different scenery, and for two and a half hours the actors will be transfigured into different people, but their aim will be the same. And they do that nearly every day.

Having done our job, we are sitting at a laid table in one of the dressing rooms. The girls from wardrobe have joined us while they wait for Uncle Gena to return from his first circuit. They are the friendliest girls, the easiest to get on with, on the technical side. We didn't invite fat Ksyukha.

They're still fuming at the manager.

"He turns some stupid little stain into an almighty crisis," Valya complains, cutting our meagre portion of luncheon sausage into tiny neat slices as only a woman can. "I was so scared I spread it all over the back. I'm taking it home to give it a good boil and be done with it."

"Yes, Victor can be a bit hard," Vadim agrees, sounding like a right old trooper. "I remember one time..."

Dima interrupts: "Let's get one down and you can tell us about it afterwards."

We have a double in each of the cut-glass tumblers. A modest repast, little more than symbolic, is laid out on a theatre poster: the above-mentioned sausage, processed cheese cut into small cubes, some bread, of course, and a few slices of tomato.

"Here's to all that's good!"

We clink our glasses and quickly gulp down the Gypsy Girl. The girls don't finish theirs.

"Aaargh!"

"Okay, easy on the food now," Vadim warns.

We munch, looking intently at the table.

"Oops!" Olya exclaims, jumping up suddenly. "I quite forgot, I have some sandwiches!" She rummages around in her hand-bag and brings out a sweaty plastic bag of asphyxiated ham sandwiches.

"Life can't be too bad, Olya," Lyokha grins, "if you can forget you've got ham! I never have that problem."

"It's all because of that awful scene he made," she explains apologetically. "Valya and I were shaking right through the performance."

"Let's forget it," Vadim frowns. "Time to unwind."

Having the girls here raises the tone a bit, as it always does when any halfway attractive woman joins a group of men who are drinking. After the show ended Vadim surreptitiously suggested to one or two of the young actresses that they might care to join us for a while, but they were in too much of a hurry to catch their bus. We're wary of getting too pally with the male actors, with two or three exceptions, or rather, we prefer not to, because most of them are queers. That's just the way it is. In my early days, when I was still only feeling my way, they would hang around me quite openly if we were having a drink in the evening. It gave you a very peculiar feeling!

People say it all began with two actors who came from the Russian theatre in Harbin after the war. They started it and it snowballed until it had spread to nearly all the "men" in the company. Another of the theatre's traditions, I suppose.

Once I very nearly landed in it big time myself. I'd been working at the theatre a couple of weeks and didn't yet have much of a clue as to who was straight and who was one of them. We were having a first night party, a real binge in the upper foyer, nothing spared. Naturally I had a skinful. By midnight or so most people had wandered off home and, as is usually the case, those who were left split into small groups and strayed off with what was left of the booze into various dressing rooms, store rooms and offices. One way or another, I found myself alone with Lyalin. He's a good-looking, simpering sort of actor, who looks the way his surname sounds. He must be about thirty-five, I suppose. Anyway, so there we are sitting in the secretary's office drinking Greek brandy out of a bottle with a long neck, and Lyalin is spinning me some yarn, droning on and hypnotising me with his high, slightly lisping voice, baring his soul to me, and there I am rocking my head mechanically from side to side, drifting off, and re-surfacing only with an effort to take another swig out of the bottle. Anyway, one time when I resurface I find Lyalin with his arms round me. He's stroking me and his face is only a couple of centimetres from mine. "Let's go back to my place," he murmurs seductively. "How about it, baby!" I take another swig of brandy, bumping him with the bottle, and then hear myself saying, very much to my own surprise, in a soft, sexy voice, "What about your wife?" For that moment, and thank God it was only a moment, I felt like a woman, a drunk, playful slapper sprawled on a sofa. I felt like I was wearing a skirt, and had a wet, hot slit between my legs, and smooth thighs sheathed in lace stockings. It gave me a shock. I came to myself and twisted so I could jump up and push Lyalin away, but he held on. Not roughly, really, but very tightly. "What's wrong?" he whispered, like a doctor inserting a needle into a patient. "What is it, sweet boy? No wife to worry about." He pressed his lips to mine and quickly slid his tongue into my mouth. It was long and cool, and sort of muscular.

Nothing happened. I got free, but in a fairly disgraceful way, like a woman coming to her senses, sobering up when she is already practically in bed. I didn't punch Lyalin, like you're supposed to if you're a man. I pulled awkwardly away from him, pushing ineffectually. I wriggled out, squealing. At least I didn't scream, or cry for help! As I was running out of the office I caught a glimpse of his expression: Lyalin had an understanding smile on his face, and nodded as if granting me a brief reprieve.

Ever since his eyes seem to be asking me, "Still not ready? Are you really still not willing? What a funny boy you are."

"Don't go, girls. Let's sit here and get to know each other." Vadim deploys his limited verbal resources to the best of his ability. "There's plenty of vodka. How about it? Eh, girls?"

"I thought that's what we'd just done," Valya replies drily, and I hear disappointment in her voice, and covert annoyance that there really is nothing doing with us lot. We're going to drink ourselves silly here while she has to take the bus to the outskirts of the city, to one of those new apartment blocks where her very ordinary husband is waiting for her in a cramped little apartment with a fractious child who won't go to sleep without its mother.

"Everything takes time, Valya," I start explaining, and nonchalantly put my hand on the back of her chair.

"What do you mean?"

"I mean, getting to know each other." I glance at her, she glances back, and for an instant I see a spark of interest in her eyes. "You see, Valya, you don't want to rush into things. You can't hurry it." I touch her warm, soft shoulder and give it a squeeze, as if urging her not to get up. "These days when everything is upside down, heaven knows, we need just to take things one step at a time."

From the street comes, "Beep, beep! Be-eep!" Fuck! Something always happens just when you least need it! Why couldn't that sodding bus have a flat tyre, or at least get its spark plugs wet?

The girls pull on their things, one a coat, the other an anorak. They grab various bags and we are history. The promising start of my deliberations is trampled underfoot as Olga and Valya rush for the door without so much as a goodbye.

"Girls... one for the road!" Dima, brandishing the half-empty bottle, makes a last-ditch attempt to delay them.

Lyokha hisses viciously, "Oh, fuck them! Let them just piss off, the bitches!"

"Ah, well, let's get jolted!" Vadim sighs. We clink our glasses and down the vodka without a toast.

In no time at all, of course, the caretaker comes shuffling in. Like most of her profession, she is cantankerous, stupid, and incessantly grumbling.

"What's all this here?" she squawks. "You've no business being in here! This isn't a bar, you know! I need to lock up ... What a fug! Something'll go missing again and it'll be me that gets the blame... Come on now, be on your way before I call the fire officer."

Resistance is futile. We take the bottles and what remains of the food, and depart. The old woman looks round the dressing room and gives the ashtray a shake to check that all the cigarette butts have been stubbed out, then turns out the light and locks the door.

"Forward, then... to Seryoga's," our leader decrees.

"Perfect, our home from home!"

As a scene-painter, Seryoga Petrachenko is indispensable. Who else would execute other people's ideas so uncomplainingly? A stage designer makes a sketch, gets it approved by the director, and brings his work of art to Seryoga. "Right," he says. "This is how I want it done: blue here, pink there, and I want it this wide and that long." Woe betide any scene-painter who doesn't do as he is told, plants a flower ten centimetres further along the plywood, or varies a colour. Shock! Horror! Desecration of the temple of art! Everything has been ruined! The stricken designer collapses into a state of deep depression.

Nobody ever has any complaints about Seryoga's work, though: he paints exactly what he is told to. The only trouble is, he drinks like a fish. He's the only chronic alcoholic I know, literally never drying out. Vodka for him is what cigarettes are for me. He needs a gulp every half hour if he's to carry on functioning.

He started drinking, as he tells anyone who'll listen, because he felt fettered, because he felt slighted, and because he was envious. "Damn it all, I'm an artist the same as him. We went to the same college, but now, dammit, look at the distance between us!" That's pretty much it, but with Seryoga's interjections omitted. "You'd think I have no ideas of my own. Well don't worry, because actually I'm teeming with ideas! Anyway, that's why I knock back one bottle after the other. I'm putting down my inspiration!"

Seryoga lives day and night at his studio, having left the apartment he inherited from his parents to his last wife and small son. He has no fewer than five children by three wives, and they all have to be paid alimony, which is why he has to daub for the theatre and paint pot-boilers on the side when he gets the chance.

You feel sorry for Seryoga, of course, but what's to be done? It's just the way things have turned out. He's not the only one bogged down. If you suddenly set him free to paint anything he wanted, he would be stuck. He goes on about all his great ideas, but I don't believe a word of it. You're washed up, Seryoga, finished. You didn't keep your powder dry.

"Hello, Seryoga, you've got visitors! Can we come in?"

"Oh, um, er, yes, please do!"

We troop in, surround the table and, without more ado, start clearing all the clutter off it. Plastic packaging and empty cans are consigned to a brightly painted bucket left over from one of the theatre's fairy tales.

"Okay, Seryoga, we're here to get slaughtered!"

"Oh, um, well, yes, it's a sacred duty, they do say."

At first sight this scene-painter's workshop might be taken for the studio of a real artist. It has all the requisite working disorder, the tubes of paint, canvases, offcuts from picture frames, and no end of the bits and pieces that artists always seem to accumulate, from seashells and chipped vases to bits of cars and lumps of concrete. On closer inspection, however, you can see that Seryoga is not the master here, but a slave, a reluctant hack. Sketches on scraps of art paper have stamps certifying the approval of higher authority, and everything, furniture, vases, picture frames, bears discreet but immediately evident white three-digit numbers, testifying to the dead hand of inventorisation.

"I hear we've got another fairy tale coming," Vadim says unhurriedly. "They say the scenery is enough to drive you crazy: a turret with three floors, a forest, a royal palace. We're going to sweat blood putting that lot up."

Andrei concurs:

"They put on a different show every evening, and fuck knows what they get up to. In the rest of the world they just put a table, a chair, a bench maybe, and away you go."

"Uh, um, er, I don't know about that," Petrachenko says with a wry smile. "The scenery, er, you know, is what gives the element of spectacle."

"The trouble is, everybody's got so used to the element of spectacle," I pipe up, "that nobody wants to just look at the actors any more."

"Well, children like it to be, um, pretty and, well, you know, colourful."

"No, well that's quite right, of course," Vadim says, putting a damper on the argument. "Do the honours would you, Dima, pour a shot all round."

We are talking shop, as usual. Like it or not, we are all firmly attached to the theatre. Although in theory none of us would mind moving to a better job if we had the chance, the theatre has a hold on us. It draws people in and enmeshes them like a spider's web; even people who have been sacked, thrown out for drunkenness, whether they're stagehands and carpenters or actors, often come back to sit in the greenroom and catch up on the gossip. They have to force themselves to leave, battling an urge to run upstairs to Victor Arkadievich's study, fall on their knees and beg him to take them back.

"How, er, um, did Larisa Volkova act today, would you happen to know?" Petrachenko asks cautiously, with a guilty smirk.

"Well, fuck knows," Andrei, who's not too bright, blurts out in reply. "We weren't looking. Although, mm, she is a bit of all right!"

The scene-painter gives a little grunt of vexation.

Without our having noticed, the Gypsy Girl is suddenly finished and we have drunk our way through most of Seryoga's private reserve. There are literally only a couple of gulps left.

It's too late to go home, and anyway we can't be bothered. Everyone is on the verge of crashing out, and even Seryoga is the worse for wear. The alcohol, which has been accumulating in him over the course of the day, has finally gone to his head, but I know for a certainty that before we fall into a drunken sleep he will treat us to his party piece. This is a speech about the nature of acting, and how he was once enchanted and deceived, only for the spell to be cruelly broken. He delivers it towards the end of every booze-up, like the closing monologue of a play, from a sadder but wiser hero.

Lyokha and Andrei, sparring between them, are meanwhile fixing a place to sleep on the floor, piling up canvases and sacking. Vadim is looking pensive and seems to be assessing how successfully we've partied and got jolted today. I am smoking my second cigarette in a row and fending off sleep, while our scene-painter is already half dozing. Dima, a sturdy lad who can take his drink, is scrupulously dividing out what is left of the booze and asking, "Seryoga, hey, tell us where you get the readies from for all this drinking. You must be getting through ten thousand a month. How do you do it?"

"Oh, um, er," Petrachenko mumbles in reply.

Vadim rallies to his defence.

"Leave the man alone, Dimentius! He's a lush, and thank God for that. Why rake things up? Let's just r-relax."

One last, good snifter and the glasses are empty. Now we can collapse. A dull, heavy itching in my head makes it feel as if it's teeming with small stinging ants. My eyelids are coming down over my eyes like rough-surfaced shutters and I have to make a big effort to push them up again. My body wants to be horizontal, on the floor. "Spill out, come on, spill out!" an imperious whisper is instructing me. It's no longer drunkenness but simple exhaustion after a protracted five-hour drinking. When you get drunk quickly the feeling is quite different, like a whirlpool, a whirlwind, a dazzling burst of fireworks, followed by an abrupt knockout. When you don't rush things, however, oblivion comes less easily. It has to fight against the mind and our foolish human obstinacy. "Spill out over the floor, spill out," I hear the wise voice whisper, but foolishly I resist. I force my eyes open, I try to get my wooden tongue to move. I'm not enjoying this. The high has burned itself out and turned into stinging ants. It is time to concede to the whisper.

I just need to lie down right now, anywhere, burrow into a pile of rags, and "spill out". I sink down and am aware of cursing and kicking from beneath me. I am silent, motionless, but still conscious, just. A tiny cell is pulsating, a faint dot is glowing, and it is looking at the lines on my eyelids. The lines are fluid and look like white-hot arcs of electricity. When will they stop? The cell tries to count them: three on the left eyelid, four on the right. No, three on both eyelids. Or four. I need to try harder.

"Um, er, life, erm, you know... art, you say? Well, yes, life. But no, actually, that's, um, that's not it at all. It's not a life, um, it's pseudo-, um, pseudo-life."

Here we go. He's off now. An eery, spectral voice appears to be coming from the ceiling. You wouldn't know it was Petrachenko but for the interjections. He couldn't cut out until he'd delivered his pet monologue, even though he's left it too late, even though he's delivering it into the void. He has to go through with it. Well, fine. I'll fall asleep to the sound of his voice, as if grandmother were telling me a fairy story, if I can just settle down a bit more comfortably.

"I could, erm, tell you a story if you, um, like, but, erm, it's a very frightening story, yes, um, about how I came to see through the theatre. Oh dear, yes, well, anyway, we have an actress, a certain, um, a very sweet young girl she is, yes, ah, erm, pretty as a picture, I'm telling you! Anyway, here she is acting, um, acting the part of a sweet young, um, girl just like herself, and she has to say the words, 'I love you!' What words those are, um, – just think about it. 'I love you!' Eh? That's really special, isn't it, something, um, you get to say, if you're lucky, just once in a lifetime, eh? 'I love you!' Those are sacred words, boys! And here she, erm, is, repeating them at every performance. Time after time! And she says them, those, erm, damnable words in a way that makes everyone believe her. The whole theatre is as taut as a string. Can you imagine it? Give it a tug and it will break."

The white lines on my eyelids become taut strings. Yes, I can imagine it. I'm even seeing it, and dancing along that barely quivering string comes the girl from the hostel, the girl on the windowsill in the old kitchen, wearing a white ballet skirt. Her legs are slender and her hair is auburn gold, but I can't yet see her face, it's turned away from me, inaccessible. She's dancing gracefully and I'm holding my breath, following her every move. I peep at her as Petrachenko provides the soundtrack.

"Um, I used to crawl up specially to the platform, um, beside the spotlights when she was saying that, and, m-mm, the tears would come to my eyes, they would, and I really believed her, I believed her and I forgot, mm, that it was all just play-acting and, um, not real, and that sweet girl was just acting a part, m-mm, m-mm, and in ten minutes she would become quite different, you know, quite a different person. All I knew then, m-mm, was that she was saying it to me, saying 'I love you!' It turned me inside out, she made music with that string. M-mm, and the next day she would be acting the part of some idiotic rabbit or a little boy, you know. She even drank with me, knocked back vodka. Who needs that? Who needs that, you know, mask? No, m-mm, it won't do, I can't forgive... you know?"

Then – silence. Total silence. All is still. No snoring, no drunken muttering, nothing. Seryoga has made it to the end of a story he's told a hundred times before, a story he's memorised like a part in a play, except that this is the part he plays in life. He's said his lines now and is sleeping. He sits there with his curly, half-bald head hanging down on his chest, his legs spread wide apart, and a thread of viscous spittle dribbling from his half-open mouth. He's sleeping, but I've sobered up and now, with a clear head, stare at his dark figure, afraid to blink, afraid of closing my eyes and finding nothing behind the eyelids.

4

It doesn't happen often nowadays, but it does still happen that I wake with the dawn, light-headed, feeling totally rested and renewed. It's a feeling, half-forgotten, from childhood.

I lie for a few minutes staring at the ceiling (which doesn't have cracks on it). My eyes don't feel glued together, don't hurt, and I don't just want to turn over and go back to sleep. At first I imagine I'm back in my bedroom in our old apartment in Kyzyl. I'm about twelve. I listen. My mother, it must be, is making breakfast in the kitchen. In a minute my father will look in and say, "Roman, up-time! You need to get yourself to school and learn something, my friend." I smile a little, stretch, and straighten my body from my neck down to my feet. People say it's when children stretch that they grow.

But I don't hear any sounds coming from the kitchen, and my father doesn't look in, so it must be the weekend, perhaps even a holiday – May Day.

I'm awake, I'm not sleeping, but I'm in a state that is more blissful than the sweetest sleep. My eyes are open, but my mind is far away in places I've left a long time ago. It's re-discovering and reliving those wonderful moments on first waking when I was a child. But then, like great dark snow clouds invading the pure blue of a spring sky, my mind brings me back to my present self. I remember where I am, what happened yesterday, how old I am, and what I can expect of the coming day. I yawn and groan and my tarry lungs wheeze, and I hear Lyokha snoring in his bed nearby. My bones begin to ache, I feel a stitch in my side, and my long-unwashed scalp is itching. I grunt, sit up, and shake a cigarette out of the pack.

Morning is when I get through most cigarettes. You have to revive yourself, restore your nicotine-dependent spirits, and only then get on with your life. I smoke my first of the day sitting on the bed, wrapped in a blanket, looking around and whispering over and over again, "Holy shit... Holy shit..." Even though I didn't manage to get hammered yesterday, I feel I've got the mother of all hangovers. I'm shattered and feel I've been shoved through a twisted, vibrating pipe. I've now been spat out the other end and am gradually recovering, rubbing bumps and bruises and getting my shook-up guts and brain back to where they're supposed to be.

I dress slowly and laboriously and get through my second Prima of the day. I roughly make the bed, grab a towel, and shuffle off to sluice my face.

Only cold water today. No, not cold – icy. I try to smooth down my hair, which makes my hands sticky and greasy. I look around the sinks for a sliver of soap but don't find any. Great. I gargle, clear my throat, and spit out dark, hard clots of mucus. In conclusion I screw down the tap, rub myself with a thin grey face towel, and inspect myself in a shard of mirror stuck to the tiles. I really ought to shave – my stubble is almost a beard – but all the razor blades are blunt. There's no point even trying: I'll only cut myself to ribbons.

The remains of last night's supper are on the table: a few potatoes in their jackets, some pieces of bread in a cellophane wrapper, salt. I sit down and skin a potato, trying in the process to catch the midges circling above the table. I breakfast to the irritating accompaniment of Lyokha's loud snoring. From time to time I look over and see his head thrown back, the chasm of his mouth from which there proceeds: "k-khh-hhh-hhh... ho-o-o... k-khh-hhh-hhh... ho-o-o ..." First the dry, toe-curling "k-khh-hhh-hhh...", and then the mucous, rasping "ho-o-o..." I feel an urge to stuff a potato or a rag in his mouth, anything to silence him, but am restrained by the thought that he may do the same to me tomorrow, if he wakes up first.

Sunday morning, but already there are lots of people about. The times when you could lie in on your days off, relax before the start of the next working week, are long gone. For many people now, working days and weekends are the same shit. The word '*uikend*' has entered our vocabulary, but for many people the reality has all but disappeared. Life has become a pointless mish-mash where you aren't doing anything worthwhile, and you certainly don't get to relax. It's one long, grey slog.

I proceed to the centre of the new part of Minusinsk.

The city is divided into two more or less equal halves by a channel of the Yenisei. In the heart of the old city are the Saviour Cathedral, the local history museum and the theatre, while the heart of the new town is the Trade Centre – the two-storey Sayan department store, a supermarket, and the vast open-air market around it.

A few years ago this was a cheerless wilderness strewn with builders' rubble and overgrown with wormwood. On three sides the waste ground was enclosed by new nine-storey apartment blocks, while the fourth side opened on to Labour Street, the main road of the city's new part. First they were going to build a sports complex on the waste ground, with a football stadium and swimming pool, but couldn't raise the money. Then they hit on the idea of setting out a park with secluded benches beneath avenues of trees, an outdoor restaurant and leisure facilities. They even got as far as clearing and levelling the ground and had started bringing in topsoil when the free market era arrived and the wilderness spontaneously turned into a flea market.

At first people traded in the open, laying out their wares on tarpaulins, oilcloth or car bonnets. Then ugly home-made kiosks appeared, put together from steel reinforcement rods and topped with roofing felt or plywood. Just recently the market has started to look positively civilised with the building of the supermarket and department store, and the erection of neat rows of kiosks with gaudy signs proclaiming "Ruslan Ltd.", "Bagheera & Co.", "Shanghai Enterprise", and rows of stalls under tin roofing. Within a few days snack bars were assembled, where traders and customers alike could have a quick bite to eat, sit down, enjoy a Fanta or a beer, and talk shop. Needless to say, a pay toilet promptly followed, a market security office, and the discreet cabin of the Trade Centre administration.

I like being there in the mornings when the traders are coming in with their carts, the vans of the serious businessmen are being unloaded, and the old women are squabbling over the best places. I used to like to go down to the banks of the Yenisei, to lie on the grass beneath the huge black poplars, watch the sluggish rippling of the water, listen to the dawn chorus and hear the occasional splash of a leaping fish. Nowadays, though, it is the Trade Centre that draws me. Tee-hee! I seem to be turning into a member of civil society, a man of Western habits. I heard someone say that in the United States, for instance, the average citizen regards going round the shops as the best leisure pursuit: not actually buying anything, just "window shopping", admiring the lavish display of clothes of every kind, size and style, the crazy stuff scattered about everywhere, and all the good food.

I've noticed when you're walking through the market with the intention of buying something you go round comparing, suffering agonies of doubt, haggling. Before you know it, you've got a headache, you've no more energy, and in the end can't be bothered any more. You just grab anything in order to get the whole exhausting business over as soon as possible. What you ought to do is just wander through the market without a kopek in your pocket. That way you can tell yourself you're at a show, or going round an open-air museum. You relax and rise above the cares of the ordinary folk bustling around you. You become an observer, free, detached, slightly aloof.

The market is a world quite different from the old collective farm bazaars I remember from childhood, with their kindly old women behind counters, and the aroma of home-pickled cucumbers, garlic, and garden strawberries. Nowadays the market provides a livelihood not just for a hundred women with kitchen gardens, a few professional cleavers of meat, and a handful of Georgians surrounded by pyramids of tangerines, apricots, and pomegranates. Nowadays, as I recently read in *Worker Power*, our local newspaper, this is how almost one-third of the city's entire population make their living. These are the muggers, factory workers, teachers, housewives, or pensioners of yesteryear. Today they sell bananas and books, clothing and cosmetics, smoked fish, biscuits, spare parts for cars, toilet paper, cassettes and cutlery, and hope to have made enough by evening to feed their families tomorrow. Only rarely now do you encounter a gardening enthusiast selling his surplus produce, and only too happy to share the secret of how to grow such large, sweet carrots, or perfectly shaped tomatoes fit for an exhibition. There they sit on their benches, crates or beach chairs, unsmiling, frazzled people, re-arranging their wares in the belief they are making them more attractive, more alluring for customers. They try to catch the eye of passers-by, and sing the praises of their goods in tones of implausible celebration: "Sweaters, sweaters – pure wool!" "Fresh-baked loaves – buy some now!" "Legal video-cassettes – all the top films of recent years!..."

Yes, early morning is the time to come, before all the heaving and the hassle. For the present, they are unhurriedly preparing for the arduous day ahead, occupying the best places, writing fresh price lists. A babble of chit-chat gushes forth as they recall yesterday's commercial successes and failures.

I sit down at the end of one of those long rows at a stall that is empty for the moment and take out a pack of Prima. I check how many cigarettes are left. Twelve. Almost enough if I'd been going to see my parents tomorrow morning, but now what am I going to do? What am I going to smoke next week? Borrowing money is almost impossible, even a measly ten roubles. My only hope is that my father won't wait until Monday to find out how I'm getting on, and will bring some food and at least a little ready cash with him.

I smoke and look around me. Many of the regular traders I know by sight. They're like the characters in a never-ending soap opera. I know their personalities, the way they do business, the way they talk. As I'm observing them I use my imagination to visualise the things I can't see. For instance, I see them fifteen years ago placidly working in a glove factory or a furniture factory, churning out shoddy products nobody needs. I see them living on an advance until payday, and then one day discovering there are to be no more advances and, shortly after that, no more paydays either. I see their factories being shut down, and them coming here, to the Trade Centre. At first, of course, they think it's only for a time, but then they realise it's forever. So here they now are, collecting goods from wholesalers and warehouses: books, cosmetics, crates of bananas, deep-frozen chickens, pulling them along on their carts, dragging them in holdalls. They get ten or twelve per cent of the sale price, which wouldn't be bad, except that day by day the bananas get more blackened and aren't all sold before they start to rot. The meat thaws out and is re-frozen a dozen times. Each morning they put it out on sale and each evening, with much cursing and swearing, stuff it back in the freezer until the next morning. Light bulbs get jarred, the ink in ballpoint pens leaks, it's only too easy to dent the packaging of expensive perfumes, and sweaters are magnets for dust.

The evenings of these people are something I see particularly clearly, their dinner together as a family, gathered silently in the tiny kitchen. They eat together not in the interests of family bonding but simply in order to share out the food equally: the grim-faced, sober husband has been dragging sacks of sugar and cereals all day; the grey, jumpy wife, her head bursting after a day at the market, is apportioning rice between the plates and, with a look of distaste on her face, pouring a thin gravy over it with occasional pieces of braised pork belly. The children don't dare misbehave. They know that if they fidget or start acting up they'll get a clip round the ear from Father, and Mother will start shaking and shrieking. She'll throw the serving spoon down on the floor and run off to her room to collapse on the creaky bed. That's not far off how it is, I guarantee.

A husband and wife are setting up their stall across from me. They look a bit the wrong side of thirty. I often see them. They're among the main characters of my soap opera. Their niche is cleaning products: detergents, various kinds of soap, Comet Powder Cleanser with Chlorinol, sanitary towels for ordinary days and for heavy days, toilet paper, toothpaste and Toilet Duck. They bring the goods on two carts fashioned from prams. Without wasting words, they deftly set out their packs and bottles on the stall. Their faces don't yet seem awake and their eyes are dull. The woman is not bad-looking, attractive but tired, probably terminally, careworn and faded from her daily sentry duty here in all weathers. These are probably the best clothes she has, she's wearing make-up and has a coquettish little beret on her head. It's generally accepted that if you look a fright you'll frighten away the customers, so you need to be as bright as the vivid packs of detergent, and not too far behind the pretty, well-groomed girls on the soap wrappers. In a word, you have to be worthy of your product. Her husband, on the other hand, is in his work clothes: a pair of old jeans, a weatherproof jacket and a discoloured ski hat. He's a yard sweeper – I know that for a fact because I once followed him. I saw him sweeping the pavements and filling containers with the contents of garbage chute bunkers in one of the nearby nine-storey apartment blocks. He's got it made. No, really. Working as a yard sweeper is pretty cool. The pay isn't bad and, more to the point, I'm told you can count on getting it paid on time. You can live on it, and even allow yourself a little extra sometimes, push out the boat a bit. That said, I well remember my own time as a yard sweeper, really just keeping the playground area clean and tidy. After I'd been working there for a month, I was convinced kids did nothing but eat sweets, throw down wrappers, and damage shrubs; trees did nothing but shed billions of leaves; and nannies, in order to torture me, deliberately missed the bins with their rubbish. Overnight the dogs managed to cover the entire area in shit. I soon felt it wasn't the asphalt I was scouring but my own brains.

This couple have the regulation two children. The son is around twelve and the daughter slightly younger. They usually come to join their mother after three in the afternoon, bringing a jar of soup and a thermos from home. She has them then till evening, sitting one on each side of her, their expression just like hers, hoping for customers.

Business is so-so, neither markedly better nor markedly worse than for other traders who are into cleaning products.

The stuff does sell. So far, at least, people still wash, clean their teeth, and launder their clothes.

The husband appears at around five, having changed into his best trousers and a synthetic leather jacket. He stands at the counter, discussing with his wife what to get for supper tonight and for tomorrow. His wife gives him money and he sets off along the stalls. He might buy a kilo of beef – no, pork would be better, it's that much cheaper, – a pack of (Russian) spaghetti, some greens, and 200 grams of mince. Over and above the essentials, he may buy an ice cream for the children, a small bar of chocolate for his wife, and a bottle of beer for himself. He returns with his purchases, magnanimously distributes the presents among his family, and primly opens the beer. For a while they enjoy dispatching their treats in silence, a blissful expression on their faces. When that is over, they return to reality and look grey again. The husband puts his empty beer bottle in the bag with the food and goes off home. He returns twenty minutes later with the carts and they slowly, as if reluctantly, gather up their wares. The children help. The market empties just as slowly, with people lethargically packing up and going their separate ways by car or on foot. Empty boxes and cartons, screwed up newspaper, rotten, squashed vegetables lie on the counters and in the passages. Beggars wander about looking for glass jars and bottles they can hand in for the deposit, or anything else that has been dropped or left behind. One man's loss is another man's gain, and they look as pleased as if they have stumbled upon treasure. The road sweepers come along after the beggars and tidy up the Trade Centre, so that in the morning it will be clean and ready for another working day.

I'm not a complete moron, of course, hanging around the market from eight in the morning till seven or eight at night. This is a composite picture I've put together from many fragments, mornings, afternoons and evenings spent there. I am an outside observer. So far, at least.

"Well now, young fellow, let me just set out my things on this end of the counter," a wiry old man suggests. He has a large bag on his shoulder and is holding a bucket covered with a pillowcase. I jump down from the counter and he immediately starts producing jars of sour cream, and packs of curd cheese and butter from his bag. He must own a cow.

Time to take a hike. I've been lost in reverie and failed to notice the market coming to life. Nearly all the stalls are taken, and there are already a fair number of customers about. Today is Sunday, so business should be brisk.

The traders are well practised in the art of attracting customers: "Socks direct from the warehouse! Pure cotton! Only twelve roubles!" "Home-pickled cucumbers! Take a bite, don't be shy!" "Anyone for halva? Crumbly halva from Krasnodar!"

The cries of the traders mix with music from the kiosks selling cassettes. There are half a dozen of these, and the result is a mind-numbing cacophony. From one of the kiosks two male voices take it in turns to call out, one thin and cloying, the other demonic:

> *Gay days. Gay days.*
> *Gay days. Gay...*

From another, the tale of Fedora and Ivan is related by a matey tenor:

> *Vanya leaned against the wall.*
> *Watched Fedora, scratched one ball,*
> *Felt today he'd be in luck.*
> *He was looking for a fuck.*

Right next to this particular kiosk some old women have set up a stall trying to sell vegetables from their kitchen gardens – late scallions, umbrellas of dill for marinating, tomatoes ripened indoors. From time to time one or other of them frowns and looks round at the loudspeakers outside the kiosk, which are

48

booming and vibrating under the strain. The old women are understandably embarrassed at having to listen to this smutty little ditty, but what can they do? This is a good spot and a lot of people come past. They'll just have to put up with it.

My parents too have been hoping to get back on an even keel at the Trade Centre. Here they too sit at a counter piled with vegetables, trading. For all their pains, however, in the end they seem only to make enough to cover their day-to-day expenses: food, petrol, the bare necessities. This seems to be true of everybody else. What my parents earn is most often spent right here in the neighbouring stalls and little shops.

When I know they're going to be at the market, I try to avoid it. It upsets me. It's just not nice to see your nearest and dearest as part of this crowd, reduced to the status of market traders always ready to cut the price, or throw in an extra cucumber, just to be sure of getting hold of those few banknotes they must have if they're to make ends meet. The insouciant observer, the slightly supercilious visitor that I usually am as I stroll through the Trade Centre, vanishes instantly, leaving only a small, saddened, helpless creature with tears welling up in his eyes. This only happens if I suddenly come across my parents with that look in their eyes, when they don't immediately see who I am and try wheedling me into buying their "lovely cucumbers, rosy red radishes, fresh, juicy onions".

I leave the Trade Centre behind and head off towards the children's playground on the other side of Labour Street. I'll sit on a bench for a bit, have a smoke, and watch the little children frolicking about without a care in the world. It would be good also to have twelve roubles for a beer but that, alas, is not on offer.

I pass the monument. A chiselled inscription reads "Places in the Krasnoyarsk Region Where V.I. Lenin Stayed During His Exile, 1897-1900". Beneath this, letters daubed in white paint on the hazel-brown granite: "Vlad woz 'ere!" A neat little sketch map is provided, indicating Krasnoyarsk itself, Minusinsk, and the villages of Kozlovo, Shushenskoye and Yermakovskoye. Just below this is a trough for flowers, which instead contains an empty bottle of Russkaya vodka.

For some reason I get quite mesmerised gazing at this familiar monument, at the tears of paint running down from that daubed "Vlad woz 'ere!" and when I move on I almost collide with a procession of local artists. They're not moving in a flock as they usually do, but walking in single file, each peering at the heels of the person in front as if afraid of losing the trail. Heading the parade is Yura Pikulin, a small, thin man with the face of a boy but disconcertingly pale and haggard. Three thin bearded individuals follow.

Yura bears before him, like the icon in a religious procession, a painting shrouded in a sheet. His eyes are as white as if he were wall-eyed, and fixed sightlessly ahead. Right now it is unlikely that Yura can see any more than the blurred outlines of the Trade Centre through the fog of a cataclysmic hangover. Assuredly he has not seen me, because he jumps a mile when I ask, "Flogging the picture?"

He stops, trying to focus, and looks me up and down before croaking, "Yup, there we are... Hello."

The artist following Yura is Shura Reshetov, a lanky man with a long, scrawny beard. He bumps into Yura and obediently stops without saying a word; the others in turn bump into the person in front of them before coming to a halt in a concertinaed column.

"You wouldn't, I don't suppose... anything to drink?" Yura asks in a parched, suffering voice.

"Skint." I spread my arms. "Not a bent kopek."

Yura gulps, frowns and walks on. Shura, Dima Kovrigin, and Sanya Missing also start up like shunting wagons. I catch up with Yura and fall into step beside him.

"What's the painting?"

"Here, look ... We've decided to realise 'The Goddesses of Ganja'."

"What are you doing!" I'm genuinely shocked. I know this is Yura's pride and joy, one of the best things he has painted.

"Oh, what the hell!" he frowns again. "A man's gotta drink."

I met up with the artists practically the day I moved to Minusinsk, more than three years ago now. Everybody knows them: a dozen thirty- or forty-year old profligates and loudmouths who, starving and penniless, stubbornly persist, through all their drunken binges, in creating things which few people other than themselves have any use for.

The artists are the liveliest section of the population of Minusinsk, with its sleepy, traditional (despite the challenges of recent years), and philistine ways. What is more, they are an integral part of this provincial little town, even though the populace aren't happy when confronted with anything striking and new, they grimace in alarm, bristle, and try to keep these alien elements far removed from their cosy little nests, and from agitating their brains under that insulating layer of warm fat. This is also the reaction of nearly all the directors of the local institutions in whose gift it lies to decide whether to foster or stifle striking new phenomena. Even though some avant-garde poets and musicians live in Minusinsk too, their closest ties are with youthful, dynamic neighbouring Abakan. That's where it's all happening, where rock festivals get organised and collections of poetry and prose get published.

For painters, however, Minusinsk is the centre, because of the art college, of course, and the local history museum. They have a gallery, which enables the artists to exhibit and reach their public. So while musicians and poets and all manner of unconventional performers from Minusinsk go to Abakan to get themselves heard and recharge their batteries, the painters of

Abakan come in the opposite direction. Right now, for instance, three of these artists are from Minusinsk, while Dima Kovrigin is from Abakan. No doubt their latest drinking spree is in honour of his visit. There is no reason to suppose it has lasted only a couple of days. Most likely they will have been at it for the best part of a week. A shorter binge, no matter how intense, would hardly have reduced them to this sort of state. For their eyes to be so white, for them to be picking their way single file like this, they must have been totally inebriated for a very considerable time.

In Dolina, the first shop the painters stumble upon, they decline even to look at "The Goddesses of Ganja".

"Let's go to Kirill's," Reshetov mumbles. "He might take it. I palmed off a couple of gouaches on him the other day. He's a sucker for porn."

"This is not an erotic painting," Yura protests, hurt, but immediately adds, "Still, who gives a toss? Take me there."

Reshetov scratches his beard, looks around getting his bearings, and leads us through the maze of the Trade Centre.

I don't like what's happening. Yura's obviously going to be upset and regret parting with his painting so lightly when he sobers up. I try to stop him:

"Don't do it, Yura, you'll be sorry afterwards. Do you really have to?"

"Of course I do." He sighs dejectedly. "A man's gotta drink."

"Here we are." Reshetov stops a short distance from the Video Rental kiosk.

Several lads are looking over the cassettes displayed in the window. The owner, a pleasant, urbane young man, is leaning out, explaining something to one of his prospective customers.

Yura unties the string. He takes the sheet off the canvas and here, in the midst of the hordes of warmly dressed people, among the stalls and the puddles and the mud, against a background of enormous containers overflowing with rubbish, the naked, dancing Goddesses of Ganja depicted on the canvas seem especially delicate and beautiful.

The picture reminds me of "The Dance" by Matisse. Seven graceful Goddesses of Ganja are circling in almost the same round-dance, but they are painted far better. They seem almost to be alive. The Frenchman painted cavorting adolescents with dark pink, whip-like bodies, but Yura Pikulin's canvas has a real plot line, real aesthetic value, a depth of thought and much to delight the eye.

In more detail, this is what's in the picture:

On a picturesque green some very beautiful girls are holding hands and dancing. They are painted in meticulous detail, and really do appear to be alive. Actually, of course, girls like that don't exist. Real girls have defects and flaws while these are faultless, all seven of them. Each one is different, but they are all beautiful. Well, anyway, they are dancing in a ring, and to one side a man is coolly lying on the grass (he looks a bit like the artist, Pikulin himself) and smoking a fat cigarette. Obviously, it's not just an ordinary cigarette, it's a joint. You can tell that from his expression and the smoke from the cigarette. The whole canvas is hazy with smoke, a light but unmistakably narcotic mist. This is the Ganja. The Goddesses of Ganja have been born from it. They are ethereal, beautiful maidens, born to indulge the gaze of the artist, weaving their voluptuous dance before his eyes and, when the time comes for the weed to lose its power, they will dissolve away.

The green grass will be empty and the artist will feel abandoned, ill, dreadful. He will get up, give himself a shake, sigh dejectedly, and trail off home, back to the reality of which he wearied so long ago, to a host of intractable problems, to his wife with her cellulite. All that will remain, still warming him, will be that memory of the beautiful, empyrean Goddesses of Ganja, and all that will animate him is the hope of seeing them again, drawing on joint after joint, and his attempts to fix his miraculous vision on the canvas. Many people, I know, have been privileged to contemplate them after impregnating their brains with hash, many have tried to paint them, but Yura Pikulin has very nearly succeeded. "Nearly" is not intended as a reproach: nobody has ever done it a hundred per cent successfully.

At last year's exhibition, Yura was invited in my presence to name his price for "The Goddesses" by someone who was far from poor (the manager of a biscuit factory), but wouldn't do it. Now here he is, himself bringing the painting to the Trade Centre and, most likely, about to part with it for next to nothing, just to raise enough money for more booze.

"Oh, well, to hell with it," Yura mutters, gazing at his goddesses as if beseeching them to understand that right now he can do no other and must part with them. "What a business." With unfocussed eyes he locates Reshetov and holds out the canvas: "Here, Shura, get him to take it! Try for five hundred."

"Why me?" Reshetov asks startled, and even shies away.

Yura frowns. "Do it, man. You know him. You said so yourself. Here, take it."

Reshetov takes the painting and gazes at the Goddesses of Ganja for a long time. He too seems to be taking leave of them, and asking their forgiveness. Then he advances on the kiosk. Yura watches him go, licking his blueing, cracked lips. Kovrigin and Missing, meanwhile, seem to have little idea of where they are or what is going on. They stare intently at the ground, trying not to fall over.

After negotiating with Kirill, Reshetov returns, leaving the painting in the kiosk.

"He won't pay five hundred, but I think it got to him."

"What's he offering?"

"Two hundred."

Yura seems to me to be deeply offended and I imagine that

now he'll take the painting back, wrap it up warmly in its sheet and take it safely home.

"We-ell... ask him to at least give us three hundred for it," he says pathetically. "Haggle, Shura. Tell him the paints cost me more than that."

"I'll try," Reshetov says, going back.

"Never mind, Yura," Missing says, suddenly returning to his senses. "The best is yet to be. You'll magic up something way better than that."

"I don't think so..."

They settle on two hundred and seventy roubles, and the money is promptly spent on two bottles of the cheapest Zemskaya vodka, a bottle of beer, a loaf of grey bread, some cigarettes and a few packs of Chinese noodles. They open the vodka in the nearest private space, behind the building materials shop, and pass it round. The beer is a chaser. I join in a couple of times.

Now there is no recognising the artists. The turbid whiteness has gone from their eyes, their faces are flushed and wreathed in smiles. "That's better," Kovrigin sighs with relief. He's a short, forty-year-old man with a bushy red beard sticking out in every direction except down. Kovrigin sighs as though he has been holding in all the fumes of stale vodka since yesterday evening.

Missing endorses this perception. "Ye-es, I feel more human already."

They take one more gulp, and then Yura screws the cap back on. "Well, Shura, your place?"

"Where else?"

The artists head off towards the nine-storey blocks. Yura turns to me: "How about you?"

"Well, no," I say regretfully. "I have to go to work. Enjoy yourselves!"

"We will. Still... we've been at it for twelve days now... time to come back down to earth."

"Well, good luck with that too."

I watch them go. Now they're walking in a tight little group, carrying the bottles and food protectively. They've found something to talk about and are arguing heatedly. They hoot with laughter. They've come back to life.

5

My potato digging trip home may have fallen through, but fate bestows on me the joy of attending Sanya's farewell party.

No sooner have Lyokha and I come back to the hostel, tired and irritable as we usually are in the evenings, anticipating an empty, boring time before going to bed with an equally empty Monday off work to follow, than our neighbour comes barging in. His shaven head bears fresh scratches and he's half-drunk and considerably worked up.

"Look at that, mates." He slaps his bald head. "I leave tomorrow!"

"So soon?" Lyokha responds without any great sympathy, preparing to lie down.

"At fucking ten hundred hours tomorrow from the army registry, and then it's bye-bye, Sanya baby, we'll be sure to write!"

I decide to cheer him up: "Don't worry, you'll be back. I had two years of it and I'm still here."

"Well, fuck knows, you were just lucky," Sanya shrugs. He takes out a pack of Bond and offers one to me and Lyokha. He lights up and, sounding somehow more intelligent, says in a different voice, "They'll stick me in that railway carriage and take me off to who knows where. Nowadays it could be any-where. They may make me a slave somewhere in Chechnya, and next thing I'll be dumped in a pit."

"Don't, Sanya, you're being too..."

"Oh, forget it!" He crushes his half-smoked cigarette in the ashtray and starts edgily disembowelling the filter. "My mates'll be here in a minute and we'll have a piss-up. The wife is getting stuff ready in there with the girls. We'll have a send-off."

Hearing there's going to be a booze-up, Lyokha changes his mind about lying down and starts pacing the room restlessly. I'm sitting at the table, smoking one of his wonderful Bonds and mechanically squashing bits of stale bread with my fingernail. No suitable words of comfort suggest themselves, only, for some reason, jeers and derision. Sanya meanwhile is getting himself in even more of a state, imagining the goings-on after he's safely out of the way.

"So I get sent off to die there, and Lena can do as she likes back here. I can see she can't wait to get rid of me!"

"Oh, I don't know," I protest. "Wives do sometimes wait faithfully."

"You reckon? In films maybe. I know women. She'll hold out for a month and then be off to get her itch sorted. I don't care, but if I find out, I'll be back here with my assault rifle and she'll know all about it!" Sanya takes another cigarette. "Who else have I got, anyway? Just Lena and little Seryozha. My God, if I find out that bitch..."

He's about to repeat the bit about the assault rifle, unless he's managed to think up something even scarier in the meantime, but just at this moment a trampling of feet is heard in the corridor and loud, obviously drunk, voices.

"Hey, mates!" He jumps to his feet and looks out into the corridor. "Hey, good to see you!"

"Hey, hey, Sanya! Fuck you!"

An avalanche of ten or so people burst into our room bearing bottles. They all head for Sanya's shaven head and tap it, shouting things like: "Soldier boy! Hang yourself quick before you get fucked! Sanya, we're here to get slaughtered! God, look at you, you bald bastard!"

When they've quite finished mocking the new conscript, his friends (and Lyokha and I with them) move to the room next door. A table has already been laid there which stretches from the window to the door. Bottles, large bowls of sauerkraut and sliced cucumber, salads, pickled herring, boiled potatoes. There's a smell of roast meat, although there's no sign of it on the table. I stand among this crowd of noisy, tipsy men and wait to be invited to sit down.

Sanya's wife, Lena, and two of her friends who also live in the hostel are busy setting out the plates, moving dishes from one place to another, anxiously counting something. Eighteen-month-old Seryozha is jumping about in his playpen and whining.

"Right, let's get going!" Sanya urges his guests. "Let's get the first one down."

There aren't enough chairs for everybody so I bring in two of ours. I feel quite light-headed already, as if I've drunk half a tumblerful. This is promising to be a very lively party. There's masses to drink. As if that wasn't enough, one of Lena's friends (whose name I don't know) from the fourth floor is really quite pleasant. I've had my eye on her for a long time, and today I've got a chance to meet her, and perhaps more than that, if I'm lucky.

Like most half-drunk people who are feeling anxious, Sanya is excited one moment, almost cheerful, and the next he's moody and brooding. His mates don't allow him to brood too much, though, and every couple of minutes they slap him on his shaven head, or his shoulders, or his back, supposedly cheering him up. Someone who is particularly active is a big, hulking fellow with a stupid face which seems not to register anything. He's sitting to the left of the birthday boy, and whenever Sanya starts looking gloomy he gives him a great wallop and then, chortling with laughter, fills up the glasses again saying, "Come on, man, drink! You aren't going to have much fun out there!"

Each person, as they clink glasses with him, feels he has to come up with some nonsense, like: "The way you manage your send-off is the way you'll serve in the army!" Or: "Two years, Sanya, is no sentence at all. Think of the lads who're locked up!" And more of that ilk.

To Sanya's right is his wife. She has dressed for the occasion and put on make-up, but her face is spoiled by the scared, anxious expression of a battered wife. And sitting directly opposite me is the girl from the fourth floor. I look mainly at her, trying to find a reason to talk to her. Almost immediately one of Sanya's mates starts making up to her. He's a stocky guy with red hair and bruised knuckles on his right hand; he has a headset round his neck and his T-shirt has English lettering. He keeps endlessly saying something to her in a booming whisper. He's smiling, and she's listening, and smiling and nodding. My ardent gazes evoke zero response.

Lyokha hasn't a care in the world. He just ladles grub on to his plate and guzzles it at top speed. How much does he think he's going to be able to drink with his stomach that full? And it looks as though the party is just getting started. An enormous bowl of meat has appeared, which results in even more intensive alcohol intake. Every three minutes there's a toast and somebody slaps Sanya on the head, heads jerk up as glasses are emptied down people's throats.

Seryozha, a small copy of his violent father, agitated by the noise and all the people, periodically does his best to climb out of the playpen. His mother feeds him another titbit and he settles down for a time.

Everybody is hammered in under an hour. Sanya is forgotten. He is dozing awkwardly on his chair and his pitiable, bluish head has fallen to the table. He tries a couple of times to regain consciousness, half raises his head, and looks cadaverously round at his guests before finally crashing out. He's no longer upset that these are his last hours of civilian life; or that the big stud with the stupid face is brazenly making advances to his wife; that one of his mates in all the commotion has pocketed his cassette; or that his guests have so completely fugged the room up that Seryozha is coughing and spluttering. Nothing is upsetting Sanya. For him, everything is just fine.

There 's no general conversation at the table: people talk in twos and threes, and are also drinking in their own sad little groups. The gingernut with the headset round his neck has his arm round the girl from the fourth floor. He's tickling her behind the ear and she appears to be enjoying it. She screws up her eyes and giggles and rubs up against him in return like a stray cat. Perhaps she doesn't fancy this red-haired man in the slightest, but he quite clearly is a city boy, and she no less clearly comes from a village, so who knows? He may fall in love with her and marry her and she'll live happily ever after, just as she dreamed in those sleepless nights in her squeaking hostel bed.

It's time for a smoking break. I extract two cigarettes from somebody's pack of Soyuz-Apollo and go out into the corridor.

The corridor is deserted and gloomy. Half the light bulbs have burnt out, and the other half are blinking with a bluish light. There's a draught. It must be windy outside.

I smoke one cigarette and tuck the other behind my ear. I walk towards the former kitchen. From behind people's doors I hear the sounds of life. There's a shoot-out on someone's telly; furious yelling where people are quarrelling, slightly muffled by an upbeat song from a cassette recorder; the crying of children who just won't go to sleep; the clatter of dishes being cleared from the table; more swearing. It's what people do in the evening. Soon it will be night and they'll go and lie down on their beds, and tomorrow there will be tomorrow. Tomorrow, they'll be faced with Monday.

A few steps before I reach the kitchen, I stop, and assume the air of an irresistible daredevil. I stick what remains of the cigarette in the corner of my mouth and narrow my eyes a little. Nonchalant, debonair, I advance. Oh, disaster.

Disaster, disaster. The ex-kitchen is empty, cold and desolate without her. The windowsill is unoccupied. The girl with the auburn hair is not sitting on it, not looking out the window. Her foot, jiggling in time to the music from her stereo, is not there.

Disaster. Today is the perfect day and this is the very moment when I am ready, willing and able to go up, say hello, and enchant her. At this moment I could be vivacious and articulate and boundlessly sociable.

I perch myself on the windowsill, finish my cigarette, throw the melted filter into the dry sink (for some reason the tap has long ago been welded down). I spit bits of tobacco at the wall tiles and pick with a fingernail at the paint peeling off the windowsill. My positive impulse has been crushed, dissipated by the emptiness of this former kitchen. What should I do now? Go back to the party, to Sanya's mates? I'm not in the mood. I know another five drinks will see me crash out and most days I wouldn't turn that down, but right now...

The truth of the matter is that I haven't really had that much experience with girls, and mostly it wasn't all that great because I was drunk. The first time was with a girl in my class I had fancied since we were in fourth grade. She used to go out with boys more grown-up than me, but I waited for an opportunity. I got it at the school-leaving party, after the certificates had been distributed and the traditional dance followed by a disco with secret drinking. She and I went up on to the roof. It was dark and very warm. June. She was wearing a pale lilac dress. I had no idea what you did or how you did it. At that time I hadn't even seen any erotic films yet. She was just curious to see how a boy with no experience would do it. I tried to undress her. My hands were shaking, I was damp with sweat and panting. She smiled, didn't resist, but didn't give me any help either. She was just amusing herself for a while. Neither of us said anything. We could hear the music playing downstairs in the assembly hall. I could barely control myself; I was ready to explode like a two-ton bomb. Then a seam snapped on her dress, she pushed me away, I stumbled and almost fell. She sniggered derisively and went back to the dance. I felt like jumping off the roof, but didn't. I trailed back home, holding my cock convulsed in my trousers and hurting from over-excitement.

After that I had some attempts, which went better, but none of it was really what I wanted or was looking for. At seventeen what I was looking for, what I was sure existed and could be found, was love. What seventeen-year-old doesn't believe that? Gradually, though, I got wiser and came to see that in reality love was something to be avoided like the plague. Love could really throw you to the wolves, as people around me demonstrated only too well. At first there's real happiness, a period of sweet bliss, when you're flying higher than the clouds, but then... Love is like the last glass of home-brew poured out of the barrel: the first two or three gulps are great, really strong and enjoyable, but after that you hit the sickening, bitter dregs. You're better off not trying it.

Sometimes, though, I'm convinced that any moment I'm going to fall head over heels in love with somebody and throw myself headlong to the wolves. It's as if I'm seventeen again. It's like an illness. I keep looking for the girl for whom I'll climb every mountain, or before whom I'll spread out like a fragrant lake. Only exist, only glance at me! I dream of soft hands, fathomless eyes, lips, and all the rest. I dream like this but feel I must be a complete freak. Lyokha tries to reassure me though. He says the main component of freakishness is a shortage of money. If you've got it there's no end to what you can do, but if you haven't you should just keep your head down. I agree, of course, but my heart doesn't. My heart has been poisoned by fairy tales about romance and rendezvous and bunches of flowers, declarations of love and ambiguous rejections. In short, all kinds of scag that only fucks you up.

I blame my parents. Of course I do. Who else? Mine are intellectuals, although, at least, only first generation. "Culture workers" educated at a culture college. The so-called 'sixties generation. As was fashionable at the time, they graduated from their culture college and went out from the big city to spread culture in a young national republic. Until they were over fifty they believed they were leading a good life. They were certain that if they worked well in their small corner, everything else would fall into place. For a while, fate was on their side.

They brought me up the same way, in accordance with their principles. Even now I know that poem, "What is good? What is bad?", by heart. No doubt until the day I die I'll have ringing in my ears such aphorisms as, "Hard work is good for the soul" and "What you keep, you lose: what you give away, comes back a hundredfold!" I heard them a thousand times from my father and mother, and once even tried to act in accordance with them. I tried to be an honest, considerate and good boy. Hee-hee, practically a girl. Families who knew us were pleasantly surprised, happy for my parents, and held me up as an example to their hooligan sons.

Almost until I was sixteen, street-life held no attraction for me. Having diligently sat through my lessons without under-standing much, but nevertheless writing down in detail everything my teachers said, having been on the receiving end during the breaks of a very fair ration of kicks and punches, I'd hurry home. I read books: silly, deceptive books. Jules Vernes, Walter Scott, Mayne Reid: you name it, I read it. I dissolved in wonder watching "Film Travel Club" on TV, and collected every issue of *Around the World*. At school and down in the courtyard the other lads called me a creep and a bedwetter; I was no good at fighting. I thought fighting was bad, unworthy of a human being, and preferred to fall down as soon as I was punched, to curl up in a ball and cover my face in order not to get bruised. I didn't want my parents to be upset by finding out I was getting beaten up. I longed to be friends with a girl, but didn't have it in me to take the first step. I was afraid of being laughed at, and anyway, I knew no one was likely to want a boyfriend who was a creep. Girls preferred boys who were strong, bold, and daring.

In ninth grade I started trying to change. I was sixteen, almost an adult, and it really was time to grow up. But you can't just suddenly change one fine day. A couple of times I did fight back, and was totally pulverised. I tried to make friends with a girl I liked in a parallel class, but she looked at me as if I were an ape, which suddenly talked.

I remember, only too well, going along on Saturdays to the school disco, trying not to fall foul of drunk, rough boys. I would press myself into a corner of the assembly hall, listening to the romantic pop songs and watching the girls dancing to the colourful flashing of the disco lights. Beautiful, unearthly creatures, they were, in leather mini-skirts, tight jeans, bare-shouldered, their young bodies writhing so enticingly. I was young too, and I cringed in my corner, afraid that the rough boys might spot me, drag me out into the corridor and, just to warm up before spending the night with girls, or to show off in front of them, punch me in the face. It did happen, often. Yet every Saturday I still went to the disco.

How I got myself ready for it! How I watched to make sure mother ironed the crease in my trousers properly. I brushed my coat, wiped my trainers with a cloth, rubbed ointment into the pimples on my forehead, smoothed and sleeked my hair. My mother was proud of me, and complimented me, and smiled so lovingly. She was sure I had a girlfriend. Hee-hee. And how I came back home, alone, through dark courtyards, almost running. Everywhere I could hear the excited shouting of young people having fun, while I was alone, angry, cowardly, but also aroused. Almost more than I could bear.

Sanya's party is over. They got pissed very efficiently, in the spirit of the times. The head of the table, which is still set and where some of the food survives, presides over a number of unfinished glasses. He is slumped in his earlier position with his head down. Lena is rocking her small son, who is listlessly trying to give her a hard time. She is looking at the wall and singing in a whisper, "Hush, little baby, lie very still". Two of Sanya's pals are still here: the big guy with the stolid look on his ugly face and some other type of whom all I can see is the tractor-tyre soles of his army beetlecrushers. Both have collapsed on the matrimonial bed and are wheezing loudly.

Without more ado I sit down, pour the leftover vodka from three glasses into one, and impale a slice of cucumber on a fork. Lena gives me a weary, unfriendly glance and again stares at the wall, intoning her nonsensical lullaby.

Of course, common decency requires that I should get up and leave, and to be a real knight in shining armour, I should shake Sanya's pals back to consciousness and take them with me. But I need a drink. Half an hour of moronic thinking and remembering has left me stone-cold sober and I need to get plastered again.

I glean another thirty grams or so for my glass and down it. I bite into a piece of cabbage and gaze mindlessly out the window. Against a black background I see the small room reflected, and me, munching.

"Aaargh..." Sanya grunts, coming to once more and ponderously raising his head. "O-oh-oh, shit..."

He looks around, rolling his bloodshot eyes. He straightens himself up on the chair and groans again, but louder this time, more meaningfully. "Oh, fuck."

"Keep it down, will you?" his wife shushes him.

In an instant Sanya is bristling,

"Aw, shut yer face!"

Then he notices me:

"Any drink left?"

"Well..." I shrug. "There was some left in the glasses."

"Gimme vodka," Sanya says, turning to his wife.

"It's finished. You've drunk the lot."

"Listen, you...!"

"In the fridge."

He tries to stand up but trips on the chair leg and all but up-ends. Without needing to be asked, I open the ancient fridge and take out one of three bottles, which perspire instantly. I move nearer to my host, fill two glasses, and look over invitingly to Lena. She curls her lip and turns away.

"Well, here's to ... everything!" Sanya jabs his glass against mine.

"Sure..."

Two slugs are enough to get him totally wrecked again. He clutches his shaven head, becomes maudlin and starts whining, "Look at me! It's all over. There's no getting away from it, no escape. That's it! A flock of sheep to the slaughter... Who goes into the army nowadays? What kind of army is it, for Chrissakes, what kind of motherland?! I... I don't wanna croak! Of course I don't... I don't wanna!"

His little son gives him more vocal support, Lena trying in vain to distract him. He wants to go over to Sanya, who looks at his son and heaves him out of his mother's arms.

"There, little Seryozha, see what it's come to. It's curtains for your dad! Tomorrow they'll put me in the train and take me away. And that's it! What's it for? It's curtains for your daddy, son!"

"That's enough!" Lena tries to take the child back.

Sanya elbows her in the chest:

"Get off, you bitch! It's all your fault, you cow!"

"My fault?! Well, who was it knocked me about every night when I was pregnant? Who was that, eh? Give him back here, you scumbag. Give him back!"

Sanya thumps her ear. I take the bottle from the table and quietly make my exit. Behind me, passions rage. Seryozha is in a paroxysm of tears, Sanya roaring, Lena screaming. No change there, then.

I think I might quietly finish the vodka off in my room and fall asleep, but no such luck. Lyokha has dragged some of Sanya's buddies into our room and they're sprawled over both beds. Lyokha is lying with his arms round some scary-looking, bear-like individual and three others have occupied my bed. To boot, there's a sizeable pool of puke on the floor.

I wander off to Ksyukha and Pavlik, thinking we could finish the remains of the vodka. Pavlik can tell me about the latest book he's read and perhaps after that we can think of something else to do. I have a feeling that, no matter how much I drink today, I'm going to be completely incapable of crashing out.

I knock, adopt a suitably cheerful expression, and hold the bottle as if I've brought a bunch of tulips, but in reply hear Ksyukha's ratty, "Who's there? We're in bed!" She sounds irritated and breathless.

I shy back from the door, the smile fading from my face. They're screwing, the shits. I look round helplessly. The corridor is empty. It's very quiet, not a soul to be seen. I wish there was somebody. I'd be glad to drink with anybody, but the corridor is empty with only the light bulbs flickering impersonally.

I take a swig out of the bottle of cloying, burning Gypsy Girl which Sanya has disguised as good quality Minus vodka and start off down to the first floor, to the one-time actor Waliszewski.

His room is a stinking hovel with a blanket over the window. The floor is covered with a deep layer of rubbish, and with every step something crunches and breaks under your feet.

"Ah, colleague!" The face of the master of this place furrows into a smile as he notices the bottle in my hand. "Come in, oh, come in! Delighted to see you, my dear boy!"

There still remain in this old soak, who has all but degenerated into a dirty animal, a few sparks of the old Waliszewski, who for thirty years in succession acted the roles of the calculating lover, the dashing hussar, the progressive party activist, the record-breaking factory worker, and other mythical figures. He was in a league of his own in our theatre. Waliszewski is said to have had hordes of lady admirers. He was bombarded with flowers not only on stage but also in his private life. The stairwell of his apartment block was written all over with lipstick; and I heard a legend that some had even poisoned themselves because of him.

Oh yes, Waliszewski had his lady admirers. He had a wife and children. But he loved young men. He belonged to the generation, which acted alongside the refugees who returned after the revolution from Harbin and, naturally, caught it from them.

Today, however, Waliszewski is just another alky, and a burned-out one at that, like most of the people I know. His drinking sprees last for two or three months at a time, and are followed by a couple of weeks of crystal-clear sobriety. At these times Waliszewski goes off to see his daughter, puts on his ancient but once expensive suit, and shaves every day. Throughout, he behaves like a true patriarch of our theatre, condescending to everyone from his great height, speaking slowly, drawling his words. He comes into Victor Arkadievich's office and discusses his stage comeback, and rummages through plays, looking for one suitable for a gala performance. Then, however, something puts him off his stride, usually the arrival of his pension, and he quickly puts away his suit, disappears into this hostel room, and is again covered in stubble. The next drinking spree closes over his head.

He occasionally makes it outside and does the rounds of his friends, ex-lovers, and lady admirers, on the scrounge, but never shows up at the theatre while in this state. That doesn't stop him, when he's drunk, from going on and on about his long lost glory days!

A year or so ago a serious attempt was made to resuscitate him. Dubravin began rehearsals for a production of "The Gentleman", about an aged Casanova, I think, and at first everything went marvellously. Before long, however, Waliszewski started drinking again, began missing the read-throughs, and then walked out completely, accusing everybody of being amateurs and complaining that they were a pathetic parody of real artists.

"Do take a seat, Roman, do take a seat. Over here," the former calculating lover fusses a little flirtatiously, sweeping the scraps off the table. "Here I am, alas, spending the evening in my own company. Mm, hmm, ah well..."

Waliszewski is just moderately sozzled, a condition which means he feels a strong urge to drink some more, rather as I do myself.

"A little bread for us, a little sauerkraut," the old man sets out our nibbles. "And as luck would have it, I've just boiled some eggs. I prefer them soft-boiled."

"Great," I nod, filling two cloudy glass receptacles with Gypsy Girl.

We hastily chink glasses without a word.

The sauerkraut is warm and not fresh, I have difficulty swallowing what I had stuffed in my mouth. Waliszewski doesn't bother with eating. He gazes at me with sad, affectionate eyes, preparing to start his usual spiel. I refill the glasses.

"You know, Roman," he sighs when the glasses are again empty, "You know, it's very hard being old."

I mumble my agreement.

"No, don't think I'm complaining!" Waliszewski shakes his head emphatically. "I'm not complaining, but... Youth... Ah, youth is synonymous with happiness! Believe me, my young friend, and appreciate it, appreciate being young!"

He only has this one topic of conversation. Well, to be fair, two: sighing about being young, and remembering his own tempestuous life and fame. You don't even really need to say anything in reply: the old geezer can rattle on for hours at a time, his eyes half closed, his head with its long, unwashed locks of thin, grey hair thrown back. All he really needs is a drink. Today too everything runs its appointed course, a monodrama of which I am the sole member of the audience.

"Oh, how I used to act, dear boy, and what a life I lived! At full throttle, breaking down every barrier, transgressing every boundary. Oh, yes!" Waliszewski says, enraptured by the memory of himself as he was those many, many years ago. "You have to break through those obstacles, every last one of them! Break free and fly, fly, fly! Alas that's something you will never do. No, no, young man! I can see, I can see you have been weary from your very childhood. You, dear boy, have weak batteries! Alas... um, yes, well... Oh, you should have seen me in my prime. For my public I was a king, a god. I reigned in the theatre! But, unfortunately, I too grew weary. There is a limit to everything. No, no, I'm not complaining! I don't regret a thing! I burned the candle at both ends. I drained life's chalice to the dregs fearlessly, never holding back, and now I have smashed that lovely vessel like a Guards officer! Yessir! I have smashed it to smithereens!"

I nod mechanically, topping up the little glasses periodically and inviting him with a gesture to drain them. Waliszewski gulps it down with abandon, as if to demonstrate how he has drained the chalice of his life.

Until five in the morning Sanya and his pals get increasingly pissed in the hostel. They run out to fetch more vodka, they yell, a few scuffles break out. They drink themselves stupid now in the raw recruit's room now in ours.

Coming back from Waliszewski, I mainly just sit on the bed, not participating in the general merry-making. I simply couldn't drink any more, but also can't manage to crash out.

Lyokha, stupefied from eating and drinking too much, keeps picking at his new pals, arguing with them, and is lucky not to get thumped. Finally they all just lie down wherever, and at half past nine go to see off the new conscript. Lyokha and I, of course, stay behind. We hear Sanya in the corridor obsessively repeating that he's a ram being led to the slaughter. It sounds as if he tries to go back to his room, but his chortling chums push him on towards the stairs. Seryozha is whimpering monotonously, and Lena says something quietly, apparently asking her husband to calm down.

A whole day in the hostel with no money, without even anything to smoke, is absolute hell. To make matters worse, it's raining outside. You don't feel like going anywhere in weather like this. Anyway where would you go? Who's going to be pleased to see me? I lie on the bed, trying to doze, or drinking tasteless water from a plastic bottle and smoking fag-ends out of the ashtray.

Waliszewski looks in a few times to see if we're boozing. In the end Lyokha gets ratty and tells him just to fuck off. He nods his head understandingly, chews his lips, and departs.

Towards evening I feel an urge to talk.

"Hey," I say, turning to my roommate. "Wouldn't it be cool if they really did put him out of his misery."

"Who?"

"Sanya, of course."

"Oh, fuck him!" Lyokha turns over, grunting and making the mesh of the bed squeak painfully. "Who needs him? Lena wouldn't shed any tears, he doesn't seem to have any folks. It's completely immaterial whether he lives or dies."

"Yeah, I guess so."

6

Every single day somebody comes in the service entrance of the theatre trying to sell something. Witch-like old women offering thick, metre-long pigtails in plastic packets, old men with battered bentwood chairs, small-time traders offering cheap panels, paints, spare parts for the bus. Today, for instance, a drunk who's always hanging around the theatre brought in a headless, badly plucked goose. He argued with the security woman in the corridor and burst into the greenroom.

"'Evening everybody!" he exclaims, bowing in all directions. "Everybody well I hope."

The actors respond offhandedly. They've already changed into frock coats and evening dresses and they're firmly made up. They've become the gentry of a century ago and right now couldn't be more distant from this sordid, unwashed little man off the street. He fails to take this in and offers his goods in a practised way, as if they were ordinary people:

"Guys, who'd like this excellent goose? Fresh as can be." The trader half opens his bag. "A really fat goose, almost five kilos! Roast it and you'll be out of this world, – m-mm!"

Kruglova's husband is an actor, but not in costume because he isn't acting today. He is tempted to go over and check it out but Kruglova grabs his arm and hisses something.

Khrapchenko, an ageing dandy in a dazzlingly white summer suit and light white shoes, his hair in a quiff, walks around the greenroom, glancing contemptuously at the fellow. The others disdain even to look.

"Yours for a hundred, how about it?" the drunk continues his patter, inviting, cajoling. "We've got guests coming to dinner, it's the wife's birthday, and no money for the drinks... Have to sell this goose here. It's a good little goose, tender as can be. How about it? Will you take it?"

The first bell. They're due on stage any moment now. Khrapchenko, frowning, goes over to the man:

"Nobody needs your... Be off with you now, there's a good fellow."

The little man looks round the greenroom disheartened, sighs disconsolately, turns and leaves.

After the performance, when they've changed back into their everyday clothing and returned to ordinary life, hurrying to get on Uncle Gena's bus, a lot of them doubtless remember the goose and have second thoughts: "Oh dear, what have we turned down! Five kilos, or even if it was just four, for a hundred roubles – that's as cheap as you'll find anywhere. We should have borrowed money from the buffet, then we'd have had meat to eat. Oh dear, oh dear!"

It's been raining almost non-stop for over two days now, a drizzly, persistent October rain. I don't have an umbrella and try to take the bus to work.

The spacious orange LIAZ buses have almost disappeared from the streets, and instead there are little PAZ buses and old Icaruses from the factories. It means their drivers can earn a bit on the side during the day, standing in for the buses of the impoverished passenger transport company which are waiting to be repaired or out of fuel. PAZ and Icarus buses display a warning in large letters: "No concessions!" The old women at the bus stops curse when they see them, and patiently wait for the ordinary, non-commercial buses, but these are rare nowadays. I wait for them too, trying to keep out of the rain beneath the roof of the bus shelter. I haven't got a kopek to spare, and walking to the theatre is really not on: I'd get soaked to the skin. Minusinsk may not be a big city but it's fiendishly elongated. On the LIAZ buses you have at least some chance of travelling without having to pay, talking the conductor round, but on the commercial ones they collect the fare when you get on, and most often it's some ex-boxer who's deaf to pleas and entirely prepared to throw out a pushy freeloader. He just repeats the same answer: "The fare is five roubles. Don't delay the bus, let people get on". He gives you a look as if to say, any moment now you'll wheedle yourself a punch in the face.

"Oh, there's one now, I think!"

"At last, thank heavens." The old ladies stir themselves.

On the opposite side of Labour Street a lopsided LIAZ crawls along, shaking and clattering like a tin can tied to a cat's tail.

"It'll be turning in just a moment," a desiccated old lady sighs with relief, leaning on her stick. She's standing almost directly under the streams of water flowing off the bus shelter roof, afraid of not getting on to the bus quickly enough.

"We've a wait yet," another woman, a bit livelier and fatter, grunts. "That's an eight. It'll do the rounds of the Trade Centre and then go on to the filling station. If we're lucky, it might be back in half an hour."

"Oh dear, oh dear."

"No, it isn't. That isn't the eight, it's a nine. You're just upsetting people," an elderly, almost ancient, man demurs. "Our nerves are in tatters as it is."

This starts up a lethargic argument, which helps to kill time. I don't get involved, although I clearly saw that the LIAZ was a number nine. As long as the bus doesn't fall to pieces in the next few minutes, we should be able to get on it very shortly and go.

Naturally, it's already packed with people at the terminus. The passengers are mostly pensioners, so inside the bus is that specific smell you get of old men and women. It's a suffocating mixture of heart drops, stale sweat, lavender, and damp, musty clothing.

I make my way into the middle of the bus where, as usual, it's less crowded. No sooner am I settled and looking out the window than I hear the voice of the conductress. She's arguing with somebody. Perhaps they've forgotten their pensioner's card or just don't want to pay. Soon it'll be me quarrelling with her.

Right beside me is a nice-looking girl on a single seat. She's wearing a light blue raincoat with a special crushed effect and her gingery hair has been lavishly back-combed to make her look taller. I try to distract myself by looking at her clean, smooth little face, for the present so unlike the faces of all the pensioners around us.

The bus moves slowly, stopping occasionally at bus stops and traffic lights, while all the time the conductress is coming nearer and nearer. She's relentlessly pushing her way past corpulent bodies and bony bodies, checking concession cards, collecting fares. On her bosom she has a pouch for money, and fixed to the strap is a roll of the old Soviet-times tickets from the days when we had cash collection boxes in buses and passengers, after honestly dropping in four kopeks, would help themselves to a ticket.

I ready myself for the fray, moving my gaze from the conductress to the girl and then out of the window. I try to look casual, unworried; then, unassailably fierce in the hope that the conductress will decide not to risk tangling with me.

But she does, poking me hard in the back.

"Has everybody here really got a ticket?"

I say nothing, and stare at a smear of dried dirt on the window.

"Young man, have you paid?"

"Yes."

"Then show me your ticket."

I sigh and turn to face the conductress. She has an edgy, tired expression, and bags of flab under her cheeks. She looks like an aggressive lapdog.

"I'm sorry," I begin pathetically. "I have no money and I have to get to work."

"Then walk."

"It's raining, and I'm late. I'm sorry."

We stand facing each other, hating each other, both waiting for something. What can she actually do? Grab hold of me and demand three roubles? In the meantime a dozen people will get off the bus who'd have paid up without making trouble. It's not as if she can turn me over to the police: I'd just push her aside and run away. She has no option but to retreat and continue down the bus, sounding even more cross as she shouts, "Any more fares? Buy your tickets now, please! You don't have to shove your card in my face, I'm not blind!"

The girl with the bouffant hair looks at me with interest, as if I've just accomplished something extraordinary. I smirk at her in response, as if to say, "One-nil to me!"

My father came to see me on Thursday. Lyokha and I were still asleep at nine in the morning. It was the weather, very soporific. It made you want to carry on sleeping. The wind was beating on the window and spiteful raindrops were pattering on the glass in a kind of lullaby.

He rapped, as always not hard but distinctly, with his knuckles. In my sleep I first took this for the rain attacking with renewed force, then woke up, jumped out of bed, and opened the door.

"Hello!"

"Hello! Still in bed?"

"Uhuh... Come in."

My father is holding a big old bag I bought some years ago before going off to study in St Petersburg. When I finished school I did make an effort. I enrolled at a building polytechnic thinking I'd meet a Leningrad girl and move the following year to study history at the Herzen Teacher Training Institute. That all fell apart when I was conscripted. I came back from the army in December 1991 with no further interest in St Petersburg or going to college. I just wanted to get back home. Now, my father uses the bag to bring me food.

"Your mother has put some things in there for you, some pies, a rabbit, some other bits and pieces. Have you got potatoes?"

"Oh, yes, plenty," I reply, dressing hastily. "Take your coat off, sit down. Let's have a cup of tea." I put the kettle on.

Lyokha turns over in bed, the mesh squeaking.

"How are you getting on?" my father asks in a half-whisper.

"Oh, much the same. Sorry I didn't make it on Monday. I couldn't come up with the fare."

"Um, yes. We need to get on with digging the potatoes. The forecast is for frost. If they get frosted we'll be in trouble."

Father takes fifty roubles from the breast pocket of his coat. "Here, we've managed to borrow some while we wait for the pension to arrive."

"Thanks."

The kettle starts stirring. I put some fresh tea in the teapot and my father continues quietly, "I would dig them by myself as mother isn't well, but unfortunately my eczema has just got worse." He raises large, knotty hands with dark red scabs on the sores. "We thought we'd come into town today. Mother has gone to the clinic about some prescriptions because her medicine's run out, and I've come round to see you."

I sigh in response, feeling both sympathetic and guilty.

"How are you getting along?" my father asks. "How are you eating?"

"Oh, fine." I try to sound upbeat. "We're not starving. Admittedly, there's a hold up with the food vouchers, but they promise they'll be issued any day now. We have performances every day, Kuprin's 'The Garnet Bracelet' is doing well, playing to almost full houses every day."

"Mother has been awarded a citation certificate for her concert on Schoolteachers' Day. Apparently somebody was there from the regional education office and liked it."

My parents work in a village school. Mother gives singing lessons and conducts a dance circle, and my father teaches drawing.

"Great." I try to be pleased to hear it. "Give her my congratulations!"

The kettle is boiling. I pour the boiling water into the teapot.

"Now we need to get back home as soon as we can," my father says. "We don't like leaving the house. We asked Valentina Stepanovna to keep an eye on it, but all the same. The Petrovs had a calf stolen during the night."

"Really?"

"They hit the dog with a pole and it hid in its kennel. Then they calmly led the calf out through the back yard. The old people were afraid to go out. They would just kill them and that would be that."

"Did they see who did it?"

"How could they? Anyway, everybody is intimidated."

We drink the hot tea in little gulps. "By the way, don't forget the pies. They should still be warm. Mother made them this morning."

"Great," I nod. "Thank you."

The room gradually fills with light. The sun breaks through the banks of thunderclouds and stares in our window. "Today looks like being mild," my father says, cheering up. "There's a breeze from the south and the sky is clear. Perhaps it'll stay warm."

"I'll be sure to come next Monday," I say definitely. "We should get the potatoes sorted in a day."

"Depending on the weather. If it sheets with rain there's no way we can dig them."

We drink our tea and smoke. "Well, I must be off." My father gets up. "Oh, yes. Mother asked me to collect your jars. The last of the tomatoes are ripening, all very wrinkled. She wants to make chutney."

I unpack the food and put the plastic bags, empty jars and lids into the bag while my father says things which he doesn't need to but which are good to hear. "Stew the rabbit with potatoes the way you like it. Mother was going to do it herself but ran out of time with the baking."

"Yes, I'll do that. Thank you. Let me see you out."

We walk down the corridor to the stairs. "Should I bring you the TV set?" my father asks. "You must get bored."

"No, no," I rush to decline the offer. "What about you? I have people around me here all the time. It's not that bad."

We go down to the hostel yard. It isn't raining, there's a feeble breeze, and small, ragged clouds dot the sky.

Redhead, our old Moskvich-412, is waiting by the porch, her orange paint faded with the years, her bodywork scratched in places, and there are a few dents. The car is almost fifteen years old and the meter is clocking up the second hundred thousand kilometres. Redhead has aged markedly in the last three years. Instead of the comfortable garage where she used to reside in the old days in Kyzyl, she now stays out in the open by the fence. My father has plans to build her a garage, but there are many obstacles. Cement is expensive, planking hard to come by. The sawmill in the village isn't working, and his health is not that good. His time and strength are given mainly to the vegetable garden and the greenhouses where he grows vegetables for sale.

"Well, so long, my friend," my father says with a positive smile, holding out his hand.

I shake the rough hand carefully. It's a bit swollen from the eczema, but still strong. "Till Monday," I promise. "Say hello to Mum."

He nods, climbs into Redhead, and presses the starter. The engine makes a dry clicking noise but doesn't start.

"Oh, oh, oh," my father sighs. "The contacts have got damp. It just rains and rains."

He opens the bonnet, cleans something with a needle-point file, and turns the ignition on again. This time the engine doesn't just start, it roars. My father hastily slams the bonnet and shouts, "We snagged the exhaust pipe again. The patch must have come off, but we'll make it home all right and I'll sort it out there. Good luck!"

"See you."

Sneezing and coughing, like a worn out, exhausted animal, Redhead reluctantly reverses in the yard and heads off through the puddles, bumping over the defective asphalt.

"Well?" my roommate enquires languidly from his bed. "Did your old man bring any readies?"

"Fifty."

"Could be worse. Party time?"

"It's for my ticket," I explain. "To go back to the village."

"The ticket won't cost that much."

"Well, but I need to buy razor blades too. Look at the beard I've grown. And we haven't got soap or toothpaste."

"Knock it off," Lyokha sits down on the bed, scratching energetically. "That can wait. Let's get a litre of Gypsy Girl. How about it, Rom?

I try to resist. I don't really like drinking in the morning, and I have to work later. There's a performance. Also, I'm reluctant to spend the money like this.

"With this meat, like classy, civilised human beings, eh, Rom?" my roommate persists. "We'll tidy the room, set the table. We can take it easy until four. I'll get it for you. It'll be great!"

I take out the money.

"Tell them, under a litre! I need sixteen roubles change. All right?"

There's a place nearby where they sell quite decent Gypsy Girl. The price is the same everywhere, twenty-five roubles a half-litre. It's all very organised. The whole city is studded with outlets where you can buy cheap booze around the clock. It's appreciable competition for the legal monster supplier, "Minal" (the "Minusinsk Alcohol"). It may all be part of the same syndicate, only targeting different segments of the population.

I'm in a good mood. To hell with the money, the razor blades and toothpaste. Drink comes first. The room is lit up with bright light and it's warm. The eternally restless dust specks whirl in golden spirals. I prepare the rabbit. In theory it should be stewed in a casserole in the oven, but you can simply boil it up in a saucepan on the stove. It doesn't taste quite the same, but it's still delicious.

When everything is going just the way you want it, when it all seems too good to be true, expect something bad in the near future. People have good reason to spit over their left shoulder to avert the evil eye, and to keep repeating, "God willing", "If nothing goes wrong". People are afraid of being too happy about anything, of anticipating anything nice. I've learnt from experience that if you're too pleased you can expect to be miserable very soon. If you find a coin in the street, you're likely to lose ten times more within a couple of days. If things are just okay, that's good enough.

I tidy the room up, and even sweep the floor. As I am coming out of the washroom with a pile of clean plates I run into a bleary-eyed, grumpy Pavlik.

"Hello there!" For some reason even meeting Pavlik makes me happy today. "How's things?"

"Oh, could be worse. Don't suppose we've got hot water today?"

"Nope. Fancy a drink?"

"When?" Pavlik's bleariness and grumpiness evaporate.

"How about now? Lyokha has just gone to get the Gypsy Girl, we've got food, what more could we need? Let's do it!"

"Thanks!" he nods and smiles. "I'll just sluice down my face." His face suddenly drops. "Oh, er... is it okay if I bring Ksyukha?"

Oh God, anything but that. I'd forgotten about Ksyukha. I shrug indeterminately:

"Sure, I suppose so... bring her along..."

Pavlik smiles.

In life you need distractions, otherwise you'll go off your rocker. That's for sure. Life is too complicated for you to go on without distractions. You need to take every opportunity.

I don't watch television much, and read the newspapers only on and off. In the last three years I haven't got through a single book from cover to cover. I have no hobbies: I left them all behind when I was eighteen, when I went into the army.

What is the army? It's not just two years discarded God knows where or what for. The army is like the last rung on the ladder of bringing up the citizen. Kindergarten, school, and then the army. Nowadays, of course, it's all falling apart at the seams and the ladder may at any moment disintegrate into a pile of rotten wood. Who knows what kind of people will graduate into adult life after that. Most likely they'll be individualistic monsters with no sense of boundaries, who've never stared into the back of someone else's head, never marched in line, and who have no idea about being quiet in class, roll-calls, institutional meals. That's when the fun will start! Nowadays there are dozens like that. I wonder what it'll be like if everybody is like that!

In order not to lose their sense of identity, people think up interests, beliefs, games, festivals. They are all a defence against dissolving into the external world. I was fortunate. When I came back from the army I saw that my earlier toy interests were silly, laughable. All those notebooks with poems about autumn rain, the confiding in my diary, those files of the magazine *Around the World*, the home-made maps of the voyages of Columbus and the Crusades. All those attributes of a so-called inner world seemed dusty and pathetic, and I had no hesitation or regret about junking them. Only, I haven't been able to find anything to put in their place. Without defences life is hard, almost unbearable, and you feel like your environment could crush you at any moment.

Defences come in many forms. Stamp collecting, spider breeding, tattoos, gardening, drinking, girls, obsessive book reading. Many people make a defence out of their everyday problems. They see nothing beyond worrying about tomorrow's bread and butter, so that tomorrow they'll have the strength to carry on worrying. It's a completely mindless whirl. Their hobbies, their work, and the meaning of life are their three-in-one, their trinity. Hee-hee. When I was young I too spent a lot of time agonising about the meaning of life. I devoured quantities of philosophical gibberish, and even tried to come up with an answer of my own. I tried to devise theories. It's only recently I realised that the meaning of life lies in getting food. The means vary, but the end remains the same. A human being is not, by and large, the least bit different from the rest of the animal world. It was all very well for those philosophers to go on deliberating about hyper-spiritual matters when they knew tomorrow was safely provided for, and that there weren't going to be any problems with grub. There they sat in their soundproof studies, sipping their cups of coffee while a ten-course meal was being prepared for them in the kitchen. Searching for the meaning of life is the prerogative of callow youths and the well-fed. The rest of us have more urgent problems to address.

Lyokha takes his anorak off as I finish setting the table.

"Why the hell have you set four places?" he asks, puzzled.

"Pavlik and Ksyukha are looking in."

"What?!"

"It's just the way it's turned out," I say defensively. "I took the dishes to wash and ran into Pavlik..."

"You utter moron!" Lyokha sits down at the table, his mood spoiled. "There's enough grub and drink for just the two of us. Oh, well. How's the meat doing?"

"Nearly ready." I sit down too, munch a cucumber, and try to make him see sense. "Pavlik looks after us sometimes, so we can't just dump him now."

"Oh, forget it," Lyokha reaches for the bottle. "You've screwed up. Let's get one down."

No sooner have we done so than Pavlik arrives, accompanied, naturally, by Ksyukha. They've brought nearly half a bottle of Minus. The rabbit stew is just ready. I place the saucepan in the middle of the table.

"What a feast!" our lady hairdresser exclaims in delight. "What's the celebration?"

"Oh, just some food turned up, and a little money, so we're celebrating."

After the second toast we start talking more freely, at least, Pavlik does. Inevitably, he starts telling us all about the latest book he has read.

"It's a great read, guys, a great read! It's called *The Hellish Trinity* by Michel Sportиs. He's French. Haven't you heard of him? It's a bestseller, and the main thing is that it's based on documentary fact."

"You don't say..." Lyokha nods sourly, pouring out the next round and plainly less than happy about our visitors.

"Anyway, what it's about?" Pavlik starts in enthusiastically, talking rapidly and fairly incoherently. "There's this brother and sister, Jean and Valйrie, and they come from a pretty ordinary family, and their parents are pretty average civil servants. So, in other words, they live from one payday to the next. Jean, well he's a bit of a yob actually. He and his friends cannibalise cars. Valйrie, though, she's a promising young poetess, very pretty, and she enrols at art school. But then their father falls ill and has to give up his job and they haven't got any money and Valйrie has to become a model. Well and there she, so to speak, comes up against the seamy side of 'beautiful life'. All sorts of twisted horrors, restaurants, riotousness, perversions. She doesn't like all that. She dreams of beauty, of poetry, of Paris. The plot is set in some dreadful little town, a kind of Shitcreekville."

Without interrupting his narrative, Pavlik downs another glass along with the rest of us and takes a quick bite of something. I can see neither Lyokha nor Ksyukha are particularly interested in what he's saying and neither am I, but what else can we do? We let him rabbit on.

"Things get worse and worse for the family. Jean gets banged up in prison for a year for being in a fight, the father is bedridden. The mother is working as a secretary for some Algerian shark but she's not his mistress exactly, only... um..." Pavlik stalls, "Well, you know, this Algerian fucks, er, sleeps with her now and again. And then he looks at her one day and see she's looking really terrible. He thinks, 'What use is this forty-year old wreck to me?' She used to take trouble over her appearance, but now with everything that's happening... Well, anyway, the Algerian suggests she ought to leave. Of course, she bursts into tears: 'I've nowhere else to go! We're almost starving!' In other words, she tells him about all her problems and the Algerian, really just being very nasty, offers to let her stay on as a cleaner. Anyway, in the end mumsy kills herself because of all the hassle she's getting."

"Could we put on some music?" Ksyukha asks, noticing our cassette player.

"It's broken," Lyokha says straight away, looking round at it.

Pavlik is hurt. "Hang on, will you, let me finish! It's a very instructive story, this is. Anyway, Valйrie, like, meets this really smooth guy, Laurent Rйmy. He's nice, from an aristocratic family, a Sorbonne graduate. He left his parents to become a sculptor, a bohemian. Well, his parents didn't understand him, right. So anyway, they start living together, getting on, and Laurent gets this idea he's one of the chosen who are above everybody else. You know, like Raskolnikov."

"Oh, Christ," Lyokha utters, dismayed.

"No, listen! These are all documentary facts, it's almost a factual account!" To give added weight to what he's saying, Pavlik raises his finger. "Anyway, he and Valйrie start living together and having it off and philosophising at the same time, and decide France is a rotten country and the people are greedy pigs, and the whole world is shit. Except Australia, they reckon. They dream of heading off there, but of course they haven't got the readies." The narrator pauses to down another glass and, without time to eat anything, babbles on. "And then Jean turns up, you know, Valйrie's brother, and he has his own ideas: they ought to kill business sharks and take their money."

"How original!" I sneer, unable to restrain myself.

"Well, that's what really happened. Anyway, he had the right idea. The three of them work out this plan of how they're going to get 10,000 francs to take them to Australia. The plan is, Valйrie will pick up some rich ponce in a restaurant, they'll dine together, drink, and then Valйrie will invite him back to her place. Where her brother and Laurent Rйmy will be waiting!"

Again I burst out: "But this is just so hackneyed. Christ, it's laughable! I've seen twenty films along those lines."

"Hackneyed or not, they did in eight geezers like that," Pavlik persists. "But what's really interesting isn't even the plot, it's the author's digressions. You find out he's entirely on the side of these kids. He's saying that was the only way they had of getting on their feet. The way he describes these geezers they did in, they're all just complete bastards, just bloodsuckers living off other people. Incidentally, Valйrie and the lads do in that Algerian who made the mother drown herself. The author is completely on the side of the kids and against rich people, especially coloured ones. He puts it down in black and white that there are so many foreigners now, French kids don't feel France is their homeland any more."

"Yes, it's simply terrible the problems they're having over there now," Ksyukha chimes in. "Nowadays their films are mainly about blacks and Algerians and about them being completely out of control."

"Well, then," I enquire in order to keep the conversation going, "Did they get enough together to go to Australia?"

Pavlik sighs bitterly, as if it's personal friends of his we're talking about: "They ran out of time. They were caught, but at the trial a lot of people spoke in favour of clemency."

"You mean they only get one year each?"

"No, they all got life." Pavlik sadly eats one pie, helps himself to another and is about to take a bite, but instead says heatedly, "That book is right, absolutely right! If you like I can lend you it for a couple of days. You see, kids have no way out other than through killing. Just look at that family: the father worked and worked until he dropped and got pathetic benefits; when the mother grew old, she was thrown to the dogs. Jean, the young guy sees how disgusting that all is and is then faced either, if he's lucky, with repeating his father's pathetic life, or becoming a gangster. Valйrie wants to dedicate herself to art but is turned into a prostitute. The state itself is created in a way that pushes people into crime. The whole society is divided into these... into estates. Like in the forest, first there is the moss, all the homeless people, the beggars, and alkies; next comes the grass, the thistles – the workers, people like us; slightly higher are the shrubs, the officials, or all sorts of intellectuals, and they get to see a little sun. Mainly, though, the sun is reserved for the trees. Isn't that the way it is? The pine trees and birches are the sharks. What are those below to do? Cut down the trees, clear a space so they can see the sun!"

I'm astonished by this disquisition. I didn't think Pavlik had it in him. Most likely, of course, it's all in the book and he's just doing his usual parroting act.

"To move from the lowest to the highest is all but impossible," he continues. "If you try to push ahead legally, those around you will soon crush you. Nobody wants to make way. That means, the only way to rise is to clamber over corpses. Look how the gangsters did it in America! Al Capone, right? He came from shit and ended up ruling the entire United States. Those kids were absolutely right. First they forced them to fill out their cheque books, and then they chucked them in the sewers. "Did you enjoy your games, pal? Well, now it's bedtime!"

"Okay, let's drink to that," Lyokha says, raising his glass. "May all of us blades of grass get to see the sun!"

"We've got to do something!" Ksyukha responds in a resolute if somewhat tipsy voice. "Nothing ventured, nothing gained."

By half past three the booze is finished and Ksyukha and Pavlik have gone. Pavlik in leaving suggested smoking dope but we turned it down, or rather, postponed it till evening. We've got to work at the theatre, putting up the devil's own scenery, and it's plain dangerous if you're too smashed. It's best to get stoned after work.

When our guests have left, we lie on our beds. We're not feeling good. Our bodies are calling for more alcohol. Lyokha is whingeing:

"Why the hell did you have to drag them in, you ьberidiot? There was just the right amount for two."

I don't rise to the bait and he soon shuts up, just sighing despondently.

The empty saucepan is on the table, the dirty plates, heaps of scrupulously gnawed bones. The cockroaches and fruit flies are already at work in their realm.

We say nothing for twenty minutes or so and then I get pissed off.

"Hey, Lyokha," I call over. "Would you like to be a tree, though? A big sturdy, spreading oak?"

"Do us a favour, shut your face!"

"No, I mean it. Like in Pavlik's theory? I would. I knew this girl back in Kyzyl. She was all right really. Her surname was Khlyustina and she said she came from an old aristocratic family. She claimed her great-grandfather had been exiled to Siberia. She was really into it. She even had a special shelf where all the books had bookmarks at pages where her name, Khlyustina, got a mention."

"Oh, what use have I got for the gentry?" Lyokha reluctantly allows himself to be drawn into the conversation. "I'm not doing too badly where I am, only I haven't got any money, any live, ordinary money just so I feel I'm a normal human being. If they even paid me the money I earn at this shitty little theatre, I'd be satisfied. I'd thank them. But all those... trees of theirs, they

88

really should all just be toppled. Cut right down at the root, with a chainsaw!"

"They are being toppled. I remember this TV series about gangsters. In one of the programs, five businessmen were killed by hitmen. They were directors of some bank or other."

"No, that's no good," Lyokha opines, raising himself on his elbow. "That's themselves toppling each other, but what we need is the people to topple them. That would be the right way of doing it. I'm a hundred percent in favour of that!" He's sounding more and more excited and my alarm bells start ringing. "Take this club that's been opened here. What's it called – 'Surf', is it? Where all these types get together, all the gilded fucking bastard youth. We ought to put ten kilos of TNT in there. That would sort them out! That would sort everything out! Admit it! We get to burn our guts out swilling Gypsy Girl, while that lot..." – he pauses for a moment to recall something, which he manages a moment later – "while that lot are lapping up their martinis. Why?!"

"Because they've got the brains to make money?" I suggest.

"What do you mean they've got the brains?" Lyokha frowns and his head falls back on the pillow. "They're just vermin, or the offspring of vermin. People like that ought to be destroyed. They're given the opportunity so they screw us and... oh, the bastards!" Lyokha rants on incoherently for a bit and then changes tack. "Take my folks. They lived the whole of their lives in Prokopievsk. I don't think they ever left the place. My dad was a miner, and both my grandfathers before him. He's been retired for ages with second-category disability. He worked from when he was twenty until he was forty-three, and then that was it. He's fifty-seven now and just a vegetable. He sits in a chair and watches the telly. He only has to move to be coughing for the next three hours. From his bed to the chair, that's all the exercise he gets. And what the fuck for, what was the point? Do you know how proud of themselves those miners are? They go into that hole in the ground like heroes. What are they proud of, the morons? The management at the mine changes every six months. They dig up the money and leave sod all behind. And the miners, if they don't get killed in an accident, then by the time they're forty they're like my dad. I got the hell out of there straight after the army. I'd rather be homeless than be like them, like that. Ksyukha was dead right – we've got to do something, take action! Sweep away all this crap to hell!"

I ask with genuine amazement, "What's got into you? You've been slobbing around all these months and now you're suddenly behaving as if you'd fallen off the stove."

"Quite simply, I've seen the light," Lyokha replies, sounding like he's top of the class and has just solved a tricky equation. "I've been thinking about this for a long time, and today I finally saw the answer. Only I'm weak, weak, do you hear, Rom? And the worst of it is that everybody around here is weak, everybody I know. There just aren't any real heroes, only riffraff."

I remember Abakan and the kids there, and first and foremost, of course, Seryoga, perpetually drunk and hence always combative. We called him the Anarchist. He wore a greatcoat over his naked body and a red parachute regiment beret with a badge saying "IRA". There he'd stand with a glass of vodka in his right hand and a Chinese fake pistol in his left. "We'll go out and kill, burn, and plunder!" he would yell. "We are the greatest and our laughter is filled with fire!" There seemed to be any number of guys like that around. I was a bit of a prat too when I was younger, went to crazy political meetings and wrote angry protest songs, until I got bored with it. Today, though, Lyokha seems just to have woken up to all that.

I look at the alarm clock. Almost four.

"Time to arbeiten. The performance starts in three hours. Get up!"

Lyokha groans terminally in reply.

7

It's a little cabin on a hillock on the bank of a pond. I faced the black, alarmingly porous old logs with green boards from the porch of our dacha before we left Kyzyl. It cheered the hut up a bit and made it look bigger from the outside.

According to the neighbours, it was built about thirty years ago for an old woman who moved away after her son got married. The collective farm paid for the building of it, everybody piled in to help, and it was completed in a week. The old woman lived there for a number of years and then died, and the little cabin has had a dozen changes of owner since. None of them took much care of it because they moved on as soon as they could find a better place to live, with more space.

Now it's my parents who live there and long for a different, cruciform house with concrete foundations. For all that, for the time being this is their home, and mine too. When I'm walking from the bus stop and catch sight of our little hut in the distance, I have a warm feeling and I get agreeably excited. I seem to sense a smell familiar since childhood and which has been brought here from our apartment in Kyzyl.

My father dreams of finding the money to enlarge the cabin, but without any great conviction. He has selected logs and put them aside to build on another two rooms. He's already got enough, but somehow never seems to have the time to get started.

I remember in the first months after we moved here my father was constantly amazed at what a sluggish, lazy, dreary way of life the villagers had. He had grand plans of making a good life for us here. "It'll be halfway between an apartment and a dacha," he used to say. Before long very little remained of those plans. To be honest, all that remains is a wish to make ends meet.

So here we are sitting at the table in the kitchen which doubles as the sitting room, so to speak, my father, my mum, and I. On

Friday I got my food vouchers and have brought half a kilo of luncheon sausage, some herring, 300 grams or so of cheese, and a bottle of Pertsovka. We decide to keep the vodka till the evening, and eat lunch in a hurry because we need to drive out to dig up the potatoes.

"I've loaded the crates," my father says. "We mustn't forget the buckets and the forks. The soil is wet because it was pouring for half the day again yesterday. We'll drag the crates into the bathhouse afterwards to let the potatoes dry, otherwise they'll rot."

"Do try to get them all up," my mother responds. "We've put so much effort into them."

The allotment we were allocated this year was pretty bad. It was good black earth but absolutely covered in weeds, mainly vigorous, prickly sow thistle. It was a thankless task pulling it out because it promptly sprang up again. We had to pull the stems out by hand together with a long root covered in shoots. Four times in the course of the summer.

My father glances at me and smiles:

"You've shaved your beard off. I warned Mother to expect you bearded and not to get frightened."

I smile grimly in reply, remembering the couple of hours I spent scraping my face with blunt razor blades last night.

"Right," my father says getting up. "Time to be off."

Mum starts fussing about, looking for things in the cupboard.

"Put on something warm, and take a raincoat. Look, the sky is heavy with thunderclouds."

Our property is too small. Redhead and our truck Zakhar almost fill it. It used to be practically impossible to get in, but when we replaced the fence we expanded slightly into the street, demolished what was left of a small shed, and moved the coal shed and firewood store into the backyard.

To the side of the property we have a tiny bathhouse and our summer kitchen. The bathhouse is still pretty solid but the roof is rotting. We had a fire last spring when the wiring in the summer kitchen caught fire, and the flames leapt from there to the bathhouse roof. We managed to put the fire out quite quickly, but the slates were damaged and nowadays they cost almost fifty roubles a piece. For the time being we can't afford to repair it.

Most of our plot is taken up by the vegetable garden. It's almost half an acre. We have five hothouses in it, we cover them with polythene from mid-April. Two of these have large heaters for bringing on early cucumbers, tomatoes and peppers. Some years they ripen at the very beginning of June.

It's hard work keeping the temperature above freezing when it's minus ten at night, and sometimes lower.

A visit to my parents usually begins with a tour of their smallholding. My father shows me what he's done since my last visit, congratulates himself on his successes and complains about anything that isn't going well. I would happily walk round the autumnal vegetable garden to see how the rabbits are doing, but right now we have other business in hand.

It isn't too far to the fields, which begin just outside the village, beyond the farmyard. Ten long, low over-wintering byres are ranged in neat rows and, from a distance, seem still to be in use, clean, and freshly whitewashed. Beneath the roofing there are small window-like ventilation openings. In fact, however, only two are occupied and a closer look at the others shows them to be in a ruinous state. The slates have been filched from the roofs and the glass in the windows has been broken. The gates are either open or have been ripped off at the hinges. The surroundings are densely overgrown with wormwood and hemp and the fences have been pushed over.

To the right of the cowsheds is a graveyard of machinery: sowing machines, harrows, rusty, half-dismantled combine harvesters, listing Kirov tractors with flat tyres. The fence around this graveyard no longer protects anything and many of its boards are missing.

My father and I carry on smoking in silence. There's no point in trying to talk anyway with the engine roaring. The truck is tossed about by the potholes in the road, and when my father changes gear, Zakhar squeals as if in pain.

The allotments close to the village are reserved for local people, while town-dwellers get the ones further out, beyond the strip of forest. Local people pay only for having the land ploughed over, but town-dwellers pay to rent a plot for a season. The collective farm no longer plants potatoes because nobody can be bothered to work in the state fields when they don't get paid and there's no machinery: the one remaining potato harvester moved to the machinery graveyard last autumn.

The fields extend along the gently sloping hill and are divided by strips of woodland. The slope is dotted with the red, green, and brown of cars, and people are moving over the black and grey soil.

"We're not the only ones who are late," my father shouts above the roar of Zakhar, cheering up.

I nod and hold firmly to the bracket fixed to the dashboard as Zakhar ponderously and cautiously lumbers over the lumps of churned-up, ploughed soil, heading towards our allotment.

Before setting to work we walk the length of the plot. The first six metres were dug by my father in August and September for food. Beyond that, amidst the half-dead weeds, are dry and withering potato haulms. At the far end, however, the allotment has also been dug up, but by some untidy person in a hurry. There are small, greenish potatoes lying about, washed by the rain.

"What bastards," my father says without surprise, almost without emotion, spitting out the tobacco fibres which have got into his mouth from the Prima. "They've stolen a couple of sackfuls." He immediately tries to calm himself and me. "Never mind, forget it. There's more than enough left for us. The potato harvest this year hasn't been bad."

It's chilly. The sun is far, far away behind the solid, endless thunderclouds entirely covering the sky. You can't even guess at where it is at that moment because from horizon to horizon all is a monotone, heavy greyness. At any moment it seems it might burst, be torn open, and snow as grey as the cloud itself will come whirling out.

The soil is damp and muddy. My fingers are soon freezing and won't bend, but even so you can't dig properly into a clump of potatoes turned up with a fork if you're wearing gloves. I keep feeling I'm missing potatoes and leaving them behind in the soil. When I've managed to warm one hand a bit, I take the glove back off and again delve with my bare fingers.

My father works rapidly and is already ten rows ahead of me. Of course, it's easier if you're only working with a fork. You plunge the tines in near a clump of potatoes, draw them up from the depths, bring out the largest tubers, and the job's done. I can hardly expect him to go digging around in the ground with his hands, which are red and swollen and covered in eczema sores.

We work hurriedly and in silence. My only thought, my one concern is for my hands which are seizing up. I rummage around in the holes, first with my right then with my left. While one hand is poking around in search of fugitive potatoes, I warm the other. It's particularly disagreeable when your fingers end up in the icy mush of a rotting seed potato, as if you've happened on a gobbet of somebody else's cold phlegm.

I'm waiting for my father to suggest a smoking break.

For the most part the tubers are large but the buckets fill terribly slowly. Or perhaps it only seems that way. When I'm tired of probing the holes, I take two buckets which aren't completely full and carry them back to Zakhar. I pour them out into the crates placed round the sides of the flatbed. On my way back, I look from side to side in the hope of seeing something to distract me.

Human figures are stooping here and there, or roaming around the field with sacks and buckets. They're doing the same as Father and I are, gathering food. Potatoes are the staple of our diet, the most important item to store. "If you've got potatoes, you won't starve": how often I've heard that said by old men, by young, well-dressed women, and by people who gave no appearance of being poor. I've noticed there aren't many potatoes on sale this year. Either there isn't much demand (most folk have a patch of land not far from the town which they've planted with potatoes), or else people are holding them back until the spring. Who knows what will happen in the winter and spring, so if you've filled your cellar, why not leave them there where they're safe?

"Well, my friend, is it time for a smoke?" my father asks at last.

"That's a good idea!"

We climb into the cab and slam the doors. We smoke the acrid, dried out Primas at one rouble eighty a pack. Occasional raindrops tap dully on the roof and bonnet. The wind gusts. My father seems keen to talk but I have nothing to say, and no wish to speak. It seems better just to say nothing, or to whine quietly and piteously. Nothing is going to change for a long, long time. Everything is going to carry on the same way it has for these past four years. We're firmly trapped in a vice and there's no getting out of it. We can, with a great effort, carry on going through the same motions, seeing the same sights, thinking about the same things. That's how life is going to be, with my parents stranded here in this declining, ruined village of Zakholmovo, and me living in a dull, dozy regional centre. My parents will keep trying from one year to the next to make some money to help me towards a half-decent life. Every winter they'll come up with grandiose plans and try to make them a reality before the next winter, using up their strength and optimism, growing older, struggling against infirmity, struggling for my sake. In the same old way I will drag on to or off the stage plywood walls, arbours, and stage-prop furniture, will try to get my pathetic highs, dream of the girl on the windowsill, or another one if I don't get anywhere with her; and will argue and play cards with Lyokha, and on Mondays come to see my parents. And that's how it will go on until something ends it.

"Why are you looking so doleful?" My father puts his arm round my shoulder. "We've collected three sackfuls already. I'll give you a hand pulling them up and we'll get through it faster."

The way he calls me "my friend" and his gesture of lightly putting his arm round me make me feel even more like howling. Trying to swallow the lump in my throat, I drag on the cigarette as deeply as I can and turn away to look out the window. The scrawny, half-naked birch and aspen trees in the woodland strip seem completely lifeless, and the people wandering through the fields look like zombies who have lost their way.

"I suppose it's autumn," I blurt in reply. "It makes you sad."

"Yes," my father sighs. "Soon we'll have to expect the snow. We still need to get in the firewood. I've had a word with Gennady, the forester, and he's promised to find us a spot and give us a saw. We need somehow to get over there and bring the firewood back."

"We'll do it, Dad, I promise. How about next Monday?"

"Health and weather willing."

The best, but at the same time the most trying, moments when I'm home are our evenings, when we're together as a family. We did all we could before it got dark and dug out almost all the potatoes. There were literally only ten or twelve rows left. The rain came on heavier and did in the end slow us down. My father said that one way or another he'd finish digging them out one of these days. We didn't bother unloading them, just left them in the truck covered with rags and a tarpaulin and hoped there wouldn't be frost overnight.

The rabbits, the chickens, the pig, Beecher the dog have all been fed, we've been to the bathhouse, and are now sitting at the table having supper and drinking the vodka. The radio is muttering hoarsely in the background and the television, which we don't need right now, has been turned off. My mother and father have no wish to watch films or the "Vremya" news programme because they have me here with them.

Mum is continually offering me one thing after another, not letting my plate get empty. From time to time my father refills the glasses. Of course, they want to know how I'm getting on and what I'm doing.

"Oh, everything's fine, just fine," I say. "They've issued us the food vouchers, twenty of them, so I've got plenty of food, a whole cupboard full of cereals and potatoes. Really, you don't need to bring so much stuff."

"And what about your roommate? Does he drink a lot?" Mum enquires anxiously.

"He's fine, nothing to worry about. Everything's fine."

"Well you, Roman, don't go drinking too much, please! How much misery that wretched vodka causes people."

"Oh no, Mum, I hardly ever..."

"What's new at the theatre?"

I really don't in the least feel like talking about the theatre. It would be nice to be able to forget about it for one day at least. I frown unthinkingly, but immediately control myself and try to sound enthusiastic. "We're doing brilliantly! They're planning a new production, some fantastic fairy tale. We get good audiences. The house is never empty. It's just a pity they don't pay a bit more..."

At this I get my mum's piteous, begging admonition: "Hold in there, please. Hold on to that job, son. No matter what it's like, it's at least a job. What else can you find in these times, and at least you have a roof over your head until we can buy an apartment."

"Yes, it's fine, don't worry," I say, trying to keep sounding optimistic. "It's not such a bad job. When I've had a chance to look around," I chuckle, "I might become an actor myself!"

"That would be great," Mum says, not realising I'm joking. "Father and I did a bit of acting after the culture college. You've no idea how it brings a person out! It's so good for your diction and your deportment..."

The overhead light has been put out and only the lamp behind the stove is still on. Father lay down to sleep shortly after supper, and Mum and I are sitting at the uncleared table, talking in a whisper.

"Perhaps we should bring you some more furniture, or crockery, or some of the books?"

She makes this suggestion almost every Monday, and I always avoid giving a straight answer. "Well, what if something happened and we just had to bring it all back? I've got all the things I really need there. I guess everything's fine."

"Well, but there's nothing worse than living out of a suitcase."

"Okay, let's think about it. Maybe later, eh?"

My mother nods before clearing her throat and evidently preparing to say something important. "Well now, there's something else I want to mention. The district education office has opened a shop and they have ..." – she struggles to find the right words – "They give you credit against your pay that's been delayed. They've got clothes that would fit you very well. The prices are a bit higher than at the Trade Centre, of course, but... not unreasonable. The school owes Father and me around three thousand roubles in back pay, so we were thinking about getting you a winter jacket, some boots maybe, a pair of jeans. I spotted a good sweater there too. All your clothes are so worn. I was washing them today, they're all frayed."

"Mu-um," I protest, " My clothes are fine."

"Wait..."

"Who cares about clothes? If they do pay you the money we'll be able to buy slates for the bathhouse, and we need new polythene for the hothouses."

"I really can't see us being paid any time soon," Father joins in. "They'll owe us the money for ages and then they'll create another bout of inflation and that will solve their problem."

"It's better to take what's on offer today, son." Mum's voice has that piteous, begging tone again. "At least we'll know our son is dressed decently."

"I'm dressed fine the way it is..."

"Do you call that being dressed?" Father smiles wryly. "In our day, no matter how hard life was, every boy had his Sunday best suit in the wardrobe, shoes, half-a-dozen ties. You really ought to have, well, maybe not a suit if they're not in fashion, but at least something you're not ashamed to be seen in when you go visiting or take a girl out."

"I'm not ashamed of these clothes."

"The trouble nowadays is that nobody seems to be ashamed of anything." Father sighs and turns to the wall.

Mum finally talks me round. I don't want to argue, and anyway I can see it is useless. I nod. What else can I do?

"I need to take the bus to the clinic again on Thursday," Mum whispers. "Let's meet up then and go to that shop. Otherwise the money really will just disappear. This is something we can do today, and God only knows what tomorrow will bring. You can choose yourself a nice new set of clothes you like. Right, son. Is that agreed?"

"Okay, okay..."

I go outside to smoke. The rain has almost stopped but the sky is black, without a single star. It's just as well. With the sky overcast there isn't likely to be a frost.

Our old, grey dog, Beecher, scents me and comes out of

his kennel. He stretches, straightens out his weary bones and whimpers quietly. I go over and pat him on his beefy, muscular neck. The dog presses against my leg, sniffs me, and continues whining. He's grumbling.

"Well, Beecher, it'll soon be winter," I say. "Snow again, eh? Never mind... there there, old doggy dog. Go back to your little home and sleep. Time for me to turn in too."

We've had Beecher for seven years. I remember the woman in the next dacha to ours in Kyzyl offered us a good, brave dog which was, admittedly, not that young. Her friends had gone away and left him and he was hanging around a house where he no longer belonged. The new owners had a dog of their own and were threatening to poison the interloper. My father drove over with the neighbour and brought him back to our dacha. He snarled and tried to attack us and we had to lock him up in the shed. We fed him by cautiously pushing his bowl through the gap in the partly opened door. He gradually got used to us, and after three days began wagging his tail slightly. On the sixth day he let us stroke him, and a day after that we let him outside on a chain. Sometimes my father would let him run free in the morning, and one time Beecher disappeared. For over a week he was nowhere to be found. He came back with a collar we didn't recognise and the remains of someone else's chain.

Four years ago we brought Beecher to our new home and for several months, while my parents were selling the apartment and completing the move, Beecher and I lived here together. I cooked the food for both of us, and played with him a lot and talked to him.

Mother has cleared the dishes off the table and is leafing through prescriptions. Her glasses make her look comical and pathetic. They unexpectedly appeared after one of her visits to the clinic. I hate it when I see her wearing spectacles. They're scary. They seem to signal the coming of old age.

"Do you want to take a look at the pills they're prescribing me, Roma?"

She hands me a slip of paper like you find in cartons along with the medicine.

"Instructions for Use," I begin reading. "Caution: Berlicort".

"On the other side," Mother says, "where it talks about side-effects. I'd better read it myself."

She straightens her spectacles, moves the paper closer to the light, and reads in a stage-whisper, stressing the scariest words:

"'The following side-effects may occur.' Here we are: 'moon face, fatty deposits (Cushing's syndrome), muscle weakness, atrophy of muscle tissue, osteoporosis.' Then, 'diabetes, disruption of sex hormone secretion, impotence, striation of the skin, cutaneous bleeding...'"

I stand listening and my sympathy is alloyed with irritation and increasing anger. I want to pull the paper out of her hands and tear it up, to do something at least.

"'... enhanced elimination of sodium from the organism, atrophy of the adrenal cortex, vascular inflammation, ulcerous inflammation of the mucosal ring of the oesophagus, pains in the region of the gastro-intestinal tract, stomach ulcers, increased susceptibility to infection, slowing down of the healing process of wounds and bones'."

Where would this end? And how could it all fit on to a slip of paper barely larger than an audio cassette?

"'...rupture of sinews, suppression of growth in children...'" Mum's voice pounds on and on at my brain. "'...aseptic osteo-necrosis of the head of the femur and humerus, headaches, increased sweating, dizziness, heightened endocranial pressure with papilloedema, glaucoma, mental disorder, increased risk of thrombosis, inflammation of the pancreas, weight gain, oedema, high blood pressure'."

There's a silence and I don't immediately realise there is no more to be read. Mum goes on looking at the piece of paper.

"How awful," I say, to demonstrate that I do have a reaction to this, although it sounds false. With the same unconvincing surprise I add, "And they're telling you to take that?"

Mum raises her eyes to me, altered, enlarged by her glasses and nods sadly: "Yes, that's what they've prescribed."

"Don't take it, please! This is... It might help with your asthma, but it's going to cause a host of other... How can they even manufacture stuff like that?!"

"Well, what can I do, Roman? Sometimes when I get an attack I simply can't breathe. A couple of days ago I had two terrible attacks – Father had to pour cold water over me to bring me back. I was fine and then suddenly my breathing stopped and I felt quite lifeless. We've got the regional dance festival coming up, and the children are so looking forward to it. I need to get them ready. I'll try it and then perhaps I'll at least be able to move around. It's a powerful drug. Anyway, what does it matter now?"

8

The monotonous, deadening beat of the *chadagan* seems not to be produced by a fingernail plucking strings but by the hoofs of a short-legged pony drumming on the endless hilly steppe, baked as hard as stone by the scorching Asian sun. To this accompaniment an incomprehensible, drowsy muttering develops into hoarse, drawling, hissing guttural singing.

Shura Reshetov has a couple of dozen records of folk music. I've rummaged through them and found the Tuva epic *Aldan-Maadyr*. It's a declining people's voluminous tale about the gigantic heroes who were their glorious forebears.

I listen to the folk music of the region where I was born, sprawled on a small, uncomfortable, home-made sofa and tapping a chicken bone on the armrest. Shura is well away, having collapsed under the table and making no effort to get up again.

I bumped into him in the morning, at the Trade Centre. He had just been paid a fee for making the signboard for a kiosk and had immediately bought a large amount of food and drink. I was invited to join the celebration. He quickly dispatched the contents of a bottle of Minus and collapsed. I have to avoid getting too drunk because I have to be at work in a couple of hours, and turning up in a state of inebriation is not appreciated. You can do as you please after the performance, but drinking too much before or during it could get you fired.

Shura on the other hand, is a free artist. He can drink when he feels like it as long as he's got the money, which evidently isn't too often to judge by the speed and avidity with which he got hammered.

The tapping of the bone on the armrest reminds me a bit of the sound off a shaman's tambourine. It goes well with the singing of *Aldan-Maadyr*, augmenting the meagre accompaniment.

Reshetov is pushing forty. He lives together with his mother in a two-room apartment on the fourth floor of a nine-storey block. The old lady is ill, and tormented by her two feckless sons, of whom the second, Victor, is currently in prison for, I think, the third time. She's frequently in hospital for long spells, that's where she is now. Shura had a family, but his wife kicked him out for getting drunk all the time and not wanting to work an eight-hour day five days a week. She doesn't even ask him for money to support their daughter. To all appearances, he's a down-and-out – toothless, shaggy-haired, scrawny, and with a shapeless, scruffy beard; and invariably dressed in tattered rags. All the money from his infrequent and not particularly large fees is spent on booze and materials for his creative craftsmanship. He quite often wanders in to cadge tacks or a scrap of canvas from our scene-painter Petrachenko, which is where I first met him. They drink and chat together, and Petrachenko's eyes reflect an unendurable pain. He probably wishes he were in the place of this scruff.

The epic comes to an end, the needle quickly moves towards the steel spindle in the centre of the record, the record player clicks and the record stops. I look at my watch. It'll soon be four, time to make a move. I go over to the table. There are several tins of barely touched food, a couple of full bottles of Minus and one half empty, the remains of a smoked chicken, some tomatoes, some oranges. Shura will be able to pig himself for a couple of days. I can't resist pouring fifty grams or so into a cup and gulp it down, followed by a generous portion of hunter's sausage. I shove an orange into my pocket and for decency's sake give the artist a shake: "Shura, Shura, get up. Move on to the sofa. What are you doing lying on the floor like that?"

"Mm-mm a-a-aaah... that's okay..."

"Well, I'll be off then."

"A-a-aaah..."

The shop assistant views us with a mixture of alarm and disdain, as if we were raiders helping ourselves to her goods with our dirty hands. If we were buying the stuff, paying her real money for it, she would clearly view us in quite a different light. She would probably be fussing around, helping us to choose; but as it is, neither she nor we know quite where we are. It's a bit like living in communist utopia.

"Just see what trousers they've got," I hear mum's sibilant voice. "Black, the way you like them."

"I don't need any trousers," I scowl. "Ironing creases... jeans are better."

"Well, they've got jeans. These are black ones too. Go on, try them."

I take the jeans and lope towards the changing room with the gait of a thief. I wriggle about in there, catching the curtains and partly opening them. The fitting room is very small. It was probably designed for the Children's World store.

"They're too small," I conscientiously confess to my mother when I come back.

She turns to the sales assistant. "Do you have these in a larger size?"

"They're all out on the rack. Take a look."

"What size is this? Forty-six." Mum starts working her way down a long row of jeans. "Here's a 38. Try these."

Once again I slope off to the changing room, suffering agonies from the look the sales assistant gives me. I'd rather wear old clothes than get new clothes this way. I really do feel like a thief.

"Do they fit?" Mum greets me by the curtains with a mixture of anxiety and joy.

"S'pose so."

"What do you mean you suppose so? Make sure they fit you all right."

"There's nothing wrong with the ones I've got," I blurt, smoothing my old ones.

"Just stop that! As it is I'm on the verge of an asthma attack. I still need to go to the chemist to get some medicine. Let's look at the sweaters. I saw a very nice one somewhere last time."

The shop is tiny, just a single room but crammed with all kinds of stuff, from stationery to children's toys to vacuum cleaners and refrigerators. It's like a TV game show where you can choose any prize you like, but only up to a certain amount, and instead of a hearty show presenter we have this surly woman suspiciously watching our every move.

"The ones on this rack are expensive," she announces when Mum starts looking at the sweaters and feeling them. "The standard ones are over there."

"Well, perhaps an expensive one is what we're looking for," Mum fires back at her and, for appearance's sake, inspects another couple before moving on to the next rack. "Look, Roman, this one is really nice. Do you want to try it?"

I pull it on. It seems okay. I should just choose everything as quickly as possible and get out of here, see Mum to the chemist's, and go and have a beer.

"Just right," I say brightly. "What about something for you? I've got trousers and a sweater – that's plenty."

"How about a pair of shoes? A winter jacket? Do stop it. Now we're here we should get everything. Look at the shoes they've got."

"M-mm, yes."

Mum starts coughing, hastily gets the inhaler out of her coat pocket and sprays her throat with the aerosol. She stands for a moment, looking upwards, getting her breathing settled. I try on the shoes.

Vadim is in the greenroom before any of the other stagehands, as usual. He lolls on the divan, smoking, and tapping the ash into a dirty metal ice-cream dish. Opposite him is the actor Lyalin, unhurriedly savouring a small coffee he has brought from the buffet.

"Good heavens, a miracle!" my team leader expresses sarcastic amazement. "You've actually come to work."

Following this not particularly encouraging greeting comes the cloying voice of Lyalin: "Hello, Rom. How's tricks?"

"Bearable."

"Well, that's marvellous, that's marvellous. Although you ought to enjoy life a bit more." Lyalin swallows the last drop from his cup, wipes his lips with his handkerchief and stands up. "Wonderful coffee, I do recommend it. Alina is being kind today. She's more than happy to serve us on credit."

"We usually prefer something else," Vadim smirks. "Coffee is bad for you."

"Who's to say, who's to say."

Lyalin leaves and Vadim hisses contemptuously after him, "Filthy queer!" He immediately turns to me. "Have you heard, Dimentius is scarpering."

"Where's he going?"

"To the cemetery."

"How do you mean?"

"He's taken a job as a gravedigger. There was a vacancy. He says the pay is serious money. We'll need to find a replacement."

"That shouldn't be difficult. We have half a dozen wannabes asking for work here every day."

"And you think we should just shove the first person who turns up into our team? What if he's a burnt-out alky, or worse, some grafter who'll drive us crazy within three days with his self-righteous stupidity? We need to find someone whose face fits."

Vadim is right. You can't just take on anyone. I volunteer a suggestion: "Why don't you air it out with the director and get him to let us decide. Tell him we'll find the right man ourselves."

My team leader nods, turns his pack of Java over in his hand, and shakes out a new cigarette.

"There's another thing..." His voice becomes serious. "A business matter. But that's for after the performance, when we can think it over calmly, without rushing. Andrei has come up with an idea we need to discuss."

The Kruglovs appear in the greenroom. The wife, fat and hideous, usually acts merchants' wives or housewives in retirement. She sails in in her usual, laughably regal manner. Her insignificant, henpecked husband makes no attempt to strut around like that, which makes you warm to him. Immediately behind them comes a dozy, frowning Lyokha, looking like the Kruglovs' good-for-nothing, mentally retarded son. This procession curls me up.

"What're you grinning at, moron?" Lyokha snarls as he comes in. "Glad rags getting to you?"

I've already shown him my new finery. He was staggered, and tried to work out, in spite of his doziness, how many litres of Gypsy Girl we could have bought instead of that pile of clothes. He couldn't believe I'd got it without paying real money. Now he re-tells it all to Vadim:

"Ace jeans, boots, an anorak with a fur collar! And he says it didn't cost him a kopek. What do teachers have to barter with?!"

"Plenty," the team-leader soothes him. "My sister works in a culture centre. Instead of money they pay them in condensed milk, tights, all kinds of crap."

"And what does the culture centre give to people who are crap themselves?" Lyokha struggles to understand.

"Fuck knows." Vadim moves the conversation on. "Dima is clearing off. He's leaving us, the swine."

The performance is at seven. Around five we start lugging the scenery out of the store in the annex into the theatre. Today is a silly whodunnit called *The Chinese Figurine* in four acts, and each has a different setting. We're going to sweat.

Dima takes it easy, which I suppose is understandable. He's leaving in three or four days, and he probably doesn't feel like putting his back into what is almost no longer his job. His heart's not in it, but he has to go through the motions.

"Come on, Dimentius. Build up those muscles," the gigantic Andrei exhorts him. "Digging holes in the ground is harder work than shifting bits of cardboard around a stage."

Dima is not one for jokes and mutters something inaudible in reply.

"You'll drink yourself into the grave there in two weeks!" Andrei continues to needle him. "I was at a funeral where they gave the gravediggers two bottles of hooch and money on top. And it's going to be like that every day."

"If only," Dima grunts, fitting a plywood wall into special grooves on the floor. "It's not blue-collars who work there now, you know, but all sorts of engineers. My uncle barely managed to get me the job. It's top-grade work."

"Incidentally, you've behaved like a complete shit," Vadim informs him. "By all means pack the job in, nobody's holding you, only you need to warn people in advance. How are we supposed to find someone to replace you?"

Dima, trying to hide his indifference, shrugs.

"Hey, I know someone!" Andrei exclaims, pleased. "He's an okay guy. My roommate. A bit young maybe, just sixteen."

"But can he graft?"

"I reckon so. He wouldn't have much choice. If need be, I'll teach him!" The giant grins and shows his mighty fist. "No, really, he's an okay lad, and he's interested in the theatre!"

"He'll work here a bit, see what gives, and pack it in," Lyokha offers his constructive opinion.

We've put all the scenery for the first act in place, and we've got the scenery for the second ready in the wings. We go back to the greenroom and collapse on our personal sofa, have a smoke, and wait.

The actors, reincarnated as the characters in the play, some more successfully than others, kill time for the minutes remaining before the start of the performance. After putting on the greasepaint and the costumes, their expressions and manners have changed as usual. The clownish Khrapchenko is now an elegant adventurer, his eyes flashing as he seeks his victim; young Larisa Volkova is ready to fall in love with Mikheev, forty years old but, for the next couple of hours, transfigured into a beardless youth.

After finishing his smoke, Vadim goes off to negotiate with the director about the new stagehand. Dima produces a pack of cards from his pocket.

"Anyone for cards to pass the time? We could play Blackjack or Seka."

"Someone's got money burning a hole in his pocket," Lyokha suggests with a twisted smile.

"We don't have to play for money, we can just play..."

"People who aren't playing for money fool around playing Durak."

"Durak if you like."

"Let's move to the bolthole."

Vadim is looking serious, solemn even. He sits to one side and observes us in turn as we throw our cards down on the piece of plywood, which serves as our card table. We're playing with partners, and Andrei and I are being taken to the cleaners.

"Oh, fuck!" my partner grumbles as he again collects a pile of cards which he has failed to unload. "This isn't a game, it's moronic. Come on, Rom, see if you can do something."

"I'll do something for him," Lyokha crows unkindly as he tosses three kings down on our apology for a card table. "Beat that and you get trumps."

The broad fan of cards in my left hand is now augmented by his kings. It's tiresome, of course, but I'm not too upset. I want to hear what Vadim has to tell us. I can see from his expression that he's now ready to reveal the idea which has visited Andrei and which it's essential for us to discuss. We don't try to hurry him, knowing that he'll talk when he's ready.

"Ho-ho, four times fool!" Lyokha flicks me on the nose with his last card. "Learn from Daddy while he's still alive!"

Andrei picks up the pack and hastily starts shuffling it.

"This time, I can feel it, the cards are going to come out right."

Our team leader lights up, admires the flame of his lighter, and walks around the little room with our eyes following him. Andrei puts the cards aside. The moment has arrived.

"Right. I've spoken to Victor Antonych about the boy and he has no objection. The second thing is that in about a week we're off on tour somewhere. I don't know where exactly, but the chief said just to be ready."

"Brilliant!" Lyokha exclaims, but our team leader quells him with a glance.

"Now, a serious matter." There's a pause. Like the Banderlogs in *The Jungle Book* we move closer to Vadim. "Andrei's had a flash of inspiration which at first seems impossible but, if you think about it, seems worth a try." He delivers another exaggerated pause for effect. "To put it in a nutshell, I imagine you all know that every Tuesday just after noon our chief cashier goes with the week's takings to the bank."

"Yep, sure!" Lyokha, always on the ball, nods agreement. "And?"

"And always, as Andrei has pointed out, follows the same route."

"She has the last four times, I know for a fact," he confirms.

"Anyway, he's had this idea of... Well, in short, relieving her of the money." Vadim is silent and looks round at us. Nobody sniggers, nobody groans derisively, we're all ears. "There's a particular courtyard..." Our team leader's voice becomes more animated, "I was there today, sizing things up... It would be a good place. The old biddy can hardly shuffle along, her eyesight is poor."

"She's as blind as a bat!" Lyokha puts his oar in again. "One time, when I was still with my wife, I went to get a form from her for the housing and she was on her own and couldn't find her glasses..."

"Hold on," Vadim interrupts him. "Everybody knows about her eyesight. In short, we'd only need to sneak up behind her, knock her glasses off, and grab the bag. The courtyard is perfect: next to an empty shack the people were moved out of recently, and surrounded by sheds and vegetable plots. There are several alleyways leading out of it between fences and it's pretty deserted. Right, Andrei?"

"Yes, absolutely!"

"So there we are. Do we give it a go? I've worked out roughly how much money she should have on her." Vadim pulls a piece of paper out of his pocket. "We usually have eight performances a week, two fairy tales and six evening performances.

Adult tickets are forty to seventy roubles, children's are thirty, so the absolute minimum is going to be forty. On average, okay? And the average audience for a performance is fifty at least. So that means two thousand roubles a performance. At the very least! Eight performances – sixteen thousand. At the very minimum. Then there's programme sales, and a lot of people renting opera glasses."

"And how about the buffet?!" Lyokha exclaims. "Just think how much money the buffet makes!"

"Half-wit," I say. "The buffet is a separate account."

"Yes, we're not counting the buffet," Vadim supports me. "If we take sixteen as a realistic figure, divide that by five..."

"Lads, I'm out," Dima stops him. "If I was staying with you, it'd be a pleasure, but as it is, count me out."

Andrei is about to start trying to persuade him, but our leader interrupts: "Forget it! If he's out, he's out. We split it four ways. That works out at, say, four thousand each, just about two hundred roubles short of twice our monthly salary."

"Which," Lyokha can't refrain from adding sarcastically, "We fucking saw when for the last time?"

He seems to be into this more than any of us. Dima has no time for the idea. He's practically left already and is looking forward to a well-paid job. Why should he take the risk? Vadim and Andrei have hatched the idea between them and are cool about it. As for me, I doubt very much that we'll actually decide to do anything of the sort. Most likely we'll rabbit on about it for while, talk about taking definitive action, and then gradually forget about it.

"All right then, lads," Vadim announces after a long, awkward silence. "Today is Thursday. We've got time to mull it over, work out what we're going to do and how. On Tuesday I'll shadow the cashier and check it out, and in a couple of weeks' time you probably need to be ready to go."

"Why drag it out? Four thousand a head isn't peanuts!" Moronic Lyokha doesn't share the team leader's caution. "We should mug her properly and the sooner the better! Only, I reckon we ought to wear masks, and different clothes. Oh! Rom has just bought new clothes. He can whack her!"

"Lyokha, if that's the problem," I hasten to parry him, "I can lend you the clothes for half an hour. We wear practically the same size. I can even buy you a pair of tights to put over your head."

"No, see, you've been chosen by fate! The very day you've got all this clobber, we're talking about this. It's a sign, a sign that you're the chosen one who's got to do it."

The door creaks and the fug of tobacco smoke swirls in a current of fresh air. Anya, the stage manager, bursts in to our bolthole, deflating us with her great goggling eyes and hissing, "What are you d-doing sitting here? On stage at the double! You've got three minutes! And get that door oiled, it's r-ridiculous."

We jump up, stub out our fags. We have to change the scenery while Larisa Volkova is out at the footlights declaring her love to the forty-year old stripling Mikheev. Her monologue lasts three minutes, during which time a sumptuous drawing room has to be transformed into a town square.

Uncle Gena takes us as far as the crossroads of Labour and Michurin Streets, about three hundred metres from the hostel.

It's already late at night, with few windows in the apartment blocks lit and almost no street lighting. Everywhere is silent and deserted. Most people were long ago in their beds and are fast asleep, recouping their strength for the coming day. Only the lights of the Trade Centre are burning brightly and music is booming in the distance. It's a beacon, an island of round-the-clock, unrestrained vitality and commercialised pleasure.

"Oh, fuck!" Lyokha spits out viciously and heads into the dark, lifeless courtyards.

I follow and archly console him. "Never mind, you'll soon be able to join the celebrations. Just whack the cashier..."

"And so I shall, you bastard. I'll do it alone if you're too much of a prat. Sixteen thousand is... I'll put the lot of them through the hoop. I'll show them how to live."

Lyokha glances over his shoulder with a mixture of hatred and envy at the glow coming from the Trade Centre. "By Christ, I'll really paint the town red!"

"Rob, get pissed, land in jail," I snigger. "What a hero!"

There's the usual scrum on the hostel porch: men, girls, things being discussed or argued about, money being counted by the light of cigarette lighters, vodka being swilled out of the bottle. The Vietnamese are chirping in their bird-language, the Chinese muttering, waving crumpled ten-rouble notes in each other's faces.

Lyokha and I slip between them, trying not to bump into anyone, not to jostle anybody and cause trouble. These slitty-eyed people are very tense, and there are a lot of them. Whenever there's any kind of bother, they scuttle out of every crevice like insects and there's no shaking them off. Even if it doesn't come to a fight they so bludgeon your brains with their "Ten! Pen! Men!" that it's worse than having your face smashed in.

By tradition, my first act is to head for the WC, glancing as I pass into the tiled box of the ex-kitchen. The windowsill is empty and bare. Once again the girl with the golden auburn hair is not there. How many evenings does that make? She's disappeared, she's gone and vanished. She just wanted to tease me a few times and that was it. The windowsill is orphaned. How warmly this despised, abandoned little space was lit by the tender glow of her presence, and now it's cold and dark again, and I'm alone again, and must seek once more among the hundreds of unfamiliar, frightening others the one I'll love and who, perhaps, will love me in return. She'll attract me and repel me. I'll see her sometimes in fairy-tale dreams and sometimes in nightmares. What I need is once more to fall in love without any hope of reciprocation. What have I to give, what can I offer? To what delights can I lead my beloved? I can't even afford to buy her a cocktail in a caфй, which means that all I have are my fantasies and all the other rubbish which substitutes for real life and real satisfactions. Of course, if you so desire, you can transform this squalid box of the old communal kitchen into a Garden of Eden populated with a dozen enchanting nymphs. You can delight yourself with their illusory love and with imaginary happiness. You can picture anything you like, but afterwards, inevitably, you have to come back to reality, look around, give yourself a shake, spit at the cracked tiles, curse, and return to the wretched, tedious life which is, however, the only one you have.

9

Lyokha is snoring his head off. I was having such a lovely dream of suntanned maidens the colour of milk chocolate on a sandy beach by an eternally warm sea, palm trees, white yachts. In the dream I was the richest of them all, the most handsome, the absolutely top dog. Women, yachts, villas, coconuts twined round me like garlands of flowers, and at times I yielded to them, and at others pushed them away. I felt more free and happy than I ever had before, whether in my life or in my dreams.

But of course I woke up, unglued my eyes and stretched, making my bones crack. I looked around, to see my roommate lying across from me, his face upturned, his jaw gaping, snoring disgustingly. His jutting Adam's apple was moving up and down in his throat.

It's cold in the room, and it smells of socks and rotting potatoes. Of the delights bestowed upon me by my dream not a trace remains. Everything is the way it always is, every morning. I recollect the things that happened yesterday. There was something, which was good and sad at the same time. Ah, yes: I met a guy I know from Abakan and he was blustering rapturously about "The Last Autumn", a recent eschatological song festival.

There'd been some twenty groups playing, he said, but nobody had invited me. I expect they just forgot. It's a long time now since I was last seen around in Abakan. When I do go there I just sit and drink somewhere with Seryoga the Anarchist or my friend Oleg Sholin who used to be our drummer, and it's a while since they bothered with festivals and social events. Even if they'd invited me to their "Last Autumn", I probably wouldn't have performed. I've forgotten the words of my songs and haven't touched the guitar for a couple of years. I'm a stagehand, a dull, grumpy, constantly hungover scene-shifter.

"O-oh, aaargh," Lyokha's snore becomes a groan; he gulps painfully, his Adam's apple dancing convulsively in his throat. "O-oh... Whassa time?"

I look round for the alarm clock.

"Half eight."

"Oh, oh. What's up?" Lyokha crawls out of the bed, grunting and scratching himself. "What sort of time do you call this?!"

"I had this fantastic dream," I can't help telling him. "I was a millionaire. Even not just a millionaire, but you know... I was sprawled in this beach chair on the sand, bronzed beauties everywhere, kind of half-castes. Yachts, painted villas, sun..." I swallow; the saliva is sour, fouled by poison from my rotting teeth. "Everything was so real, as if I was there. Can you imagine it, I owned everything. I could do anything I wanted, anything at all. There was a little marble table in front of me with pineapples and coconuts."

"Shitty death!" Lyokha barks. "You're just trying to upset me, you bastard! And I was in a bad mood to start with."

He pulls on his trousers, picks up a sheet of the local newspaper *Worker Power* off the floor and goes out. I turn to face the wall, put my hands under my cheek like a little child, and screw up my face. And then again I can see the golden sand, the young half-castes in their revealing bathing costumes, the yachts, the villas, the coconuts. And I'm healthy and wealthy and powerful, lolling in that chair and groaning with pleasure; only now none of it is alive or real. It's like that painted board in the park in Abakan next to the photographer's kiosk. I and the half-castes have black holes instead of faces and anybody who likes can shove his lousy, unshaven snout in there.

Somebody gives a quick, glancing knock on the door, opens it and rushes in. Panting, an unfamiliar footfall. I jerk round even before I have time to open my eyes, sit up, fists clenched, ready to fight.

It's only Pavlik, but he's almost unrecognisable. In place of the earlier moulting sheep there's a scared, whimpering little dog standing on three trembling legs.

"I blew it! I can't do anything right!" The room is instantly full of his lamentation. "That's it, I'm done for, guys. I've had it! Oh, those swine, those scum. What am I going to do now?"

"What are you on about?" I asked, pulling on my clothes.

"Rom, I'm finished, I've had it," Pavlik wails. He collapses on to Lyokha's unmade bed. "I've really landed in it now!"

"Landed in what?"

I shake two cigarettes out of the pack, one for me, one for Pavlik, and we light up.

"Rom, you won't believe it... Somebody offered to let me make a bit on the side. A clear seven thousand. Hell! I just had to courier some hash from Kyzyl to Krasnoyarsk."

"Ouch!"

"Well, I talked it over with Mom, Ksyukha, that is. We needed the money. We decided to go ahead. Lots of people do, they make a living. I agreed to do it and off I went. They gave me a thousand in advance, and a bit for the journey... We spent the money straight away, of course. Winter boots for Ksyukha..."

"Now I feel better!" I hear Lyokha exclaim, full of profound satisfaction which, when he sees Pavlik, immediately evaporates, as is usual when he finds someone in our habitation who has brought neither food nor drink. "Oh, hello." He shakes hands with our guest unenthusiastically and asks him to get off his bed.

Pavlik removes to the chair and resumes his whimpering: "Anyway, I've landed in it now, lads, there's no escape. I'm completely up the spout like the saddest mug that ever lived." He crushes his fag-end in the ashtray and repeats to Lyokha everything he's just told me, while I put the kettle on, straighten my bed, and start clearing the table. Lyokha sprawls on his bed, staring at the ceiling and barely reacting to his visitor's tale of woe.

"Anyway, I got on the bus and went to that bloody shithole, Kyzyl!"

"Why's it a shit-hole?" I demand, miffed at this affront to my hometown.

"Well, but to land in it like that! You've no idea the shit I'm in!" Furrowing his scrawny forehead, Pavlik starts adding up: "They charge seventy roubles a gram, so how much is 500 grams? Five hundred times seventy, um, um. Oh, I don't know." His lips move, he tries to count on his fingers, but can't work it out and we're in no state to help him. In the end he shrugs.

"Anyway, there's sod all chance I can pay it back. So, I arrived in Kyzyl early in the morning, right? I decided to take the night bus because that would be more convenient. I met up with the guys and got the goods, five bars of 100 grams. I sat down to wait for the Krasnoyarsk bus in the cafй next to the bus station. Hadn't brought any hash with me, transparently sober, scared even to drink a beer. I looked like a completely innocent, intelligent young man reading Stephen King."

I look at Pavlik with his pinched face dried out by years of smoking dope with his physique of a dystrophic adolescent and can't help smirking. Luckily, he doesn't notice because he's too tied up in telling his story.

"I was one of the first to get on the bus and made straight

for the back seat. I shoved the parcel with the hash under the seat. You know, on those old Icaruses, where they have the engine, the seats are always beaten up and have loads of rubbish under them. Anyway, the guys told me that was the safest place to store it. Everything was going fine, right? I went to sit in the seat shown on my ticket. I was sober, clean, and well-behaved. Off we went. It was night already, and dark and quiet in the bus and I dozed off. Everything was going fine. The next thing I knew my shoulder was being shaken. Lights, commotion, a cop standing over me. 'May I ask you to come this way for a check, sir'. We were stopped at the Yermakovskoye customs post. You know the one?"

"You bet!" I respond readily. "That really is a dire place. They give me a right going over there every time, down to my socks."

"Well, there you are." Pavlik sighs and retrievs his cigarette butt from the ashtray. "They went all over me too, and made a thing about my passport not having a residence stamp in it, but then they let me go and even wished me a good journey. They checked one or two others at the same time. Everything was fine, but I was praying to myself, 'I just hope they haven't sniffed out my stuff.' Then, just as I was going to get back on the bus, they said, 'This way please!' and waved a bag with two wraps of about five grams each under my nose. 'Is this yours?'"

Pavlik is suddenly silent. He sits there for ages hanging his head, with the cigarette stub smoking right beside his fingers.

"Well, and then what?" I prompt him, wanting to hear the rest of his story.

"Eh?" He starts, raises his haunted eyes to mine, takes a drag in disgust, burns himself, and shoves the butt back into the ashtray. "They framed me, in other words. Quietly, without a lot of fuss. They took me back into the customs post, took my passport, and shoved me in a cage. I started denying these were my wraps and they told me to shut up. I could see they were just itching to really beat me up. Then they dragged in some Tuvans from the bus and made them witnesses. They said they'd found drugs under my seat. The guys nodded, signed, and went off and I saw my bus leaving. 'What are you doing!' I yelled. 'What's all this!' 'Shut it,' they said. 'Sit down and stay put. Wait.'"

"They don't give an inch," Lyokha chimes in. "When you're in the sobering up station it's a waste of time arguing over whether you're drunk or just half-drunk."

"You're comparing this to the sobering up station?! For heaven's sake, I had half a kilo of hash on that bus. It was more than my life is worth!" Evidently feeling the full impact and hopelessness of his situation all over again Pavlik almost shrieks, "What am I going to do now?! They'll demand all that money back from me! How can I possibly repay it? Oh, hell, I've really landed in it."

When he has calmed down a bit he continues his tale. "The sergeant came and took me into his office. He was a young lad, almost younger than me. I could see straight away that he smoked hash himself, I guarantee it one hundred percent. He was into it for sure. Anyway he took me into his office and started giving me the runaround: 'Confess honestly. What do we need forensics for and all kinds of shit? Taking swabs from your gums, your larynx, wipes from your hands. Come on, just write down where and who you got it from.' I told him, 'But it's not mine, don't you understand! You think I'm such an idiot I'd chuck it under my own seat? I'd have hidden it a bit better than that!' Anyway, I said I do smoke sometimes, occasionally, but I don't cart it around on me. In short, we went at each other for a bit, and then he suggested I'd write a statement that I'd been discovered with less than half a gram on me and with that amount, he assured me, it'd be no big deal, I'd just get fined eighty-six roubles and be released."

Lyokha guffaws.

Pavlik smiles too, but bitterly.

"Well yes, I thought that too, that it was just one of the tricks the filth get up to. He wanted to catch me out. Of course I told him, 'I've heard about the new law that now if you have even a grain you get the book thrown at you. Let's not do this. It's not my grass, and that's the truth.' The sergeant shoved the criminal code across to me. 'This is what we work by and none of those new directives have the force of law yet. Look up Article 224, Section 1, and read it.' Well, so I agreed."

"What are you saying!" I exclaim in amazement. "And you mean the sarge didn't stitch you up?"

"No, it all turned out pretty well. I paid the fine, they took me back to the customs post, and they even found me a lift. And here I am back home."

"You were lucky."

"I reckon it would've been better if they'd put me away. Now what's going to happen? I went straight back to look for the guy I had the agreement with but he wasn't home. Then I came here and Ksyukha was out too, and I'd left the house key here so as not to have more on me than I needed. A-aah." Pavlik gives a long groan and hangs his little balding head despondently, but quickly raises it again and jumps up out of the chair. "I'll go and look again. She may be back. I expect she spent the night with her aunt. If she's not there, let's have something to drink, just to raise my spirits. It's enough to drive you crazy."

"Good idea, let's do that, Pavlik!" Lyokha agrees, instantly becoming livelier and kinder. "You need to release the tension."

Ksyukha wasn't home so the lads went off to get the vodka. Pavlik wanted to buy the Minalu stuff but Lyokha persuaded him to buy a litre and a half of Gypsy Girl, and some sausage to go with it.

They left me to get the food sorted.

I peeled some potatoes, of course, and went off to wash

them. I'd boil them and with salted cucumbers and sausage they'd be just perfect.

I found Lena in the washroom, the wife of conscripted Sanya. She was busy with potatoes too, digging out the eyes and cutting them in two.

"Hello there!" I feel my lips part in a charming smile.

Lena glances at me, looking oddly frightened, and nods.

"Hello!"

She has changed in the course of this past week and a half without her pathetic, debauched husband. She seems fresher, straighter, like a half-withered flower someone has put in a jar of water.

"Heard from Sanya?" I enquire.

"No, not so far."

"Ah well, the first few days there you don't have time for sending news back home," I explain as a former soldier. "You're only interested in working out how to stay alive."

"Uh-huh."

A thin, close-fitting dressing-gown with baby elephants is tightly drawn round Lena's substantial figure. I feel restive, and an almost forgotten excitement begins to disturb me. I look out of the corner of my eye at her full, white legs and her plump knee which the hem of the dressing-gown is stroking as if it were a live thing.

"How's Seryozha? Getting bigger?" I produce another question to keep the conversation going.

"Yes, of course."

"He must be missing his father."

"Ha, you think he'd be sobbing his heart out." Lena scowls, "What did he ever get from him? I've sent Seryozha off now to my parents. I want to redecorate the place."

"Quite right. You ought to change your surroundings. Once you've rearranged the furniture it's easier to get on with your life."

I hear that dull sigh again.

"Well..."

Encouraged by that "Well", I say in my protective male voice, "Let me know if you need anything. I'll be glad to help. I'm completely free during the day, and any other time, of course, when I'm not out at work." It doesn't even sound like me speaking, but somebody bolder and stronger who has suddenly awakened inside me. "I can paint and wallpaper, or mend furniture for you..."

Lena forces herself to look up from the saucepan. That fear is still in her eyes, but also something else which makes me smile and give her a wink.

"Thank you... If there's a problem..." She goes back to concentrating on halving the potatoes.

"Right, then," I bid her farewell. "All the best, neighbour!"

She starts and I sense she's in two minds whether to look at me or not. Instead of a glance she limits herself to a nod.

Lyokha and Pavlik are discussing something, genuinely agitated, but I don't hear what they're saying. My mind is busy going over the details of my encounter in the washroom, my imagination embellishing it with new and highly seductive details. I feel that if I were even to touch this young female, tormented by loneliness and an alcoholic husband, she would melt in an instant, moaning with desire. Yes, just walking away like that was definitely a mistake.

"You need to explain everything to them clearly," Lyokha was advising. "They're bound to understand."

"They'll understand it all right, and you'll find me with a hole through my heart."

"Oh, come off it!" Lyokha always views life optimistically when he has a hundred grams of vodka inside him. "You're worrying too much..."

Am I imagining it or do I really hear a slight sound coming

through the wall from Lena's room? As if somebody were scratching on the wall, quietly, timorously summoning me. I listen intently but am hindered by the voices of Pavlik and Lyokha.

"You have to fight, lads, for life. I realise that now," our visitor is saying. "I've tried to get money too easily, and fate has punished me. We must struggle."

"What do you mean struggle?" Lyokha asks, clearly interested. "How, exactly?"

"How, how... Do you remember I was telling you about those guys in France?"

Through the wall I hear the unmistakable sound of furniture being moved. I imagine Lena has finished her potatoes by now and returned to the decorating. With renewed force I feel that desire to be beside her, to see her, to see that strange fear in her eyes. I am confident now. I'll be resolute, I'll do it...

"Drink without me," I say getting up. "I'll just.... Don't wait for me."

Lena asks anxiously from behind the door, "Who's there?"

"It's Roman, your neighbour. May I come in for a moment?"

The bolt is slid back and the door opens a little. Lena peeps out through the crack of light.

"Excuse me, please... May I come in?"

I almost force my way into her room. Lena retreats slowly, a bit at a time, as if she's being pushed. She's both trying to resist this invasion and enticing me in further and further from the door.

"I heard you moving furniture. Perhaps I can help," I mumble. "After all, I have nothing to do... as it happens..."

My eyes probe her face, her neck, her hair, her cleavage in the neckline of her dressing-gown. She's staring at my forehead. Her lips are trembling, she has probably realised what I'm up to and is going to scream. I want to soothe her with my gentle murmuring: "Before I go to work... there's ages yet... Let me help with anything heavy... We've been living side by side for so long, and we've never... Lena, let's..."

I prepare to put my arms round her. I've noticed that half the bed is piled with rags and half is empty. I finally break loose from the chain which is holding me back and take off. There is no stopping me.

She continues to retreat.

"No," she says, but doesn't scream. She's asking so submissively and hopelessly that I would have to be a complete cretin to do as she says.

I grab her and press her to me, my face almost hitting hers. I feel neither her lips nor her cheeks, and my own lips seem to have disappeared, leaving behind only my jawbones and teeth.

"Wait, wait!" She turns her face away, exposing her ear and cheek to me. She tries to pull away but without much determination, as if unsure of herself, forcing herself.

I push her down on to the bed. The bedstead squeaks wearily as it takes our weight. Beneath me is a soft, warm, trembling body, so alive. I quickly run my hands all over it, stroking, squeezing, kneading, and my hands are trembling too, icy fingers burned by the heat of another person's skin.

"Please..."

Her eyes are shut tight, the eyelids wrinkled, her hands on my chest. She could push me away or kick me but doesn't do so. She's cringing there, waiting. I undo her dressing-gown and one button gets torn off. For a couple of precious seconds I look at the blue disc with its holes, not knowing what to do with it, then, coming to myself, throw it on the floor. I ought to say something, to keep soothing her, but no words suggest themselves. There's only gasping, an honest, genuine gasping given by nature as one being possesses another. How many of them there are, concealing themselves beneath heavy clothing, all wanting each other, famished, almost crazy for it but yet not able to make up their minds. They walk past each other not daring to signal, not daring to say openly what they're thinking. The idiots.

I do it all quickly and confidently, as if nature herself really is controlling me. How could it be otherwise? In me right now there's not only myself but someone else, strong, aggressive, aroused and erect in a matter of seconds. There's no pacifying him, no deceiving him. He's going to win, and will crush anybody. In her, in the body beneath me right now, in her too another has emerged, another who frightened her there in the washroom. She felt that other becoming alive and tried to resist but couldn't. They, those others, have overcome our foolish timidity and pushed us down here on to the bed.

Her soft, damp warmth sucks me in. I sink into her completely. Time expands and stands still. I'm in an enormous whirlpool, like a woodchip with no will of my own, spinning faster and faster, wanting only one thing – to plunge into the very centre of this maelstrom and be consumed by joy. To be stifled, to perish, to explode – what do I care?

"No, stop! Wait!" Lena has come to her senses and is doing something beneath me, her face to one side. I can see only her ear, then her left eye squinting at me, imploring me. "Stop! Don't come in there."

"Quiet, don't talk." I try to get back, I seek her lips. I want them to suck me in again but they're no longer responding. They've become tasteless and dead.

"Don't come inside me, do you hear?"

Down there something contracts, becomes coarse, dry now, and rough.

"Not inside me, please. Do it on my belly."

I'm only me again. That strong, invincible person has vanished as if he never existed. My arms, legs, back have regained their usual weight and are aching. I slide off the woman, off her ossified body in which I've lost all interest. I look between my legs at a small, limp appendage, hide him in my shorts and pull my jeans up over them.

"What?" Lena seems surprised.

I turn round. She's lying on her back with her dressing-gown wide open. Her skin is a yellowish white, her body running to fat and looking crumpled. I just need to get back to Lyokha and Pavlik as soon as possible. They probably still have some of the vodka left. I realise that everything is very straightforward, or perhaps complicated beyond all understanding. I take a step towards the door. Lena grabs my hand.

"Wait!"

"What is it?" I pause, skulking.

"Wait, don't go away." Doing up her dressing-gown, Lena goes over to the table.

On the table is a bottle, a frying pan with potatoes, and some pickled cabbage. I start feeling a bit better, and even manage to mutter, "You drink on your own?"

"Sit down!" She hastens to fill me a glass right to the brim. "Drink!"

"What about you?"

"I will too, I will too."

We drink together and I follow it with some of her tasty garlic-flavoured potatoes. Lena bursts into tears. I know the way she cries. I've heard it through the wall many times when she and that husband of hers were fighting. She cries shrilly and very loudly, gasping and trying to speak at the same time. Even now, when her husband is not there and no one is having a row, she cries in exactly the same way, sobbing, choking, and trying to speak.

"Well, so I drink. What of it? There's just been so much, so much I've had to put up with... I thought... What does it matter? The things he's done, the things he's done to me!"

"Come now, calm down," I say with a frown. "Take it easy."

"No, wait... there is no one else I can tell... Please!"

It's the usual. Not very nice, but familiar, and as a result I return completely to my normal state. I fill the glasses myself, and drain my own without more ado. Lena sobs, chokes, forces words out through her spasms, and I look around at the disorder in the room and her attempts to redecorate it.

"He, he so... degraded me. There was never a day, not a single day he left me alone. What kind of life is that, what kind of... Seryozha's so highly strung because of that... he understands everything, he sees it... And me, what kind of future..."

"Well, yes," I nod understandingly. "It's hard."

"Look!" Lena shows me her shoulder. "There's what he... do you see?" Just beneath the collarbone is a round, lumpy scar. "He did that with a screwdriver!"

"Oh, dear. Drink up, Lena."

She seizes the glass and pours it down her throat, coughing and choking. I thump her on the back.

"Eat something. Calm down."

"I went to the shop," she starts telling me, stifling her sobs. "I left Seryozha with him. I got stuck in a queue for cheap minced meat. I was stuck there, and Seryozha was acting up, and when I got back Sanya shouted, 'Where have you been, you slut?' and then he went at me with the screwdriver. And what's more, he was sober. When he's drunk, though, oh, oh, oh!"

More sobbing, choking, stifled words. I've had enough and get up.

"Okay, Lena, I'll be off. Things to do. Forgive me, okay?"

10

I was early getting to the theatre today, at around eleven, straight off the bus from seeing my parents. I left my bag in the bolthole and made myself at home on the sofa in the greenroom. Yesterday was hard going. We were getting in a supply of firewood, combing the fire breaks in the forest. We piled Zakhar high but on the way back got stuck in a swampy bit of the road. We had to unload the truck and shove branches and bits of wood under the wheels. In short, we got back home at ten in the evening, chucked the logs down by the lean-to, and collapsed into bed. Now my body feels leaden and I can barely lift my arms. I don't feel up to shifting even the lightest scenery.

I was sitting on the sofa waiting for the actors, the stagehands, and the others to start arriving, but Petrachenko came in and led me off, mumbling and nodding enigmatically.

So here we are in his studio. A bed, a little television on the wall, a table piled with junk, government-issue paints, canvases, awkward-looking stage props, inventory tags...

"Um, er." The master and slave of these premises is in a quandary. "Sit down, erm, erm, sit down over here. Let's have a drop to drink."

"No, no," I move away. "Vadim will kill me! Let's do that after the performance."

"Well, I'll just have a little one." Seryoga pours some Minus into a glass, downs it and chases it with water.

"I've decided, erm, to give up, erm..."

"Give up what?"

"Well, you know, drinking. I can't go on like this."

He gives a heartfelt sigh, staring at me expectantly, waiting for my reaction. I, of course, decide to support him: "Well, that's very good. Give it up."

Petrachenko has a bit more to drink and starts dreaming out loud: "When I give it up, erm, I'll sort everything out. I'm going to put a partition here." With a sweeping gesture he divides the studio in half. "This bit I'll live in, you know, paint my pictures; and this will be for everything else. Rom, it's time to sort my life out, absolutely sort it out!" Seryoga looks at the bottle and in his eyes I see determination and anger. He picks it up as if he's going to smash it against the wall. "Come on, Rom. Drink to that, eh? To me start on my journey!"

"Well," I cave in, "only a tiny drop. Fifty grams at the outside."

The gurgling of the vodka mingles with the grumbling of the scene-painter.

"Oh, what a long time it's been, erm, since I was properly dried out. For the last five years or so I've been in a kind of haze, ever since, erm, erm, since I left my last wife, Svetlana. That was it. Well, right, let's go!"

We clink glasses.

"Seryoga, to your success!" I convey my good wishes in a formal toast of exhortation.

"Thank you. I'll succeed. I've decided to."

We clink glasses a second time and then drink it down.

"Erm, er, sorry, there's nothing to eat with it." Petrachenko rustles food wrappers and pushes plates and tins around. "All I've got is water. Oh, Rom, you, erm, don't make my mistakes. You're still young, erm, get out of all this. It really does wreck everything, it turns everything to ashes!" He gets to his feet and shakes the almost empty bottle. "How many of these have I got through in my time? Oh, oh, oh."

I smoke and look at our scene-painter, and I simultaneously believe and don't believe that he really will give up drinking. Only, what kind of state will he be in if he doesn't imbibe his daily couple of bottles? What will he do if he succeeds? If he doesn't drink for a day, if he sobers up, he'll go out of his mind.

As if to underline my doubts, Petrachenko produces a new half-litre bottle from the cupboard.

"That's it," he announces. "The last one! We'll put it away and that'll be that. Forever!"

"Don't you think it might be better not to?"

"Oh, come on, this is the last one. Come on, Rom, let's knock it on the head!"

Again that gurgling, and again Petrachenko's dreams.

"I'll make up for lost time, believe me. I'll catch up with

myself. After all, I've got the canvas, erm, to hand, all the materials I need, there are the paint tubes waiting for me... Hey, I'm going to do amazing things!"

We clink glasses resolutely.

I put the glass to my lips, intending to down it in one without taking a breath. I'm all ready when suddenly the door opens.

"You're boozing again, you cunt!" Our team leader rushes at me, his face distorted with rage. "I warned you last time..." I can see he's about to thump me, but Petrachenko, bless him, intervenes just in time.

"Wait, Vadim, erm, don't be angry. I, erm, am having a celebration!"

"What the hell are you celebrating?"

"I'm giving up, erm, giving up the demon drink forever. Forever, Vadim! Sit down, erm, and let's have a drop. Ritually, to me start on my journey."

Vadim sits down, grunting testily, watching the transparent aromatic fluid pouring into his cup. With every drop his eyes become kinder and warmer.

"Have you forgotten, then, that today's Tuesday?"

A little unsteadily, the team leader and I leave the scenery workshop.

"No," I say. "Of course not. Why?"

"Why, why? We're supposed to be following the cashier. Or are you wanting out of it?"

"Not a bit. Let's go, let's tail her."

Andrei is hanging around the security booth looking tense and very upright, as if he's one minute away from a duel to the death; his eyes are fixed on the stairs to the first floor where, among all the useless offices, there's the accounts department.

Vadim gives him a shove and orders in a menacing whisper, "Relax!"

The giant instantly goes limp, his muscles deflate, he sways on his thick legs, and his eyes stray over the walls, the worn linoleum on the floor, and the dusty cornices up by the ceiling.

The security woman is enthusiastically tucking into pork scratchings and buckwheat porridge out of a litre jar. She pays no attention to us.

"Where's Lyokha?" the team leader asks me. "It's five to one already."

"I don't know, I haven't come from the hostel."

"Shit, we agreed on this!"

I'm beginning to feel very uncomfortable. I feel as if, when the chief cashier does appear, Vadim is going to shout, "Get her, boys!" and we'll carry out a very public, noisy, bloody robbery. I wriggle my shoulders to shake off the goose pimples running up and down my back but it doesn't help. I take out a cigarette and slowly knead it.

Just then from upstairs we hear gasping, the rustling of a plastic mac, and slow, tentative feet testing each step on the staircase. Vadim turns to stone, his eyes like Andrei's three minutes ago, fearless and determined, registering a crazy readiness to pile in. He immediately remembers himself and assumes the appearance of someone who just happens to be standing outside the security post, an inoffensive, rather bored person of no consequence. The footsteps are meanwhile approaching, growing louder and more distinct. The prey is being driven towards the guns, until: here she is, our stout, elderly chief cashier, over seventy, wearing enormous spectacles and carrying her invariable imitation crocodile bag.

She creeps lower and lower, gripping the banisters and positioning first her right then her left foot on the next step. She advances, like a sapper crossing a minefield, slowly but resolutely, for what is probably the five thousandth time.

Coming abreast of us, she looks us over suspiciously through the lenses of her thick spectacles, recognises us, and creeps on. She stops at the security point and declares, as always, in a voice that is firm but rasping, because she's so ancient, "I am going to the bank."

The security woman detaches herself from her jar, licks a stray grain of buckwheat from her lip, and looks up at the chief cashier. Their semi-cadaverous eyes make repeated contact and a spark of recognition flares.

"Yes, yes, fine," the security woman nods, shoves her spoon into the jar again, and the chief cashier continues on her way.

Out of the door, on to the street, following her traditional Tuesday route to the bank.

Lyokha didn't turn up to work at all. I find him back at our room, naturally on the bed. He's lying as usual on his back, staring at the ceiling, but his face is subtly changed: he's sporting a magnificent, browny-blue, swollen black eye which is fairly hideous, but also quite comical.

"Who treated you to that?" I enquire as I take off my shoes.

"Knock it off, scumbag," my roommate growls quietly. He sniffs the air and a hint of envy can be heard as he growls, "you rat, you've been drinking!"

"Yes, we had quite a booze-up with Petrachenko. He's decided to give up drinking, so we were celebrating..."

I judge it best not to pry into how Lyokha earned his punch in the face. He could turn nasty, and in any case he soon gives up and starts telling me himself.

"They finally turned the fucking hot water on, so I thought I'd wash my socks and shirt. The washroom was full already, packed with women all shouting at each other. There was only one sink free. Everybody in there was washing clothes. Anyway, I took that one."

"And?" I encourage my roommate, even as I rejoice that the hot water is finally on.

"In came some slitty-eyed Chink or Vietnamese, you can't tell one from the other, and started kicking up a fuss because no sink was free. He shoved me, maybe by accident, maybe deliberately, and I shoved him back and he fell over. He was just a little squirt. I don't reckon I pushed him that hard. Anyway he jumped up and started jabbering in his chinky lingo and ran out. I got on with washing my clothes and suddenly half a dozen of them came running in, including him. Well, shit." Lyokha gingerly touches the affected part of his face. "We're just about to go on tour, and here... well... Has anybody said when we're going?"

"This Friday."

"Oh, fuck!"

I lethargically set the table. I've brought plov from the village in a saucepan, and some pies. I need to eat and go to bed. Yesterday's saga with the firewood took so much out of me I'll need more than a week to recover. Then there's the tour in Sayanogorsk, which is going to be hard work.

"Want something to eat?" I ask Lyokha as I take the warm plov off the cooker.

"You bet."

We fish rice and pieces of meat out of the saucepan in silence. I guzzle the plov while Lyokha eats cautiously, occasionally fingering his black eye.

"What do you think," he finally asks. "Do you think they'll take me on the tour with an eye like this?"

"Unlikely, to be honest... Although Dimentius has handed in his notice and the new boy, Igor, starts only tomorrow. They might well take you. At least you know what to do and how to do it."

In Sayanogorsk, the town beside the Sayano-Shushenskoye hydroelectric station, the culture centre is twice the size of our theatre, and the stage is in proportion. To make the scenery look right you need experience and familiarity with the stage. Lyokha and I have been there ten times already and have a fair idea what we are doing. "Of course they'll take you," I say, confidently now. "What choice do they have?"

"That would be good... Oh, by the way, I came across that floozie of yours!" Lyokha returns to life.

"What floozie?"

"You know, that redhead, from the windowsill."

Now this really is interesting! Of course, I don't let on. I ask casually, "Where did you see her? Back on the windowsill?"

"No. Wait for it!" Lyokha, instantly forgetting his sufferings, can't wait to tell me. "Well, after those chinks had done me over, I ran to Pavlik to borrow seven roubles to get some lead water. It's really good for stopping swelling. Pavlik wasn't there, so I went round to see Lena, you know, Sanya's wife. She lent me it and I ran to the chemist's at the Trade Centre and who do you think I saw beside the kiosks? Three guesses!"

"Okay, you saw her there. And?" I ask intrigued.

"Well, hey, listen to this. They were out of lead water, so I bought a pack of Java cigarettes instead. I was on my way back when, suddenly, there she was. All painted up, wearing a short skirt, jiggling about to the music from one of the kiosks. Smoking. Wearing a pair of really expensive tights and looking ... phwoar! She got even me hard just looking at her! Anyway, I stopped over to one side, watching what was going on. I don't even know why. Anyway, up come these couple of bruisers. They were huge, and clutching litre bottles of Ferrain wine in their maulers, and bagfuls of grub. They haggled with her for a bit, she nodded, gave them a smile, God be damned what a smile, and the three of them went off together. They got into a Lada-9 and drove off. Get it, Rom. No?"

"Get what?"

"Are you a moron, or are you a moron? She's a straight up and down hooker. You should've got stuck in while she was here. I bet she's got the clap by now."

Needless to say, Lyokha's tale has not left me unmoved. I'm ready right now to race to the Trade Centre. I shake a fag out of the pack, and feel around in my pockets looking for a lighter. Lyokha scratches himself and grins derisively:

"'She's a real sweetie. We ought to get to know her. Just barely sixteen.' Oh, you sad loser. You missed out! You screwed up big time."

The town is covered in grey freezing fog. All colours other than grey have faded. Even the lurid advertising boards have turned grey. It's difficult to breathe: the frost scorches your nostrils and throat. You have to hide your face in your collar.

The fumes from car exhausts hang above the street in a suffocating shroud; the soot from coal fires first rises from the stove chimneys of the nearest log cabins then sprinkles black flakes over the pavement.

"Well, ain't this something," Lyokha drawls in amazement, burying his hands deep in the sleeves of his anorak. "Real brass monkey weather!"

It's uncommon for the temperature to plummet below minus twenty at the end of October, and to make things worse, there's no snow cover. The cherry trees, plums, cultivated Victoria strawberries are likely to freeze to death. My parents earn most of their income in the summer from selling strawberries.

We're walking to the theatre, of course, going to work. From time to time we slip on puddles turned to ice and curse. We're following our usual route to perform our customary routine functions. It's hard to carry on when every cell in your brain is desperately shrieking, don't do this! What's the point? Just drop everything, run away, be different! Find something else, for heaven's sake, something new!" My legs, meanwhile, continue to propel me forwards, along a pavement I've walked a thousand times before.

I glance at the infrequent passers-by, at people in cars with their headlights on. All their faces are crying out the same thing, but all of them are walking, driving, hurrying forwards to a place where they have to be. It's only in fairy tales that you fall over and become transformed, that you put on seven-league boots and in a trice find yourself in a land far, far away; you make a wish and – whoosh! it comes true. In real life you have to scrape along as best you can. Changes for the better are a matter of luck, and some people never have any.

A bus comes along. It's the No. 120, Minusinsk-Abakan. In half an hour I could be there, in a different town. I could try to put together a pop group, write some new songs, make a demo tape in a decent studio, send it to Novosibirsk or Moscow and get myself known. Or something like that. For heaven's sake, I could spend my whole life in this pathetic way. The bus pulls up, the doors open, hissing and scraping. Shall I just jump in and go?

"Well, are you coming or not?" Lyokha shouts, sticking his ugly mug out of his collar. "What have you seen there? Your little floozie?"

I catch up with him without a word and we stagger on.

I was here yesterday, and today I came here again before work, searching, hoping... and now I'm doing it again. I didn't wait for Uncle Gena and his old boneshaker. As soon as we'd cleared the scenery away after the performance, I caught the bus to the Trade Centre. I paid the bloody conductor five roubles, but she isn't here. She isn't here again.

Both yesterday and today I got on Lyokha's nerves, asking him if he was sure he'd seen her by the kiosks. Had she really been jiggling about in front of those men, and had they rented her and taken her off? At first Lyokha replied "Yes" calmly enough, but then he started telling me to go fuck myself. That means, he wasn't making it up.

And so, as soon as I finished work, I rushed here. But she isn't here. She isn't here.

Most likely it was just a one-off. She'd got fed up with the hostel, her tiny room, the windowsill in the old kitchen, tired of her stereo, and decided to blow away the cobwebs. Chances are they'd gone off with her and abused her, hurt her, brutally murdered her. Perhaps she's lying now in the city rubbish tip in a black bin bag, or in the pine forest with a few branches thrown over her, or in some cellar. Or perhaps I've just turned up too late at night.

But I keep hoping. Stupidly, sincerely, I keep hoping. Sometimes I walk very slowly, almost crawling along. At other times I practically run, the length of the kilometre-long row of kiosks. I'm looking for her, wanting her, angry but ready to be delighted. There are plenty of women around, young girls, teenagers, but now even the prettiest of them leaves me cold. I need only that girl, the girl from the windowsill, the girl with the golden auburn hair, small and fragile and needing me to put my arms around her and cherish her. I need to look into her eyes. I've needed to look into her eyes for a very long time.

Meanwhile, the Trade Centre is partying round the clock, noisy, unstoppable, indefatigable. The stalls may be almost empty, but the kiosks, the cafŭs, the mini-markets are in full swing. From time to time cars drive up and muscle-bound men in tracksuits and mink fur hats buy booze and expensive food. They're getting ready to mark the end of the working day in a worthy fashion. But what about me? I search through my pockets and pull a few coins out of the detritus and count them, blowing away bits of tobacco from my hand. I scowl and slip them back. There isn't even enough for a tub of ice cream.

Once again I wander along the pavement, bumping into girls I don't know and don't need, into couples blinded by love, into guys wearing tracksuits and mink fur hats. I sift through hundreds of faces, trying to pick her out, a small human being, a small, vulnerable human being. In a moment I am going to see her, and put my arms round her, and we'll both be saved. We'll warm each other, we'll hide. We'll go away, escape together, she and I, to a place far away, forever.

A few times I think I've spotted her. It always happens

when you really, really want to see someone. I rush towards the glowing mirage, bump into people, get hissed at and tut-tutted at, loudly sworn at, accused of being a drunken ass. I really don't care, they can call me what they like. There she is, that's her! I run towards her, slipping, and jostling people. But it isn't her, it's someone quite different. My mistake. And again I search and am driven crazy by hopes which are soon dashed. I run tirelessly along the pavement, rushing towards mirages, and running fearfully away from them.

You could make a fool of yourself that way from now until morning. For a hundred thousand years. You could spend your whole life doing it.

11

There are almost no old people in Sayanogorsk. The town didn't grow out of a remote village in the taiga, but rose ready formed with its bright five-storey apartment blocks divided into symmetrical regions with shops, schools, nurseries and cinemas conveniently to hand.

It stands on the banks of the Yenisei, some fifteen kilometres upstream, its hydroelectric station one of the most powerful in the world. Sayanogorsk is surrounded on all sides by the Sayan Mountains overgrown with pine and larch forests. Up there the Yenisei is raging, angry, hemmed in by cliffs, and that's why, some thirty years ago, they decided to build a hydroelectric station. First surveyors and geologists were sent out, then came construction workers.

At the same time as they constructed the hydroelectric station, they built Sayanogorsk. There were no settlements nearby, only the decrepit dugouts of Old Believer hermitages and hunters' cabins. It really wasn't a hospitable region with its high mountains, and a winter that, although it wasn't particularly severe, lasted from late September until the middle of April. Even in May there is snow on the mountaintops.

Hordes of romantic young people came here from every corner of the Soviet Union, and many settled; others, having built the hydroelectric station, went off to new construction projects.

There are several sanatoria nearby where the citizens of Sayanogorsk and visitors from Abakan, Krasnoyarsk, and Novosibirsk were meant to rest and recuperate, but they are all empty because the local aluminium factory is hard at work polluting the environment.

This is, nevertheless, a beautiful region, and the town itself is toy-like; or rather, it's like a scale model in an architectural exhibition. It's compact, pleasing to the eye, and neat. It's the exemplary capital city of one of the Soviet Union's "projects of the century". Its broad, straight thoroughfares are nearly all named after the cities from which construction teams came to build the hydroelectric station: Moscow, Leningrad, Kharkov, Kiev, and Odessa.

People live on memories of their romantic youth. They often gather on Barren Hill on the outskirts of Sayanogorsk where their tented encampment once stood. They make campfires of pinecones, play the guitar, and sing life-affirming songs. Every three months a literary and news magazine called *Midstream* is published, featuring poems, stories, and reminiscences of the earliest pioneers, essays about the Yenisei, the taiga, and the history of the Sayanogorsk region. *Midstream* first appeared, I'm told, as a wall newspaper which was glued up on notice-boards at the "crossroads" of the lanes in the town of tents; later, with the appearance of a printing press, it grew in size, added illustrations, and was printed in more copies.

Our theatre is often invited here. The town has a population of around thirty thousand, and a great many of the inhabitants have college education. They are intellectuals trying desperately to break down the wall dividing the old, fairly large cities from such artificial settlements as Sayanogorsk. It really does stand in the midst of the mountains and the taiga, seventy kilometres from the railway line and over a hundred from Abakan. People feel cut off from the mainstream of life, and stew in their own post-romantic juice.

In the old days, people say, theatres came here from all over the USSR almost every month, circuses, zoos, and all sorts of exhibitions, but that's dried up. We're nearer to Sayanogorsk than other theatres, so two or three times a year we have to get ourselves together, load up our ancient ZIL truck with scenery, and go there. That's in effect the only touring we do, other than outreach to villages in the Minusinsk district, and taking part in the annual drama festival of the Krasnoyarsk Region.

We're sitting in the back seat of the bus, the four stagehands – Vadim, Andrei, me, and sixteen-year-old Igor in place of Dima. Lyokha has been left behind because of his punched up face, and in any case he has concussion. He worked for one day and then started being sick. We're all suffering as a result of not being allowed to light up: a couple of elderly actresses can't stand tobacco smoke.

Uncle Gena makes periodic five-minute stops. The company bundles out of the bus and we quickly smoke a cigarette whilst admiring the view.

"It's wonderful, it's simply wonderful! How I wish I could have a warm little house here, with a bathhouse," Semukhin fantasises as he gazes down at the bottom of the ravine and, assuming the character of Trigorin in "The Seagull", continues in an infinitely weary voice, "To rest for a year or two. To sleep, to sleep..."

Khrapchenko, our company jester, brings him down to earth: "The bears won't let you. You might find fighting them off every night rather too much of an action holiday."

"Can there really be bears here?" Kruglova asks in disbelief. "The road is so near..."

"Darling, don't you remember that bear which wandered right through the middle of Minusinsk in 1985?"

Our director, Dubravin, announces edgily, "Ladies and gentlemen, it's time to move on! We were two hours late in setting off. Please get back on the bus!" Grinding his cigarette into the snowy gravel, he's the first to climb back on board.

The main topic of conversation today is the disappearance of Ksyukha, our hair stylist. Nobody knows anything for sure, but there is no shortage of guesswork and rumour mongering. Some of it is complete nonsense, to the effect that Ksyukha has done her partner in (that is, Pavlik).

"She wouldn't have killed him, but there's something fishy going on," Vadim who is sitting next to me mutters. "What were you saying had been going on at the hostel? Hey, Rom?"

"I've already told you," I respond lazily, but nevertheless tell him again in a mysterious whisper and not without a degree of satisfaction. "Waliszewski ran in to see us last night and said, 'Ksyukha's room is crawling with police'. Lyokha told him to bugger off, but I went to have a look. Sure enough, there were half a dozen cops, everything had been turned inside out, they were carrying out some sort of little packets. Her guy was into weed, perhaps it was something to do with that."

"Mm, yes." Vadim leans closer and whispers right in my ear, "This incident might mess up our plans for the chief cashier!"

"Why?"

"Fuck knows, it's just a feeling... at all events, it isn't going to help."

"I suppose not," I mutter. "Most likely..."

"Incidentally, how much money you've got on you?"

"None. Where would I get it from?"

"Well, that's great!" the team leader exclaims in amazement and turns to Andrei. "Andrei, got any dosh?"

"About thirty roubles, no more."

"Something tells me this is going to be a grim little trip.

Well, what can we do?" At this point he remembers the new boy. "Hey, Igor, how are you placed financially?"

Igor, a very thin boy who seems to be frightened by something, answers evasively, "I've got a little, for emergencies."

"No, don't think I'm... It's just we need to celebrate your joining the team. Going away on tour is a great start! We should celebrate it properly." Vadim gives the boy a wink. "This evening we'll go to the banks of Father Yenisei, make a fire and... Do you know what the Yenisei is like here? It's a wild beast! We'll sit, talk together, toast some bread over the fire..."

"Stop it, Vadim!" Andrei smacks his lips, and strokes his stomach with an enormous hand. "Or I'll hit the bottle before the performance."

Vadim's promises about the outing and the campfire came to nothing. The whole three days we were working frantically, and the weather wasn't up to much anyway.

We had two performances a day: fairy tales in the morning and something for the grown-ups in the evening. They all involved loads of scenery, and we had to drag it from the truck some two hundred metres to the culture center because it's in a park and nobody had thought to provide vehicle access. We were swearing like troopers.

On top of that, for the whole three days we bore the burden of their manager, a stout, red-faced geezer of about fifty. He would come into the smoking room where we stagehands were killing time while the actors were on stage, and start going on and on: "Life is not much fun here, lads, not much fun at all. We all had faith, we lived in hope, and now it's all over. Hope is the greatest evil, the worst folly. If it hadn't been for that things might still have worked out right for us. We could have moved away while we still had the strength, settled down somewhere normal. But we were full of hope, and now look at us. Oh, oh, oh..."

We patiently sat there listening dully to this guy, whose once expensive suit was scuffed and worn now, with a ridiculously bright tie hanging down over his chest. At times he looked like he was suffering from the mother of all hangovers, at others he just seemed terribly weary. His bloodshot eyes appeared unseeing, and his face too was covered in a cobweb of purple veins. He had thin, pale lips, and clumps of stubble on his throat.

He would sit there, chain-smoking Opal cigarettes and rambling on deliriously, "Hope is a great evil, it destroys people. How truly we find that expressed in 'Faust': 'Cursed be Hope! Cursed be Faith; And cursed be Patience most of all!' Not bad, eh? Those are immortal words." He taps another cigarette out of his pack, listens for a moment to the artificial voices of the actors, and shakes his head. "There, the theatre is packed again. Do you think it's because people are enjoying life here? Do you think they have any alternative this evening? Alas, no. They have no options. Emptiness, emptiness... The shelves of the bookshop are completely bare: they don't even send us crime novels any more. Television? The national channel is the only one with reasonable reception, and what are you going to see on that? Action films, soap operas? We can't appreciate those, we don't know how to. It's as if we're in a sealed jar. Oh, boys, boys, thank you for coming here, for not leaving us to suffocate completely. We need to see someone occasionally..."

Vadim whispers to me, "Do you think we might be able to touch him for a couple of bottles? We could sit somewhere after the performance and unwind."

"Unlikely," I whisper in reply. "I doubt whether he drinks, and if he does, I bet he does it alone."

"Um... quite possible."

"The worst of it, lads, is that we're ruining our children. They already despise us, they find us ridiculous." The manager abandons the melted filter of his cigarette, takes out a new one, and seems to be trying to remember which end to put in his mouth. "They don't just laugh at us, they don't just hold us in silent contempt, they say quite openly, 'You idiots, why ever did you leave Moscow? What was wrong with life there? Did you think about us and what sort of life we would have here? It's obvious,' they say, 'not difficult to picture. You grabbed your rucksacks and took off for God knows where, and now what are we supposed to do in this dump?'" The manager casts his bloodshot eyes over us, and lights up again. "That's how it is... but could we ever have imagined... We came here to build a town, a real town of our own where people would be genuinely themselves, without all the dross, without the weight of the past, in order to live happy lives! We knew we'd have to create everything from scratch, but at least it would be clean. You understand, don't you?" He nods at Vadim. "You're a grown man, you probably still remember your elder brothers going off to build the Baikal-Amur Railway, to Yamal, to this place. There was so much noise about it at the time, every day bulletins broadcast from the construction sites as if they were reporting a battle from the front line. Ah, but now... there's just the emptiness and a bitter taste. Hey ho, we've landed back in all that old dross! We are ashamed to look our children in the eyes. We've cheated them. And they have every right, every right to despise us, and to ask us to give them the money to get out of here. So be it! Our generation has had its day. There are no more pioneers of Sayanogorsk, there's no more of that proud tribe who loved life. We carry on, we work here like prisoners of war. We've even got, lads, we've even got..." the manager lowers his voice and almost hisses, "our own psychopath. Yes, yes! Haven't you heard? He attacks pregnant women at nightfall, kicking them in the stomach... Have you really not heard? There were articles in all the papers, special reports, we're famous for it the length and breadth of Russia!"

"I read about it in *Worker Power*," young Igor says, excited and fearful.

"There, you see? It was in *Izvestiya* too, and in the *MK Gazette*. Could we ever have imagined such a thing back then? Our dreams and aspirations were so pure."

From behind the door to the stage and the auditorium comes a sharp, deafening explosion of applause. It goes on, unstinting, for a long, long time, not lapsing into the usual rhythmical hand clapping but with everybody applauding in their own tempo, putting their hands together for the cast in complete sincerity. Then comes the stampede of the actors as they hurry to their dressing rooms for a rest and a smoke before the second act. We head the other way, on to the stage. It's our turn to work.

I look round and see the manager pulling a face as he lights up his tenth cigarette in half an hour. He rubs his red, tormented eyes as if he would like to gouge them out.

They have put us up in their one and only, but very classy, hotel. It's a slender, twelve-storey glass and concrete tower such as you might find at the seaside in Sochi. At our request they've given us rooms on the first floor: many of the actors are afraid that such an unusually high building, unoccupied for a long time, could collapse. If that happens they'd prefer to be closer to the ground.

Vadim, Andrei and I occupy one triple room, while the luckless Igor finds himself sharing with Lyalin and Khrapchenko.

"I'm sorry," our team leader said to him, his voice untypically hesitant. "There are no four-bed rooms. With those guys you need to be a bit... Keep your distance. Especially with Lyalin."

Of course, after the first evening's performance we had a party to celebrate the start of the tour. A little banquet was held in the hotel restaurant. The mayor of Sayanogorsk came, and officials from the Department of Culture, several prominent citizens, and the red-faced manager of the culture centre. There were speeches, a poet from *Midstream* read a poem; our Dubravin did his best to respond worthily, and promised to bring us back to the "glorious city of hydroelectric engineers and romantics" practically every quarter. There wasn't much food on the tables, and in place of vodka there was nine-proof red wine, so we soon repaired to our own room to have a proper party. A blizzard blew up outside and the glass in the enormous windows groaned under the gusting wind. There was no question of an outing to the banks of the Yenisei or making campfires.

"This is more like it," Andrei says, watching Vadim and me setting out the bottles and the food we bought in the local "24 Hours". "Down there you didn't even feel you were one of the family. You were just waiting for them to get tired of talking nonsense and be ready for a nice glass of that grape juice."

Our team leader has a cheering announcement: "Larisa Volkova has promised to come. I nicked a bottle of Isabella for her specially."

"A party always goes better with a few girls," Andrei grins. "We should have invited Olga from Wardrobe, or that one who's replaced Ksyukha."

"I did, but they said no."

"Oh, what bitches!"

Incidentally, before our departure they had to comb the hairdressing salons of Minusinsk to find someone to replace the missing Ksyukha. They found a girl (not bad-looking), and managed more or less to show her the ropes. She's okay. If Ksyukha is in serious trouble, the new girl may stay on, in which case I'll endeavour to establish relations...

We don't go at the drink too hard, each of us is tacitly waiting for Larisa, one of the pleasantest of the actresses, to arrive. Whenever Petrachenko starts in on his renowned monologue about the treacherous nature of the art of acting, it's Larisa I imagine. She acts her roles with such feeling that I, along, I detect, with many other people, am almost moved to tears. Such unsettling feelings begin to pick at my heart that I quickly move away from the stage in order not to see her, or hear the words contrived by a long-dead author, which she is bringing to life so passionately for the twentieth or fiftieth time, and sincerely experiencing them. People say she's very talented and has become almost irreplaceable in the three seasons she's been at the theatre since graduating from drama school. She's engaged in almost every production.

We hear the sound of many feet on the hotel's carpet runners, and voices.

"The banquet is over," Andrei guesses. "They've agreed to open a branch of the theatre here!"

"Yes, and it'll be you who gets to stay in glorious Sayano-gorsk," our team leader promptly needles him, "as local director of scene-shifting."

Andrei is trying to think up some suitably witty rejoinder when there comes a knock at the door. Vadim leaps to his feet.

"I can only stay five minutes, boys," Larisa warns even before she has come in. She assesses the room from the doorway. "Oh, what wonderful apartments you've been awarded! De luxe! Tatyana and I do have a twin room, but really... the walls are so stained, and the wallpaper is coming away."

You would think that in Minusinsk she lived in a snow-white palace with pools and baldachins. Vadim fawns upon her like a lackey.

"Over here, Lara. We've been keeping the wine specially for you. How was the banquet?"

"Call that a banquet! Ugh!" the actress wrinkles her pretty little face. "Not too much for me," she says, stemming the flow of Isabella into her plastic cup. "We have a fairy tale tomorrow morning which is hard work. Somersaults, running about... The children's productions use up more energy than serious plays."

Vadim is plainly infatuated and, to the best of his limited ability, pays her clumsy compliments. Andrei is in competition with his team leader. For some reason this begins to get on my nerves. I feel an urge to blurt out something unexpected and rude. I look at Larisa's face, expressive, attractive, and young, but already being spoiled by the greasepaint. I listen to the sweet, melodious, but artificial and irritating voice in which she shares her creative plans with us.

"This summer I intend to enrol at the State Institute of Theatre Arts. Dubravin has agreed. He's convinced I have talent."

"Immense talent!" Vadim corrects her.

"Go for it, Lara. That could really lead somewhere!" Andrei promptly piles in.

"If I make it in Moscow I'll try to find a job there. Why come back? But," Larisa gives herself a little shake, "let's not try to second guess the future."

"Absolutely," I say, pouring more vodka for the guys. "Let's just drink to great expectations!"

"Not for me... I can't," little Igor, who has got smashed without anyone noticing, pipes up. He tries to stand, almost loses his balance, and clutches at the back of a chair.

"Wait, Igor my friend, just this last one. Come on, for expectations! It's a sacred toast!"

"No, I really can't... I need to sleep..." Staggering, hiccupping, Igor leaves the room, and shortly after that our actress gets up to make her exit.

"Time to get some rest. Tomorrow I have a demanding fairy tale."

"What's this! Look how much wine we've still got left, how much food!" Vadim proffers her a plate with slices of yellow-skinned apple. "Larisa, just a little more! Let's get to know each other better."

But she leaves. We drink our way through the vodka in silence, then the Isabella, put out the light and go to bed. Our team leader begins in a voice tinged with anger to fantasise about how and in exactly which positions he would shag Larisa Volkova. Andrei and I join in. It becomes incredibly arousing, almost as if it were happening. The girl seems to be in the next bed right now, having it off with Andrei or Vadim, and next she will be underneath me or, better, on top. A naked Amazon on a young stallion. Trying to move as little as possible, I rub my mighty, engorged cock in my fist and quickly come onto the edge of the sheet. I fall asleep, feeling the hot, smooth, firm body of a beautiful girl beside me.

Late on Sunday evening we returned to Minusinsk, but put off unloading the truck with the scenery until Tuesday. Completely knackered I dragged myself to the hostel and there, naturally, found Lyokha. The black eye had almost gone from his face, but now he had another problem.

"Why now? What can I do to help them?" He starts moaning even before asking how the tour had gone. "Empty their bedpans? Oh, fuck, shit!"

"What is it now?"

He reads me a telegram: "'Come to say goodbye. We're very ill. Have sent money for fare care of theatre. Mum.' What do you make of that?"

I don't say anything. I'm taken aback, but at the same time pleased that Lyokha might be away, if only for a week or two, leaving me with a room to myself. In order to make some kind of response, I say, "Yes, it doesn't sound much fun."

Lyokha immediately deluges me with talk: "Perhaps I should just forget it, what do you think Rom? Get the money and send it back, eh? Send a telegram to say I'm working and there's no way I can go? I'll rot there, Rom, I can feel it! What's there for me to do there, I ask you. Absolutely zilch. Go down the mines, do you think? I do have a licence, I suppose I could drive a truck, but... is that really on? I'd go completely out of my mind from boredom. I don't want to leave here. So what if they're my parents? They've screwed up their own lives and now they're asking me to go and help them last a bit longer. Shit, I want to live myself! If we make a go of it with the cashier, I'd like just once in my life to live it up. I shouldn't go, should I? Fuck my filial duties! When they were conceiving me, were they thinking about me? I didn't ask to be born, but since I have been... why should I have to suffer too?"

"Hang on," I say, trying to change the topic. "Have you heard any more about Ksyukha?"

"I don't give a fuck about Ksyukha! I've got enough shit of my own to deal with!"

But, when he's let off steam, Lyokha as usual starts enthusiastically in on other people's problems. Today, they're those of Ksyukha and Pavlik.

"That moron has finally read more than was good for him. He won't be doing that for the next five years or so. Apart from his case notes! What happened? They did try mugging a 'bloodsucker'. I heard all about it at the theatre and in the hostel, but I couldn't believe it, it was just too hilarious. Really, like in a bad film. Apparently Pavlik had some pal with a car, right? So the three of them go round to this businessman's home one evening, Pavlik, Ksyukha and his mate. They pull stockings over their heads and whip out toy pistols, you know, those Chinese ones you can't tell from the real thing. So, anyway, they barge into this businessman's house, get him and his wife on the floor, tie them up, search the house, find maybe fifteen thousand roubles and some bits and pieces, and scarper. They might have got away with it if the traffic cops hadn't flagged them down, completely out of the blue, wanting to check their papers. They stepped on the gas and the cops went after them. They've really landed in it, the woman from the box office told me; seems like her son works in the prosecutor's office, bear that in mind, dickhead! They think Ksyukha will get a suspended sentence, but Pavlik is really in the shit. The more so because they found weed in his room. Pretty clever, eh?"

"Well, yes," I sigh. "They are truly remarkable idiots."

"Hold on, though, that isn't all there is to this story. There's a moral in it. I've been slobbing around here for three days now, thinking. You just need to be smart if you're going to do something like that. Smart! That goes for our business with the chief cashier too. Only we, the four of us, should know anything about it, and we mustn't lose our nerve or let anything go wrong. Let's face it, if they'd done everything right they'd be in clover now, but at the last moment they fouled it up themselves."

Relieved that Lyokha has finally got off the subject of his imminent visit to his sick parents, I undress and fall on to the bed while he dreams on.

"You have to focus on what you're doing, reduce the risk to zero. If they'd held on to that fifteen thousand, that would've been five thousand for each of them. Pretty clever, eh? On top of that there was some gold there, and some other valuables. If we play the cashier right we'll be sorted. It would be good to have anything at all! We can't even get our hands on a hundred roubles at the moment. Nobody's going to hand us money just for fun, and the fact is, we need to live!"

12

It's quarter to midnight and an icy wind is blowing from every direction at once. For some reason I decided to walk home from work, to get some fresh air. Oh, dear! Now I'm cursing myself for a fool, pulling my head down into my jacket collar, clenching and unclenching my stiff, cold fingers.

The streets are dark and deserted. The windows of the log houses have their shutters firmly closed, held with steel hooks securely bolted to the walls inside. In the yards dogs on chains growl, spoiling for a fight; barbed wire runs along the top of endless fences. These are safe strongholds: nobody is going to get in there.

I can't go back to the hostel. I'm fed up to the point where the very thought of it makes me sick: whingeing Lyokha, the crazed ceiling, the smell in the toilets, the flickering of light bulbs, and that empty windowsill in the kitchen. But where else can I go? Whatever made me think it would be a good idea to walk? But something did. I need a different destination, anywhere but the hostel. I need to break out of this old, tired routine. I need to change into someone new, someone nobody knows, not even me. Especially not me.

I stop at the corner of Labour Street and Michurin. I see the lights of the Trade Centre shining ahead of me, the colourful Christmas garlands in kiosk windows twinkle enticingly, but that is not where I have to go. Nothing in the Trade Centre is meant for me. The girl with the golden auburn hair is not there. Perhaps I can't find her because she's not meant for me either but for a different kind of person. Well, to hell with her.

I look dully up. The sky above is colourless, not black, not white, not high, not low. I don't know what it is. Something falls out of it occasionally, which might be rain or might be snow.

I pull a pack of Prima out of my pocket and am about to light up when I realise that I haven't the least desire to smoke. What I want is something else. I shove the cigarettes back in my pocket. Am I ill?

I wish I could just go to the nearest entrance, knock on the first door I see, and say, "Hello! I've come to see you." "Oh, do come on in! Welcome! We've been so hoping you'd come. Let's be friends!"

"Hey, great to see you!" Shura Reshetov gives me a twisted, but sincere smile. "Come in, come in, just at the right time."

"May I?"

"Yes, yes! Come right in."

Shura's "just at the right time" is a little disturbing, since it implies he's planning either to hit the bottle or get stoned, when what I need right now is something quite different. How long I've been waiting for an unhurried, half whispered, heart-to-heart talk by the light of a table lamp or, better still, a candle. To talk all kinds of childish nonsense, and hear the same in return, all night, right through till morning. And then to watch the dawn, amazed, enraptured. Such nights have been left far behind, back in the non-drinking times when I didn't particularly think about girls, but thought, until I trembled with excitement, until I gave myself a headache, about the meaning of life, about how the telephone works, or a television, or a tape-recorder; about whether the universe has an end, and if so what it might be like, and what might lie beyond it. That's the kind of nonsense I am longing to think about right now.

Shura seems to be hearing what I'm thinking. He smiles kindly, like a really close friend, and nods. "We'll just enjoy each other's company and take it easy. This is the last day of autumn. It will snow tomorrow."

"Snow?" I am pleased to be so surprised. "How do you know?"

"It's just the weather. All the signs are of snowfall." As he brings me into his room he says, "You know, Rom, when you total it all up, I've spent more years than one living out under the open sky. You can't become an artist if you're going to stay inside: you need air, freedom."

He's completely sober and suddenly seems much younger, in spite of his beard and his wrinkles; he seems strong even though he's thin. He feels very close to me at this moment, just the person I was reaching out to a quarter of an hour ago as I stood on the corner of Labour Street and Michurin.

"Take a seat," Shura says. "I'll bring us some tea. Herbal!"

"What kind of herbal?" I ask in alarm.

"Herbs from the taiga, medicinal. It's really good for you. Every sip makes you feel better, clears your head. You wait and see. I'll just infuse it."

I don't want him to go just yet; I give a half-smile and, myself not sure quite why, begin to feel irritated.

"Yes, that's an amazingly simple explanation. You're in such a good mood today; Petrachenko has been off the bottle for several days now; and something is brewing inside me, as if at any moment shit is going to seep out of every orifice, but leave me afterwards as pure as a newborn baby."

"It'll be winter tomorrow, that's why we're hankering after purity. How could we not put a damper on all the hustle and bustle, not reflect a bit? It's the voice of nature. I'll just make the tea and we can talk about it."

Shura leaves the room. I take out a cigarette and look for an ashtray. There's none to be seen. Hmm, can Reshetov himself really be so immersed in his rest cure that he's given up smoking? Oh, to hell with the lot of them. One moment they're groaning and drunk under the table, and the next you'd think they were all saints. I strike a match and suck into my throat the warm, acrid smoke of a Prima.

I stretch out on the sofa and look at the bulky stand for paintings which takes up the whole of one wall. Among the canvases, new frames and old stretchers riddled with nail holes I can see the green sailcloth folder Shura keeps his gouaches in. It contains a bright little fairy-tale world, almost unreal.

I tap the ash into the cigarette packet, where there are only two or three smokes left. I have two packs back home, that is, in my room at the hostel, and that thought cheers me.

A painting he's begun is leaning against the back of a chair. Blue-white cliffs with snow clinging to them, long scraggy larch trees with dark-green, almost blue, paws on the sparse branches, which grow only on one side of the trunk. A dirty reddish sky hangs low over the Earth, punctured by the treetops. The lower part of the painting has not yet been touched by his brush, and there the naked canvas gleams with priming.

"Here's the tea," Shura says in a friendly voice as he brings in two large mugs covered with saucers. "I've been detoxing myself with it for three days. It's great stuff, it's got all sorts of minerals. I don't even feel too hungry."

Steam is escaping from beneath the saucers and the air is soon filled with the fragrance of the herbs. It reminds me of the pantry in my grandmother's house with bunches of herbs hanging from a beam in the ceiling. They had a strong, pleasant smell which made my nose tingle and my head spin slightly. I started imagining something mysterious and moss-covered, living beings in dark corners, not scary, but warm. And then, there's a sense too of the trees of the taiga in autumn, before the coming of the frosts, and that too is mysterious, quiet and kind, unhurriedly readying itself for a long, placid sleep.

"I haven't been out to the taiga for a long time," I say. "When I was little my parents often took me to look for mushrooms, or berries, or just for the ride. When we were on tour to Sayanogorsk we stopped in the hills. It was good there, but it made you feel so unsettled..."

"The taiga beckons us, it calls us," Reshetov nods. "It can be our salvation." He lifts the saucer from his mug and loudly slurps the boiling hot tea, smacking his lips before continuing, "The taiga is our main oxygen supply, where we get our energy from. The pine forest around Minusinsk is no more than a grain of sand, a pond, while the taiga is an ocean. You can walk in it for a month and feel you've barely taken a dozen steps. That's because it's so vast, but a month spent in the taiga can have more meaning than an entire life spent indoors. All our wisest men have gone off to the taiga."

I sip the sweet, tart and, to tell the truth, unappetising tea and put my mug back on the table. I'm not warming to this talk about the taiga. It sounds artificial, cloying, too purposeful, somehow. I'm tempted to say, "If you were dropped right now, Shura, two hundred kilometres from the nearest human habitation, how big a thrill would you find that?" I bring the conversation a bit more down to earth. "You've become a teetotaler then?"

"Well no, why..." Reshetov seems to have picked up on the sarcasm. "I'm just taking a break, mm, cleaning myself out. I'm clearing the toxins out of my body and my brain." He again starts philosophising. "What really matters, Rom, is not whether you're drinking or not drinking, smoking hash or have never tried it. That's not the real issue. What ultimately matters is whether you're in control, whether you have a grip on the reins. You say Petrachenko has stopped boozing? Well, thank God for that. But why? What is he giving it up for?"

"He's going to paint," I reply. "He's got creative ideas, concepts. He's finally had enough of painting scenery."

"Um, yes, that work of his is not very rewarding. But you see, the real issue is not whether you drink or not, but whether you're free. Seryoga lost his freedom and is unlikely ever to regain it. Even if he hands in his notice as a scenery painter and packs in all his old ways, I still doubt it." Reshetov sips his tea and hems and haws, looking for the right words. "You see, erm, even though I do hit the bottle, and on occasion smoke dope till I'm completely out of it, nevertheless, basically what I do is paint. I might seem to be on the most appalling bender, disappearing from view for two or three months, but when I resurface I take a look to see what I've got. Whizz, bang, wallop! I find I've got several new paintings. I have no recollection of when or how I painted them. Somehow, you see, it just happens, as if you were a sleepwalker or something."

"Not bad," I grin. "Unconscious creation."

"What do you mean, unconscious? Quite the opposite. It's a profound consciousness, which you can't get away from, can't escape. It's a vital necessity, like eating or breathing; although, life itself can take a turn where you suddenly find that it's all over. Or some higher power just decides to cut the thin thread that holds you and then, like Petrachenko, it won't matter how much you drink, there's no way you'll ever be able to re-tie it."

"You're right about that, Shura. When I was younger I used to write poetry, songs, and other stuff. We had a band, even gave a few concerts. But somehow it never came to anything."

Reshetov sighs sympathetically. "That was a big mistake. Perhaps it was what your life is for, your vocation."

"Perhaps," I agree, but immediately drive the thought away and say, without knowing whether I really mean it or not, "No, it was all just childish nonsense. Who needs poetry. By the way, where's the ashtray?"

Shura seeks it out beneath the sofa. It contains the relics of a dozen joints.

"You really were going at it before you gave it up!" I say in amazement. "Smoking this amount would convert anyone to tea drinking."

The artist frowns, his mind focused right now on something quite other than joints.

"You see, Rom," he says in a serious voice, sounding almost like a teacher, "you need to have something different inside you, a kind of inner centre not related at all to routine matters. You can't live on mere, barren routine. That's like a living death, choosing to decompose. Do you see that?"

"I see what you mean well enough, but for Christ's sake, what if you haven't got that centre? What then? I'd just like to get away somewhere, to get really far away," my secret bursts out. "To go to St Petersburg... I studied there for two and a half months before I was drafted, at a building polytechnic, as a tiler. At that time it was so easy. You just got on a plane and in six hours you were there. You went to any trade school, showed them your documents, and they gave you a bed, food three times a day, and a stipend. But now..."

"I've had my own dreams," Shura sighs, "almost since I was a child. I've never been further than Krasnoyarsk. I want to go to Tibet, or Japan. You can't imagine the kind of places there are in Japan! They are still just the way they were before the Europeans arrived. The real Japan is still there. I'd like to marry a Japanese girl and live in a bamboo hut, and sit painting in tranquillity, meditating."

"Hey, Shura, show me your gouaches. Go on, the ones in the green folder."

He looks at the stands, suddenly alert, mentally browsing through his works, but then dismisses the idea.

"It's not worth the bother. These are all sketches, Rom, just pathetic forays. You have to try a hundred times before you come up with one real success. If you're lucky."

"Go on, let me see them. Stop playing hard to get."

Reshetov reluctantly takes the green folder from the stand and puts it down on the floor. He unties the ribbons and, as usual before displaying his work, gives a slightly embarrassed explanation, grunting and smoothing his beard.

"They're mostly on Southeast Asian themes. Only fantasies, I'm afraid. They date from different years, some of them new and some I painted ten years or so ago. Some are pure gouache, some are mixed with watercolours, oil paint, bronze."

He takes out the first picture, moving the unfinished painting off the chair and saying as he does so, "Here's one I started, for some reason. It should have Lake Oy down here. It's in the Sayan mountains. You may know it."

"Of course. The Kyzyl road runs right past it."

"Ah, yes, of course. It came back to me and I decided to paint it." Reshetov looks at the painting with an eye both critical and affectionate. "Really I'm just wasting paint. No one is going to buy it or even take much notice of it. It's just another landscape; and yet I needed to paint it. Something was hammering away in my head saying, do it, paint it. So here it is."

He props the painting against a leg of the stand and puts a gouache in its place.

"I don't have a title for this yet... well, for a working title let's call it, 'Planting Rice'".

People in pointed straw hats are bent over, standing knee deep in mud, with bunches of green leaves in their hands; a water buffalo harnessed to a plough is straining its thick neck and laboriously moving across the swampy field. Tones of brown and grey predominate, with only the delicate greenery of the seedlings to cheer the eye. On the next sheet a languid, blooming Thai woman is lounging on the patterned cover of a settee. Her eyes are half-closed, and between the fingers of her right hand she's holding the long stem of a delicate pipe; a shoe with a pointed toe is suspended from the very tip of her little foot. The whole room has pink and crimson petals scattered around it.

"An opium dream," Shura murmurs, concealing the picture with a new one and, animated once again, comments, "This is Lhasa. It's a town, the capital of Tibet."

"I know, I know. I got 'Very Good' in geography."

Small, ground-hugging houses built from stone slabs and with flat roofs look like children's building bricks. The windows are black slits. The little houses climb up the mountainside, and instead of orchards there are stunted, leafless trees. In the distance is an austere, snow-covered peak which looks like both Everest and Fujiyama.

"It's impossible to live on unadulterated earthly reality," Reshetov returns to the conversation aborted half an hour ago. "Above all else, beware of ending up there with no escape. Remember that. You'll never be able to climb back out! It's better to be stark, staring bonkers than to be completely, invariably sober. I need to break out, I really need to break free, to breathe in that oxygen again. Tomorrow somebody has promised to bring me a customer who needs a new signboard for his shop. I'll paint it, he'll pay me, and I'll be off to Mount Tepsei."

There's this Mount Tepsei about thirty kilometres from Minusinsk, on the banks of the Krasnoyarsk reservoir. It's a favourite spot for artists. They have a dug-out there with a stove built of stone, and there are fishing nets hidden away somewhere. It's where they go to recover from civilisation.

"You see, on Tepsei time moves quite differently," Shura drones on, and his slow, muffled voice already seems to have taken on a mystical, ethereal quality. "A day is a whole lifetime there. It draws out over a long, long time and every minute is different. You experience so many sensations and thoughts. Smoking a joint just doesn't compare. Our ancestors had the time in the course of their lives to unravel a vast number of secrets and think an incredible number of thoughts, and that's why there were true sages among them. But what do we have nowadays? People cram their brains with complete rubbish and, just as you understood nothing when you were born, so you die a fool."

"Okay," I interrupt. "For a couple of months you can live blissfully at one with nature, but then, let's face it, you start missing a WC, your bath, the telly. You have to admit, gas is a lot more convenient than a campfire."

"Oh, wow!" Shura jumps up, switches off the light, and pulls back the net curtain. "It's started! The snow is here!"

I stub out my cigarette and stand next to him.

Outside the window, large, shaggy flakes of snow are falling. The night air has become dense and white and the nine-storey apartment block opposite has disappeared. You can't even see the light from its windows.

"I heard somewhere, or perhaps I read it," I say, not really knowing why, "that while a snowflake is falling it's a miracle, unique and beautiful. But once it has fallen on to a snowdrift it's just snow, just something that makes it difficult to move about."

"Yes," Shura responds vaguely, reluctantly, and in his eyes I see a childish delight.

It only sharpens my irritation and makes me say spitefully, "Here you are, Shura, convinced that giving yourself over to art is the way to keep yourself separate from reality, not to become sucked into it. That's all very well in theory, but actually it's a form of weakness, ordinary, straightforward weakness. It's like the way they draw ostriches in cartoons. They've got someone chasing them and they run and run until they're exhausted, and then they stick their head in the sand and kid themselves they're hiding. You're no better. Certainly you are an artist, and a good one at that, but Lhasa, and Fujiyama, and your Thai woman... the truth of the matter is that you can't afford to go there yourself in reality. Or take our actors. They're constantly trying to cobble together a world of their own, and afterwards, when they've got their strength back, they return to reality. The audience are just the same. Ostriches, all of them. I'd like to do it myself, but somehow... Okay, Shura, forgive me for coming out with all this stuff to you. I'll go home. I have to go to work tomorrow."

"Fine," Shura nods with what seems like concealed relief. "It looks as if I'll have work to do tomorrow too, if my customer turns up. When I've got some money I'll buy a stack of food..."

"And go off to Tepsei to hide," I finish for him.

Reshetov turns on the light and goes into the hallway to see me out.

In the corridor, almost opposite our door, Lena is sitting on her heels, ceaselessly rocking to and fro as if an undetectable wind is buffeting her and trying to knock her over. Above her stands that lump from Sanya's send-off party. He's scowling at Lena, plainly seeing his last hopes of spending an agreeable night with a woman draining away. Her face, on the contrary, looks younger, pink but hostile. Her lips are trembling. Slightly to one side of them is Lyokha, sleepy and cross.

"She's had too much to drink again," the hulk explains despairingly. "I've been doing my best for the past two hours but I just can't get her into bed."

"Evidently," Lyokha responds tonelessly.

For a time the three of us stand looking at Lena in silence, expecting her to do something, but she just carries on rocking to and fro, facing upwards and with her lips trembling.

"Any news of Sanya?" I ask the hulk.

"He's still in training, learning how to wind his leg wrappings.

He'll take the oath on 23 February, apparently. Then it will be for real."

"Bastard," Lena forces out of herself. "It's all what he... it's what he... the rat!"

"You should see the letter he suddenly sent Lena. She showed me it, on five sheets of paper," the hulk continues, and his speech is unexpectedly articulate given his Neanderthal appearance. "He's asking her to come, to forgive him, you know, well, for being such a bad husband."

"The stinking rat..."

"But she," he nods at Lena, "has taken her son over to her folks and, look at her..."

"Couldn't be clearer," Lyokha says suddenly, with evident glee. "This is her way of taking revenge on her beloved hubby."

"Fuck knows what's going on between them," the hulk says with a heavy sigh, bends over Lena and tries to get her back on her feet. She resists lethargically.

"No... don't ... it's better... it's better like this."

"Okay, pack it in, Lenochka. Get up now. Let's go to bed," the hulk booms, trying to make his voice sound tender. "You'll be able to sleep."

She makes a more determined effort to pull free, now almost beating the guy with her little fists. He holds her and tries to calm her down, but this proves to be a mistake: Lena suddenly ceases her muttering, her eyes become round, and an instant later a disgusting fountain gushes out of her mouth. I rock back instinctively. Lyokha exclaims, "Oh, great!"

The giant lets go, pushes Lena back to the wall, and with aversion starts wiping off his wet jacket with the side of his hand. "What the fuck is this! What are you doing?"

Disturbed by the noise, the neighbours stick their heads out of their doors but nobody has the guts to say anything.

Lena curls up on the floor, retching and writhing. Slimy waves reeking of vodka and gastric juices continue to emanate from her. It looks as if she's downed a good three litres, with nothing to eat. The hulk stands dismayed by the wall opposite, looking alternately at his jacket and his puking lady. He looks as though he might be about to snap and kick her head in with the square toe of his shoe.

I've seen enough and go into our room and start getting undressed. It's bedtime. I listen for a long time with a mixture of fear and curiosity to hear the punch, immediately followed by Lena's hysterical screaming, the bellowing of the hulk, and above it all Lyokha's appreciative chortling.

13

There is a 'flu epidemic in Minusinsk. The hospitals are reported to be overflowing and to have no medicine. In every issue of *Worker Power* they publish the bank account number of a charitable fund for buying medicine. At the theatre more than half the company are off sick and performances have been cancelled for the next two weeks.

On top of that, we've had An Incident. We were celebrating the birthday of Tanya Tarosheva, one of the actresses. I'd had nothing to eat since morning, very quickly got legless, crawled to our bolthole, collapsed on the bed and crashed out. This proved to have been very wise. After the booze-up, that queer Lyalin lurked on the stairs waiting for Igor, grabbed him and started kissing him. Igor tore himself free and told the guys. Vadim, Andrei, and Lyokha, predictably enough, decided to take matters into their own hands and overdid it. The result is that Lyalin is in hospital with a broken rib, concussion, and something else besides. He's rumoured to have complained to the police.

Lyokha got the money his parents had sent and today went off to see them. He had to go through Abakan because trains don't go out of Minusinsk in a westerly direction, so I decided to keep him company and finally go look up the lads there.

They've had plenty of changes and unpleasantness of their own. Oleg Sholin's mother has died of cancer, Seryoga the Anarchist has split up with his wife, and the guys are living together now in Sholin's three-room apartment. On the money they had, they bought twenty kilos of peas and ten loaves of bread. The Anarchist dried the bread into rusks, and now they eat a kind of pea porridge twice a day, so they're not starving.

Sholin is standing by the window looking distracted, I am sitting in an armchair enjoying a filter cigarette I cadged off someone in the street, and the Anarchist is sprawled on the sofa wearing his old Central Asian housecoat with the dress uniform epaulettes of a colonel and a parachute regiment red beret, with an IRA badge, on the back of his head. He's reading passionately from a thick notebook:

"And now the last soldiers of the Irish Republican Army found themselves trapped. They were holed up in the ruins of the port of Belfast, heroically repulsing attack after attack of the blood-crazed British executioners. From the bay a relentless hail of fire from naval forces rained down upon the fighters. Exploding mortars had scythed through them, but those still alive asked for no mercy. "Liberty or death!" they whispered through cracked lips. From atop a huge crane in the port the green, white and orange tricolor fluttered, the symbol of free Ireland."

"No, that's it, she isn't coming," Sholin announces and turns his back on the window.

"What?" Torn from his reading by this remark, the Anarchist gives Oleg a wild-eyed look of bewilderment, then understands and shrugs. "Stay cool, Schollinberg. Where else is she going to go?"

"No, no, I've lost her."

The Anarchist gives a thoroughly unconvincing sigh of condolence and turns to me to announce, for what must be the fifth time in the hour I've been sitting here, "See? My novel. Nine days of tireless work. The working title is *Freedom!* I plunged right in on the first page, and just this morning I resurfaced when I wrote the final full stop. I am re-reading it now."

For the fifth time I reply, "Well done, well done, Seryoga." No other words come to mind.

"Right." He's satisfied with my meagre praise and sticks his nose back into the book, trying to find his place. "Right: 'The predatory flocks of the Queen's helicopters circled overhead...'"

"Seryoga," Sholin begs in a pained voice. "Let's listen to it later. I can't take it in just now."

The Anarchist obediently closes his notebook and drops his head on to the pillow. Oleg wanders about the room, stopping often at the window, looking out into the courtyard and, not seeing what he desires, turning away. He wanders about some more.

The apartment is furnished as it was when his mother was alive. The untidiness is, of course, considerable and the air heavy with cigarette smoke, but nothing has really changed. The possessions and furniture tell of intimate family life. Inanimate objects do, after all, last a lot longer than people.

There's a sideboard containing twelve place settings of the best china, crystal liqueur and wine glasses. An old-fashioned sewing machine decorated with stars and sheaves of corn stands on a little lace tray cloth that's still quite clean and almost fresh. Along the walls are two bookcases with that same selection of books you found in the Soviet period in every intelligentsia family: the brown twenty-five volume Collected Works of Gorky, the green Chekhov, the equally green Dickens, the light-blue Blok, the lilac, three-volume edition of Bunin, sundry tomes from the Library of World Literature series, and the paper bindings of the series "Classics and Contemporaries". In the corner the enormous plywood and glass carcass of a Ruby television stands on slender legs.

"The way it's turned out, Sen," Sholin tells me, "I now rank as a complete orphan. I have nobody, absolutely nobody left."

Even just two or three months ago he was a well-fed, clean, fair-haired youth. I made friends with him on one of my very first trips to Abakan. That time I'd decided to look in on a rock festival, and ended up taking part in it myself after asking some young musicians I bumped into if they could accompany me. Sholin was a drummer and thumped along with the song. After the performance he and I shared a bottle of port wine and he invited me to stay the night at his house. I remember, he was a freshman in the physics and mathematics department at the local teacher training college. Even drunk he spoke in a cultured manner, using lots of clever words and constantly slipping into formal speech. Within a few years he had lost his entire family. First his grandfather, who was an announcer on the local radio, died, then his father, and now his mother had too. She worked in a research institute studying the history of the ancient Khakass and, even when she was already very ill, carried on writing. I saw her several times when I stayed overnight at Sholin's, and on each successive occasion she looked more like a dead person. Oleg nursed her for two-and-a-half years, intercalating from college, but she died of stomach cancer all the same.

He was left a three-room apartment. They had obtained it, I heard, not long before and now – bang, bang – he was the only remaining one of the four people who had been occupying it, at the age of twenty.

All these tragedies changed him a lot. He suddenly seemed gaunt, taller, his hair had quickly grown long and unkempt and stuck out in all directions as if he had a dirty yellow wig. His face was the mask of a martyr, wrinkles furrowing his mouth and forehead. His activity came in bursts. He would start, make several quick movements, and then freeze as if becoming oblivious; then there would be another burst, a half-minute of activity, and then again this stupor. You felt embarrassed looking at him, as if you were staring at an invalid or a cripple.

"Mmm," I murmur my condolences, and the Anarchist, bless

him, quickly moves in with consolation: "Don't think about it, don't dwell on it. You can't bring them back. You need to throw yourself into work of some kind. You should write something too."

Oleg grunts bitterly, sits down at the table, and starts rolling a cigarette.

"Mum bought this tobacco," he reflects, "to kill greenfly at the dacha, and now here I am smoking it."

The Anarchist stirs restlessly on the sofa before again picking up his notebook and leafing through it. He turns to me and asks, "Can you suggest where I can get my *Freedom!* published? This is a major book. It needs to be read by the people."

"Oh, Lord," Sholin frowns. "What an idiot."

"Okay, Oleg, it's not you I'm talking to, actually."

It looks as if Oleg and Seryoga are really beginning to dislike each other, something only too familiar to me after a year and a half of mutual torment with my own roommate. The best way of making an enemy is to live cheek-by-jowl with someone for a long time. In the end you'll be ready to kill him.

Cramming a fag-end into the overfull ashtray, Sholin gives a start:

"That's it, I can't stand this any longer. I'm going! I have to find her!"

"But for Christ's sake, where are you going? Do you at least know the address of this Zhenya of yours?" The Anarchist explodes. "Some object you've found for your passion! She isn't even up to much!"

Sholin isn't listening. He's in the hallway putting his shoes on and nervously fussing with his jacket.

The door slams. He's gone.

"Who's Zhenya?" I enquire.

"Oh, he brought some bird back the day before yesterday," the Anarchist tells me. "He was in that far room with her a full twenty-four hours and wouldn't let me in. Then she left and said she'd come back this morning. He's been running around since six o'clock going on about her. You know him, suffering is what he does best. Let's talk business instead."

"What business?"

Seryoga exchanges his horizontal for a sedentary position, fidgets with the notebook, glances into it as if seeking the first words of a speech, and only then begins: "I have to warn you straight away, Sen, that I'm deadly serious. I rattled on a lot about this in the past, and at the time it really was little more than chatter, but now I'm serious. In a word, I propose we go to Ireland."

The Anarchist has this obsession. He's constantly taken by all sorts of grandiose projects, but the main one has always been to make his way to Ulster and join the Irish Republican Army. When he was little he was watching television and saw a child who had been disfigured by a plastic bullet, then Irish hunger strikers in prison, and ever since he's been obsessed. He bought a dozen badges printed "IRA" and pinned them all over his clothing, studied books about weapons and, as he had no way of rushing off to that faraway isle, contented himself, so far only verbally, with preparing terrorist acts against the Glorification Pentecostal Church in Abakan, the Governor of Khakassia, Tolkienists, and Zhirinovsky's far-right "Liberal-Democratic" Party. Nevertheless, now and again he starts going on about travelling to Ireland.

"Just think, Sen, just ask yourself what kind of situation we're all in," he says in the tones of a maniac. "What future do we have here? Let's face it, none. Tell me, what do you have to look forward to? Or me, even more so. And Sholin too. That's why we absolutely must perform a definitive act. All great people at one time carried out what seemed at first glance to be an act of madness and – soared to the heights! Think about it: we get on a train, travel without tickets, and we're off. First to Novosibirsk, that's only one day's travel! I have a friend there from my days in the army. We'll rest up, and then it's on to

Sverdlovsk. Okay, I don't know anyone there, but they say there are plenty of unofficial groups there, and they'll help us. Okay? From Sverdlovsk to Moscow is another day. Let's do it, Sen! From Moscow to Minsk. People travel round the world without money, and here all we're talking about is a measly eight thousand kilometres. Poland, Germany, France – we can walk across them. And then we're at the Bay of Biscay. We'll requisition a yacht, the place is full of yachts, and head for Ireland. Shall we do it? Say yes!"

The Anarchist leaps off the sofa and stands there in the middle of the room in his housecoat with its epaulettes, that beret on his head, bearded and haggard and looking like the soldier of some tiny, unknown army fighting its way across the mountain ranges of the Pamirs. His comrades are despairing, they have lost hope, but the Anarchist is cheering them on, firing the red-hot bullets of his words: "Let's join the IRA, let's fight the sacred fight for freedom! We must in the end be victorious! Rom, understand, only victory will do! I've seen again, the situation is growing tenser, punitive action is being taken. They're trying to totally crush them, simply eradicating a people. The Irish are now the least numerous population in the whole of Europe! It's as if they were living in a concentration camp! Let's go, Rom..."

"Tell you what, why don't we go to Chechnya instead," I try to laugh it off. "It's nearer, more real. What difference does it make where you get killed?"

"It's not death I'm talking about, for heaven's sake." Seryoga loses some of his panache. "I'm talking about fighting for freedom, for Ulster."

Outside the window is a snow-covered courtyard with small poplars, which look like the skeletons of strange animals, children's swings, a horizontal bar, and benches for young mothers and old age pensioners. It's enclosed by three nine-storey blocks while on the fourth side there's a shop and kiosks offering a large quantity of vodka, wine, and good food. I remember a film in which a man, crazed by poverty and from being sober for too long, rushes into a shop, gulps down a litre of vodka and scoffs a complete saveloy sausage before collapsing. In prison he doesn't feel particularly bad about his impulsive act, taking the view that, for a few moments at least, he was happy.

There's absolutely nobody about, which is odd for the middle of the day. Outside everything seems sleepy, frosty and still. On one branch of a poplar tree sparrows are sitting motionless side by side. You feel they might at any moment rain down like little frozen packages on to the snow. I scrutinise the courtyard, the windows of the next apartment block, the pavement, without knowing what I'm looking for.

I avoid talking to the Anarchist. I have little time for his empty speechifying. He's going nowhere, as he knows perfectly well. He's just arousing himself and deluding himself with these grandiose plans. Novosibirsk, Moscow, Warsaw, Paris... Perhaps I should just go back to Minusinsk, tidy up my room, and get on with useful activity of some description.

There comes a ring at the doorbell, impatient and repeated. The Anarchist goes to open it.

"That'll be Sholin. Can he really have found his missing Zhenya?"

Instead of Sholin, however, we have an unexpected guest, Yura Pikulin. He looks unbelievably desiccated, stooping, frail, like a burned matchstick. You feel that if you were to kick him he would disintegrate.

"Hi, hello!" He forces the hoarse greeting out with immense difficulty and hurries to the nearest chair; with every breath he groans, "Oh, ah, have you got anything to, ah, smoke?"

"We have tobacco," I reply, "for exterminating garden pests, but I could make it into a roll-your-own."

"Oh, please do. Only as little paper as possible, or otherwise, ah, I'll be sick."

"How did you get into this state?" the Anarchist enquires. "Have you been beaten up?"

"Nobody beat anybody up. It's the mother of all hangovers. We been going at it for three days there... at Kovrigin's," Yura tries to speak coherently. "We drank through a whole thousand roubles, my entire advance. I only came to today... ah, and... not a rouble left. They told me... I was buying champagne, Smirnoff, beer... ah... it's a blur... mixing cocktails..."

"Seems clear enough," the Anarchist nods enviously. "Sounds pretty wicked."

"But, but now, well," Pikulin stretches out his arms which are shaking all over the place. "I don't suppose you'd have... anything?"

"Um, if only."

Pikulin accepts the roll-your-own, greedily inhales a few times, and chokes on the smoke.

"Hey, I've written a novel," the Anarchist can't resist boasting. "A whole novel in nine days! Ninety-six sheets of my notebook covered in small handwriting."

"What's it about?" Pikulin asks without the least interest.

"It's about Ulster, about liberating it from the occupation forces."

"Ah, yes, of course. You haven't got over that yet, then?"

"It's not something you get over, Yura, it's an ideal!"

"Ah, yes... Yes, of course..."

It's getting dark, slowly but inexorably. The snow has taken on a bluish tinge, the skeletal poplars stretch out their hideous dark bones even more starkly, but the walls of the apartment blocks have become whiter, the rectangles of the windows standing out on them more sharply. In some of them there's a kind of yellow, cosy, comfortable light, while others display a cold, dead blackness.

The Anarchist has just finished his latest passionate speech about Ireland, summoning us to pack our essentials and rush to the station. Pikulin and I keep mum.

"You're making a big mistake, lads, a big mistake by not saying yes," the Anarchist tells us in dismay after a long, awkward pause. "There's nothing for us to do here, nothing at all. Not for me, not for Sen, and not for you, Yura. And we really must take Sholin with us, otherwise he'll be out in the street."

"Why in the street?" Pikulin asks, suddenly taking an interest.

"Of course he will... Someone is already taking this apartment off him. Some bruisers turned up and offered to exchange it and pay him a cash adjustment: a one-room apartment and seventy thousand. You can guess what kind of an exchange that is. The minute he signs the documents they'll just chuck him out."

"What does Sholin think about it?"

"He doesn't seem the least bit bothered. He's in shock after his mother's..."

Yura fidgets in his chair, and re-lights the stub of his cigarette.

"Are these serious guys or just the usual riffraff?"

"They look pretty hard, only you don't see much of them. They act through intermediaries. There's one who turns up, says he's Andrei, an agent, just wants to be helpful..."

For a few moments Pikulin sits and thinks, while Seryoga the Anarchist gazes upon him as if he were the saviour of mankind. Then Pikulin starts talking in a serious, businesslike voice.

"Right, here is what I reckon. I know a guy in Chernogorsk, that's a little town about ten minutes bus ride from here..."

"We know, we know."

"Well, anyway, I know some people there who operate in the local wholesale market, and have outlets here as well. Tsedekovich is the top dog. Have you heard of him? Stas Tsedekovich. Well, never mind. In fact, think yourselves lucky. They have a very "authoritative" office. If I have a word with Tsedekovich he won't turn me down. How about you, Seryoga, are you up for it?"

"You bet, one hundred percent, but you'll need to get Sholin to agree. He just grunts at everyone's suggestions."

Yura shrugs.

"Why should we even tell him about it? Right now he isn't up to fighting his corner. We'll do everything ourselves." Then, with a change of tone, Pikulin asks piteously, "Sen, have you got anything to eat? My guts are shrivelling."

"We've got some peas soaking. We can cook them."

The mention of food evokes a feeling of hunger in me also. I quickly suggest to the Anarchist, "I'll put them on if you like."

"That's okay, I'll do it."

Sholin reappears at about six, drunk and knackered. He staggers in, clutching at the furniture, makes it to the sofa and falls heavily on to it face first. He lies there for a bit, turns on his side and starts snoring.

"Oleg! Oleg!" Pikulin shakes him. "Tell us where you managed to get drunk!"

"Leave him," the Anarchist frowns. "Let him sleep. Why don't we go through to the kitchen?"

We spoon the pea porridge out of a common large bowl like members of a patriarchal peasant family. Squelching those which have not been boiled long enough, I survey the great variety of kitchen utensils hanging on the walls and standing on the shelves. What an immense amount of stuff they bought, and all of it is quite useless now, except for the saucepans and spoons.

"I'm going to live," Pikulin purrs. "I feel better already. Great stuff."

"Sustaining the organism?" A ghostly Sholin is standing in the doorway and looking at us with bloodshot eyes and reproachfully shaking his head. "You're quite a sight. You really haven't evolved much above animals."

"Sit down and join us, do," the Anarchist responds in the tones of a solicitous auntie. "Get your strength back."

"Thank you, I don't feel like it."

He does, nevertheless, sit down at the table and pulls a cigarette out of the back pocket of his jeans. It's broken. Sholin puts it back. With seeming reluctance, he starts telling us about his expedition into Abakan.

"I've been practically all over town, in search of people, love, joy, anything like that. Kolya Kidienkov is about to travel round the world, Manankin is preparing a new television program, and treated me to the vodka."

"Hang on a minute!" the Anarchist exclaims. "Kidienkov is going round the world? Where'd he get that sort of money?"

"He's not doing it on his own, he's going with that Tuvan folk music group, 'Cheltys'. Throat singing."

"Lucky bastard!"

"Let him go, let him see the world," Sholin shrugs dismissively. "My destiny is here in this beloved, accursed town. This is my planet, this apartment is my country, its rooms are my cities."

"When those bruisers chuck you out, you'll have neither country nor cities," I comment mentally, making an effort not to snigger.

If you have neither the opportunity nor the energy to travel round the world there is always the, admittedly rather pathetic, fallback of moving from the main room to the kitchen, and from the kitchen to the main room. Doing so does have a slight refreshing and energising effect, at the same time as helping you to settle.

We finish the porridge and move. Pikulin lies down on the sofa in the posture of a dead body, with his hands crossed on his breast; the Anarchist busies himself rolling a cigarette, and Oleg, who by now has sobered up slightly, for some reason starts showing me a scuffed, crumpled photograph from a newspaper.

"There," he elaborates. "See what a family we were. Observe

how intelligently we are looking into the future, only, as it turned out, we were looking into the grave."

The photograph shows a rather portly but fit-looking, elderly man with a mane of grey hair, a handsome young couple, and a chubby-cheeked, smiling three-year old boy in a fur hat on the husband's shoulders. They are all looking confidently and joyfully in the same direction, and above them is written in the form of a firework set piece, "Happy New Year, 1980 to All Our Friends in Abakan!"

"That's my grandfather, Vasily," Sholin murmurs in a creepy, unsettling voice. "That's my father, Yury, and this is my mother."

"Hiya, everybody!" A cheery, young voice cuts through the fetid air. "How come your door is open? Aren't you afraid? Oh, I see, you're being sad again."

"Mm, yes, Natasha, what is there to be happy about?" the Anarchist sighs. "Night approaches and we're still sober."

"Well, great! Let's hope it stays that way!"

Natasha is fifteen and lives in the neighbouring apartment. Like most girls of her age she is fresh, likeable, and bewitching. She skips into the room and sits down on a free chair, announcing, as if it were the most heartening news in the world, "I've just been swimming! I persuaded my parents to buy me a six-month subscription. I had such a good swim, it was wonderful!"

We are acquainted, I can say, having met her here several times when Sholin's mother was still alive. Natasha helped Oleg to look after her. I admired her when she was a little girl and, obviously, still do. So here I am sitting on the corner of the sofa, holding my breath, my face half hidden in my hands, and peeping between my fingers at Natasha's legs sheathed in black nylon tights, through which the whiteness of her skin just barely shows. I try to imagine the skin on her legs, smooth, hairless, without veins or blemishes and, I imagine, as people used to say, the colour of ivory. I'm not too sure what colour that is, but it's a nice expression. From her legs I run my gaze higher and higher.

It touches her long fingers, the angular corners of her elbows, caresses her throat so free of wrinkles, without a single centimetre of surplus skin. I proceed cautiously to her face.

The face is the most important aspect of a person, the most important and the most vulnerable. I think the Muslims are right when they compel women to hide their faces, to protect them from the sun, dust-laden winds, and the eyes of strangers.

"Natasha," Sholin whinges, "Sunshine, please warm us. Help us overcome our latest bitter disappointment."

Natasha smiles encouragingly and lights up an aromatic cigarette. Sholin and the Anarchist promptly cadge one off her, and I get both of them to agree to save a bit for me.

"Well then, Oleg, what disappointment was that?" Natasha enquires.

"I've come today to the realisation that there is no such thing as love."

Natasha giggles.

"And what did you find in its place?"

"In its place? Well, there is, if you'll forgive me, sexual attraction. More or less strong, protracted or brief. There was a girl here yesterday, really quite likeable and very intelligent. We enjoyed each other's company, intimately, for a day and a night, sometimes talking, sometimes... well, you know... When we were talking, and we were talking about elevated subjects mainly – art, literature – I couldn't really discriminate between what she was saying and what I was saying myself. I kept wanting to kiss and stroke her. I wasn't listening, I was admiring her, fantasising. I'm absolutely certain that is how it is for everybody. After a certain amount of time, it's over and people are strangers again."

Natasha flares up. "For some sad men, maybe, but for women what matters is something else!"

But I liked what Sholin said. After all, I feel those same desires when I'm next to an attractive girl. Like now, for instance. So I ask rather nervously, "And what is important for a woman?"

The doorbell rings. Irritably muttering something, the Anarchist goes to open it. Pikulin half rises from the sofa and whispers a simple prayer, "Let it be someone with vodka. Let it be someone with vodka."

The Anarchist looks into the room with a worried expression. Behind him looms a gaunt, tall, very young lad with a neat haircut and wearing a bomber jacket. He smiles at Sholin, who obediently goes to him.

"Let's go into the other room."

They leave. The Anarchist remains standing half in and half out of the room.

"Who's that?" Pikulin asks, peering suspiciously. "Eh, Seryoga?"

"One of those I mentioned. About the apartment again."

"Those swine," Natasha sighs. "You ought to report it to the police. They're taking advantage of Oleg."

"We could always try to sort things out ourselves," Pikulin says, rising from the sofa. He looks out into the corridor, and shouts loudly, "Hey, visitor, come in here, will you!" He looks round at the Anarchist. "What's his name?"

"Yura, don't get worked up about it!"

"What's his name, I'm asking?"

"Andrei, I think."

"Andrei, hey, be so kind as to come in here for a word or two!" Pikulin sits on a chair in the centre of the room and crosses his legs. "Natasha, could I trouble you for a cigarette?"

"I've only got two left."

"For effect! Just to look right!"

The girl reluctantly parts with a cigarette. Pikulin casually lights up, probably imitating some film hero. He waits a minute or two and then shouts again, "Andrei, my friend, don't keep me waiting, it's not polite!"

"Perhaps this isn't such a good idea," I say. "After all, it's between them."

"He's coming," the Anarchist hisses.

Andrei comes into the room, with a weary, despondent Sholin behind him.

"Hello, Andrei!" Pikulin exclaims, brazenly eyeing the middleman. "How's life, how's business?"

"Good evening."

"Everything okay? Well that's splendid. I wanted just to explain one or two things to you, Andrei. Do sit down, make yourself at home."

The boy looks scornfully at the small, unprepossessing man on the chair and turns to Sholin: "What's this?"

"Don't give me that, sweetie pie. You understand perfectly, you shit!" Pikulin explodes. He jumps up and immediately finds himself in front of Andrei. "L-listen, soldier, and remember what I'm saying. Understand? Tell your bosses this little property is already taken. Your riffraff are out of business here. This is my patch! Understand, little fellow, understand? And my name, for your information is Tsedekovich, Stas Tsedekovich. You haven't heard that combination of words? Too bad, too bad, sweetie pie. Remember them now. Your bosses should know. And if there are any other little misunderstandings, we'll have to get more closely acquainted. You understand me? If you do, you're free to go."

Andrei, having listened calmly to this emotional outburst, shrugs and says in a cloying voice which has an undertone of menace, "Fine, I'll pass that on. That's clear. Goodnight," and, with a slight bow, he leaves the room.

The door slams.

"Well then, was that convincing?" Pikulin canvasses our opinions. "He got the message. You won't be seeing them again."

"You shouldn't have done that," the owner of the apartment responds in a toneless voice, sits down on the sofa, and puts his head in his hands. "Anyway, who cares... I'm tired."

At this point the Anarchist comes to his senses.

"Yes, Yura, you shouldn't have done that. You'll go away today, or tomorrow at the latest, but what about us? Did you think of that?" He goes over to the window and stares out into a darkness punctuated with lights.

"In the middle of the night the whole gang may turn up and mangle us all just to make an example."

"It's sorted," Pikulin says, refusing to be discouraged. "Stop moaning!"

For some reason I throw a little brushwood on to the fire: "He's right, everything may blow up now. Let's get out of here and spend the night somewhere else."

"Guys, everything's fine!" the impetuous Pikulin shouts. "I've done everything by the book. You have to put those bastards in their place. Natasha, tell them! They got the message, they know who Tsedekovich is."

"God, I feel like a drink." Sholin takes his hands from his face and looks at the girl. "Natasha, I get my welfare payment in a week's time. Any chance?"

"I haven't got any money."

"Mm, right..."

Seryoga the Anarchist meanwhile analyses the predicament in which we find ourselves.

"There can be no retreat. We must prepare to defend ourselves. They won't let this pass, they'll be back." He looks round the room and straightens his beret. "There's no time to lose! Right, they'll roll up in their ride to just under this window. They'll start coming up, which will take them no more than one minute. First of all, we'll need a look-out on the balcony. Volunteers?"

Pikulin scowls and gives a contemptuous shrug.

"Oh dear, here comes the IRA."

I have my eye on Natasha, who has gone quiet and looks distraught, which only makes her all the more lovable. I feel an urge to heroic deeds, to defy the mafia. I imagine us fighting ogres built like cupboards. I am rescuing Natasha, lowering her to safety on knotted sheets. No, it'd be better if I deflect a pistol aimed at her, shield her with my body from being struck by a chain.

A war-like cry breaks from my lips: "Let them come, we'll fight off all their attacks!"

"Well done, Rom! Right, how many of us are there?" The Anarchist starts rushing round the room. "One, two... five people! Natasha, you'll be the nurse. There's a pillow-case on the bathroom floor we can use for bandages. Sen, Yura, Sholin..."

"I really can't be bothered. I'm tired."

"An end to defeatism! This is a matter of life and death; or of your independence, at least!"

"We can pelt them with bottles," I say, pointing under the dining table. "There must be thirty of them there."

"And I'm good at throwing knives!" Pikulin is finally fired by the imminence of battle. "From any position. I'll hit a target ninety per cent of the time."

"Excellent, Yura, brilliant! We'll fight them off! How much can we be expected to put up with, after all? Liberty or death!" the Anarchist shouts, continuing to rush from corner to corner. He leaps over to the sideboard. "Hey, friends, help me move this over here, it'll provide excellent cover."

I readily catch hold of the other end of the sideboard. I strain and heave, and in passing catch a glimpse of the expression on Natasha's and Sholin's faces. The girl is frowning as she watches this commotion, and Oleg is listlessly picking bottles from beneath the table. The legs of the sideboard scrape over the parquet, the crystal tinkles piteously.

"That's enough, you idiots!" Natasha's patience snaps and she leaps up. "You oafs!"

She pushes Seryoga out of the way, making the sideboard rock perilously. Some wine glasses fall over on the glass shelf.

"What a bunch of idiots you are! Don't touch anything! Sit

down!" Natasha's shouts rain down on us like a long burst of gunfire. "Sit down, I said!"

Pikulin flops down in a chair, his eyes wide with astonishment. I put down the buffet and straighten up.

"Sit down, and don't touch a thing! I'll be back in a minute."

Sholin mutters, "Where you going? To the mafia?"

"I'm going to get some money for you idiots. You've completely taken leave of your senses! The best thing is for you just to get drunk and go to sleep."

"Will you really do that for us, Natasha?" Pikulin seeks reassurance in a reedy voice which sounds as if he's coming to after fainting.

"Only don't be a bunch of idiots. And you, get all that crap off yourself."

"Okay, okay!" Seryoga looks deflated and quickly pulls the beret off his head and starts undoing the belt of his housecoat.

"Right, I'm off. I'll be literally ten minutes."

"Perhaps we should go together?" Pikulin makes a move towards her. "Well, so we don't waste time at the kiosk..."

"I'll go by myself. They sell it to me. All you have to do is sit here and keep quiet."

"Fine, Natasha, no sweat. But, you know, maybe buy cheap stuff... so we get two bottles... or one and a small one."

The door slams. Pikulin goes over to the table and starts clearing a space. The Anarchist has hung up his housecoat and his beret in the corridor and returns in a T-shirt emblazoned with the word "BOSS".

He sits on the sofa, and sighs deeply.

"We're surrendering, then."

"At least we're getting a drink out of it."

I start rolling a cigarette. I'm beginning to feel a warm, surging emotion. If Natasha brings one bottle that'll be over a hundred grams each, which is not a lot admittedly, but if she brings two...

"Let's at least move the sideboard back," the Anarchist suggests tentatively, but is immediately overruled by a shriek from Pikulin.

"No! Don't touch anything, for God's sake!"

"After we've had a drink, I'm going round to the Tolkienists," Seryoga growls. "They are idiots, of course, but at least they have a life. They fight battles, they make all kinds of swords. They have energy, and I may be able to fire them with the ideal of freedom. Shall we go, Sholin? They've got a basement, under the Victory Cinema. I went down there once or twice to work out where would be the best place to plant explosives. Mmm, I was thinking of blowing the lot of them sky-high. It's a perfectly tolerable place to live. How about it, Sholin?"

Sholin smiles wearily in reply.

14

Our little cabin is snowed up to the windows. There are impassable snowdrifts everywhere, almost up to your waist. It seems as if the earth is trying to blanket itself as warmly as possible against the frost, the wind, and in general against this trying November world.

Already from the causeway I can see my father clearing snow in the courtyard with a plywood shovel, turning over great piles of the stuff. He's working steadily and unhurriedly, knowing it isn't something you can rush. Smoke is rising from the chimney in a dense, straight column. For some reason they've started heating early today. Usually they warm the hut up shortly before going to bed, at about eight at night. It isn't five yet.

It's overcast and the pine forest beyond the village looks like an uneven wall painted with thick, dark-blue oil paint. Above the forest, masked by the storm clouds, is the blurred suggestion of an old, dying sun.

I make my way along the bank of the pond to our little house, following a narrow track trampled between snowdrifts swept into the hollow. You'd never believe that only three months ago there was a beach here, and girls in skimpy swimming costumes were splashing in the warm water, and then sunbathing on the golden sand. Cheerful music played from tape-recorders, and in the evenings the bank was covered with fishermen who, now and again, would pull out a small carp. At night a campfire would burn under the birch tree, and the young people would be drinking spirits, caterwauling songs. Until dawn their shrieking disturbed the dogs in nearby yards and kept people from sleeping and regenerating their strength for the coming day. In the morning the cows were driven down to the pond to drink before a long day's grazing. Now, however, there is dead silence and cold, white monotony.

"Well, hello there," my father exclaims. "What brings you here today? We weren't expecting you."

He drives the shovel into the soft snowdrift beside the garden gate, takes off his mitten, and runs his hand over his brow damp with sweat. "They've cancelled the performances because of 'flu," I reply. "So I can come and spend a couple of days with you."

"How are you?"

"I guess okay..."

"Well, that's the main thing. Your mother will be very pleased to see you. I'll just finish off here and come in too."

"Where's Beecher?" I ask, noticing the empty kennel.

My father sighs.

"Well, there we are. Our old friend passed away, four days ago. He howled the whole night, evidently wanting to go away, and in the morning I found him beside the kennel. We've had a word with some people we know who have puppies, although they're very small yet. It's not good not having a dog. You can't sleep soundly. You lie there wondering if there's someone outside."

"What a shame. That's a great pity, of course," I say, shaking my head.

The familiar, mouth-watering smell of home, a compound of the aroma of food cooked by my mother's hands, of dough, fresh oilcloth on the table, and dusty books; the smell of clothes and things near and dear to me since childhood. In the stove dry firewood crackles merrily and the flue roars as hot air rushes up it headlong to freedom.

"Why haven't you got the light on?" I ask, clicking the switch to no effect.

"Oh, they're blaming extreme weather again," Mother replies in a bright if rather forced tone. "There was a storm the day before yesterday and they say the electricity poles have been knocked down for several kilometres."

"Really? I don't think we had anything like that in town. How are you managing?"

"We're getting by. Father has rigged up a battery to a small light. It makes everything a bit cheerier."

Mother takes the lid off the saucepan, trying to see into it through the thick, scalding steam. I get my lighter and illuminate it for her.

"It's been trying to boil for half an hour but just can't get there. On the other hand," Mum immediately accentuates the positive, "it's much tastier on a live flame."

"Sure," I agree darkly. "Is there anything I can help with?"

"No, that's fine. I'd rather you told us what's going on in town. The last few days we've been completely... no television, no radio. Thank God, they're still delivering the newspaper."

I cudgel my recalcitrant brains, trying to think of something to tell them, but Mum beats me to it.

"Have you heard about Kashin, the mayor of Kyzyl? It was in yesterday's issue of *Worker Power*, an announcement that he's gone on a hunger strike."

"Over what?"

"Over being prevented from doing his job and because Russians are being harassed in all sorts of ways. I'll find it afterwards, you can read it yourself. Oh, it's finally boiled! I've used up two armfuls of firewood, and they still haven't brought the coal. I ought to have gone to complain more often."

We have beef stew and potatoes for dinner. Above the table a low-powered car light is suspended which emits an unsteady, diffuse light but does nevertheless help to dispel the unsettling, total darkness.

"Father has earned us three kilograms of beef," Mother announces proudly. "He and Gennady hauled firewood for somebody and they paid him in meat. I've cut off a piece for you to take back, son. If you put it between the frames of your double-glazing it won't go off, God willing, in weather like this."

"It's really time we got round to slaughtering the pig," my father says. "Winter is on its way like it or not, and it's time we did it. Do you think we might tomorrow?"

"Fine by me," I say, trying to sound as if I'm raring to go, although the very thought instantly takes away my appetite. It isn't the pleasantest of activities. I overcome my squeamishness and ask briskly, "Are the blowtorches ready?"

"I checked them a couple of days ago. They'll do the job."

"Do you think we ought to ask someone to come and help," my mother suggests anxiously. My father dismisses the idea.

"Oh, we'll manage ourselves. What's that," he winks, "to two grown men! We'll butcher it, I'll go and get some spirits, and we'll have a feast fit for a king. Eh, Roman?"

"Sure."

With no light there's nothing to do. It's too early to sleep, you can't browse through a book, and conversation with my parents isn't flowing too freely.

I wander round the smallholding, try to shovel snow but can't really see where to throw it, and my heart isn't in it. There will, after all, be a new snowfall tomorrow or the day after. I stand next to the empty kennel and see Beecher's chain and collar on the roof, his bowl, and a gnawed bone. In a month or so a new occupant will come and live here for a few years, and then the next. The same will be true of the cabin some time.

I sit down on the porch and light up. I hear faraway sounds in the night, indistinct and disturbing. I try to tell who or what is making them, but can't. Incidents from the past float into my mind, and there's plenty to remember after twenty years of conscious life. But actually, how conscious has it been? You drift from one day to the next; some changes occur, of course, and all the time you're hoping for something, only to see afterwards that you were kidding yourself. Either you were deceiving yourself, or someone else was.

There's deception every step of the way. For example, for a long time (and come to think about it, to this day) I've been deceived by my parents, with the best of intentions, needless to say: by an excess of tenderness and love, by an abundance of sweet things to eat and various spectaculars. What do I remember most vividly from my childhood? The appearance in our house of the New Year tree, decorated with colourful baubles, tinsel, garlands and sweets, and with a shining star on top. Only the evening before, the main room in our apartment was ordinary, with everything standing boringly in its place; and in the morning it had suddenly been transformed into an unexpectedly bright, festive, unrecognisable world. I looked around enchanted and asked how it had all happened, and my parents told me, "In the night Grandfather Frost came and brought the New Year tree and the toys, and there's something for you over there in that red sack". I squeezed under the fir tree, pushed my hand into the sack and found presents. And afterwards? When Mum took me out for a walk she tried to make sure I didn't see the bare grey fir trees piled next to the rubbish container in the yard. Then, when I was about eight, I discovered it was really my father who brought the fir tree, and let it thaw out and spread its branches in his study. I found the box with the Christmas decorations on top of a cupboard, and thus something essential in myself was lost. I remember one time when I didn't feel hungry I was being difficult and turned away from my plate. My parents told me a chocolate medal would appear under the plate, but only after I'd eaten my soup or porridge. I did as I was told, and became the possessor of a round piece of chocolate wrapped in golden foil. "How did that get there?" I asked in astonishment, and was told, "It's a magic plate. It only gives medals to boys who eat up their dinner!"

At the end of summer and in the autumn my parents often went away for several days to pick mushrooms and berries. They travelled deep into the taiga, and left me with my aunt. When they came back, they'd give me a tangerine, or a chocolate, or a piece of Tula gingerbread. Again I was amazed and wanted to know how they'd found such tasty things in the forest, and they would explain they'd been put on a tree stump by a little rabbit specially for me. I had behaved well while they were away, hadn't I? Much later, when I was in a forest myself and saw a tree stump, I couldn't help feeling excited and hoping I might find a present on it from a little rabbit.

In the evenings Mum liked to tell me about the magical city of St Petersburg; she made me fall in love with it. Later, when I tried to actually live there between the end of my schooling and the army, I realized it was about as accessible to me as the exhibits in a museum: "Don't Touch!" "Open: 10.00-19.00 hrs"; and St Petersburg turned into the same kind of deception as the little rabbit and Grandfather Frost with his red sack of presents.

I was deceived by the nannies at nursery school, by Yuri Senkevich with his "Film Travel Club" on television, by my teachers, by girls at discos, by the lines of that poem which said all jobs were honourable and you could choose whichever you wanted. Our teacher, Natalia Grigorievna, made our history lessons so interesting. She really tried to make us into educated, cultured people, worthy citizens of a great country. When I came back from the army I heard she'd packed in school teaching and was getting down to business in the real sense of the word. She'd set up a chain of shops called "Exotic Fruit". I bumped into her one day in the street and didn't at first recognize her. She looked younger and was wearing a pink tracksuit. Her voice was not exactly coarser but it had become more emphatic, and her sentences were like bouncing balls. Instead of history, civic values, and the Battle of Borodino, Natalia Grigorievna now started telling me just as enthusiastically about kinds of tropical fruits which had never been heard of in our Siberian, Asian Kyzyl. She intended to have people eating mango, kiwi, pineapple, guava, and avocado. She told me how many invaluable vitamins they contained. I plucked up courage and asked, "And what about school? The False Dmitry, the Battle of Borodino, Count Rostopchin?" Natalia Grigorievna dismissed it all, as if I'd reminded her about some long-forgotten piece of foolishness.

Yes, deceptions peck me every day from every direction. That girl on the windowsill, sitting there for a reason. And there was a reason why I saw her, lonesome and waiting for her prince to come. When I was ready to be transformed into a prince, to become my real self, when I was ready for true love – she disappeared, the windowsill was empty, and that tiled box of a kitchen was cold and scary, like the shaft of a dry well. And what about all those actors of ours, with their seductions and illusions? What about Seryoga the Anarchist, who spent so much time trying to enthuse me with his ideal, daft as it might have been. It was at least an ideal but now it seems to have flown away like a punctured balloon.

I flick away my cigarette end. The fiery dot describes an arc and falls, tiny sparks scattering and disappearing. Shit, it's landed among the wooden planks! I jump up and go over to where it fell and spend a long time looking for it. I prick my finger on a nail, I turn over the boards. Where is the damned thing? Even a pathetic fag-end can't land in the snow for me. It has to cause all this hassle.

The door to the porch creaks and I hear my father calling, "Roman! Rom, where are you?"

"Don't worry, I'm here."

"Why don't you come in? We thought we'd lost you."

"Just coming." I put the board back down. Well, fuck the fag – what will be will be. "I'm coming. I'll just go to the toilet."

"Okay, fine, it's time to go to bed. Tomorrow we need to stir ourselves good and early if we're to deal with the pig. We'll be hard at it for quite a few hours and the days are so short now it's dark before you know it."

Our hefty pig has had no piglets and has lived for just under nine months now in a cramped, dark lean-to built on to the end of the rabbit hutch. In March, I remember, it was a neat, playful little pink bundle, but now it's a lazy carcass grunting greedily when it sees a human being.

My father likes giving names to everything: cars, cold frames, fruit trees, to say nothing of living creatures. Every pedigree rabbit is called something: one is Prig, another Whitie, a third is Crosspatch. The pig never got a name. Throughout those nine months it was a creature of no importance and went almost unnoticed; two times a day we poured the nauseating slop into its trough and quickly went on to other matters, not listening to it slurping the food and putting on weight. Only now, as we let it out into the yard, do we see it as a live being.

It plants its feet firmly on the grimy, trampled snow and slowly turns its head on its fat, wrinkled neck. It looks around, accustoming itself to the fresh air and daylight. You can feel it's tense, and ready to defend itself at the first sign of aggression on our part. Its clever, beady eyes watch us and it seems to know why my father is tying a noose in a rope which has its other end attached to a beam under the woodshed roof; why Mum is holding an enamel basin; and why I'm laying out knives, blowtorches, and rags on the table. Yes, it knows all right; and yet it can't believe that people who've fed it from its infancy, who cleaned the manure out of its dwelling, and threw it dry straw to lie on, could want to hurt it.

"Right, I'm ready," Father says in a soft, quiet voice. "Shall we start?"

"Oh, God be with you, my dears," Mum sighs.

There was a time when my father couldn't bring himself even to cut the head off a chicken, but now he kills rabbits a dozen at a time, knows how to skin an animal properly, how not to puncture the gall bladder, and what is edible in the belly and what is not. Ever since we moved here, every autumn we had to deal with a pig. Village life is not sentimental: if you don't want to get swollen with hunger yourself, you need to know everything, what to do and how to do it.

Cautiously, trying not to make any sudden movements, Father moves towards the pig, murmuring something in an ingratiating, almost tender tone of voice, stroking it behind the ear. The pig soon relaxes, trusts his stroking, and begins to grunt appreciatively. My father's movements become bolder and more confident. He tickles its ear with his left hand, even as a long, broad hunter's knife appears in his right. I stand at the ready. The pig has completely stopped worrying, and lies down closing its eyes blissfully. My father unobtrusively moves it until it's lying on its right side with its left legs slightly raised.

Continuing to tickle it and talking to it kindly, he almost sits on the body. I tighten the noose on its back leg and also prepare to fall on it. Mum is nervously shuffling from one foot to the other, standing some distance away, holding the basin for the blood. It's a joyless morning, the sky densely covered with leaden clouds from horizon to horizon; the snow is heavy and not new, as if this were not mid-November but March. The air is surprisingly warm, dense, and somehow steamy. Or perhaps I'm just imagining it.

"Everything's fine, everything's just fine," my father lulls his victim, and she responds with a sweet, grateful wheezing.

He turns to me and in a different, anxious, serious voice, as if we are facing a fight we might lose, asks, "Ready?"

"Yes."

"Well, then..."

A short gasp from the depths of his chest, the flash of a dull steel mirror, and something crunches and bursts. The relaxed heap of fat beneath me turns to stone in an instant and jerks in a way that makes the rope as tight as a bowstring. Our ears are immediately pierced by a thin squeal more terrible than anything a human being could utter. The pig tries to jump up but we sit on it, pinning it to the ground with all our strength.

"H-hee-ee-ee-ee!"

"Oh dear, I've slipped up a bit," my father shouts over the squealing, and twists the knife under its shoulder blade.

"Never mind!" I reply. "It'll soon quieten!"

Its attempts to stand are weaker and weaker, and the squealing is replaced by a laboured wheezing. Its body goes slack, no longer blissful and loving but caught in the impotence of death.

"Galina, put the basin here!"

Mum runs over and pushes the basin under the pig's head. The knife blade slices through its throat and from there the thin, crimson blood gushes out as if under pressure. Convulsions run over the body in waves, as if the blood is being pumped in waves.

"You can let go," my father says. "Get the blowtorches ready."

I rush over to the table, groping in my pocket for the matches, although there's no particular hurry now. The risky moment, the actual killing, is over and ahead of us now is the wearisome procedure of singeing. There is worse to come: the eviscerating, trimming off of lard, the butchering. It's really not much fun, but at least we'll have meat to see us through the winter.

Dealing with the pig has taken up the whole day. At last Mum is cooking supper and my father's gone to buy spirits. I feed the rabbits and let the chickens out of the coop into the yard. They can peck the intestines and the drops of blood, frozen like berries in the snow. Now I'm sitting on the low wall of earth by the cabin with my mittens under my bum, smoking and relaxing.

The sun has completed its truncated November trajectory and is creeping behind a low mountain covered in aspen brushwood. The thunderclouds are darkening, filling up with moisture as night falls. The colours are disappearing, muddied and effaced by night as it enters its dominion, leaving only black and greyish white.

The village is drowsy and lifeless, the pond empty, the smoothness of the snow incised by the dark lines of paths. They seem just to be waiting for someone to walk along them, but nobody is going anywhere just now.

Here, however, is a sign of life. I instantly half raise myself. Down the nearest street across the pond a stocky little ginger horse is dragging a broken sleigh with no sides. A lad I don't recognise, standing unsteadily on a straw mat, is clutching the reins, simultaneously urging the horse forward and holding it back. One moment it rushes forward, the next sits down on its rear legs, obediently stopping.

"Gee up, you she-devil!" the boy yells in drunken vexation, eager for a wild sleigh ride, and lashing the horse's back with the reins. "Gee-up, you fucking pain in the arse!"

The animal jerks forward, making the boy stagger backwards and thereby tighten the reins. The horse stops again.

"For Chrisssakes, go, you...!"

Along the whole length of this uneven progress the dogs are barking themselves silly. The dogs from all the neighbouring streets join in until half the village is in uproar. Only our smallholding is quiet. We have no dog now, no one to warn us of danger.

The table is lit by the car lamp. Pork is sizzling appetisingly in two frying pans, in one of which there is meat and kidney, while in the other is the liver. On a large plate there are velvety yellow potatoes which seem steeped in butter. To crown it all there are salted cucumbers, tomatoes, cabbage, home-made bread... and a bottle of vodka.

"There, all our own work," my father announces proudly as he fills the glasses. "Well, apart from the flour and the spirits. But normal people have always regarded drinking as a luxury, and we could grow our own corn if we wanted to. In principle, if you have land you don't really need money."

I'm tempted to remind him just how much money was spent on feeding the pig, on the polythene, the irrigation hoses, but don't want to spoil his good mood, so I nod my agreement. Father raises his glass: "Let's drink, my friends, to all that is good. So far we've kept our heads above water, and may things be no worse in the future!"

We clink glasses, gulp down the burning liquid, and chew with relish the fresh, tender meat redolent of pine smoke. "Out of this world!"

For some reason it's just as we are embarking on our feast that my memory decides to replay the process by which we came by this meat. Once again I take in the thick, oily smell of bloody innards, see the carcass with the roaring, blue jet of flame from the blowtorch scorching it; see the bursting blisters on the scorched skin. For some reason I start trying to feel disgust for the meat of the animal so recently slaughtered with my connivance, but it doesn't work. I feel no disgust. The knife, the guts, the reek of scorched bristle, the axe crashing down on the animal's joints, the smoked pig's head, deprived of its tongue but smiling blissfully on the block, seem perfectly natural, as normal as this bodily function of eating, as the need subsequently to excrete superfluous matter from the body, and the sounds and smells which accompany the process.

"Take it from here, son. This is mainly kidney," Mum says solicitously. "Let me get some for you. I know how much you like it."

"That's all right, Mum," I say, and start energetically picking pieces of sliced kidney out of the frying pan myself.

After two more glasses of the potent vodka I start feeling really good. One after the other, like sunflower seeds, I toss the tight little vine tomatoes into my mouth, bite into them with pleasure, and swallow their juicy, salty-sweet flesh.

My father is a bit drunk and flushed and declaims an unhurried monologue: "Well, in the old times we lived much worse than this in material terms. Life was harder, but against that people's morale was high. Especially after the war. I was just a little boy then but I still remember how it was. My father came back from the war with a terrible wound. In fact, he was sent off to hospital in Krasnoyarsk as a hopeless case. And what happened? He later got married and looked after three children not too badly at all. He built a house, a bathhouse, a chicken coop. We had a goat, then a cow. In 1957 his war wounds finally got the better of him and he died. He prepared us for life and died. And how we toiled! My sister's work record dates from when she was eleven. Everybody around us was working hard. Shirkers were not regarded as human beings. I can say that with no exaggeration. It was only later people started going soft on them. But at that time we were all working like ants in an anthill, everybody was. How could it be otherwise? If we hadn't, we'd simply have ceased to exist as a nation." My father refills the glasses, raises his, and solemnly proposes, "Let us drink to that generation. To the fathers of your mother and me, to your grandparents, Roman! You never knew them. They died young because they didn't spare themselves."

The alcohol affects him in different ways: sometimes when he's drinking, my father is irrepressibly optimistic. He looks forward to a good summer and the dawning of a better life in the near future. Other times his speeches paint everything in the darkest colours and he foresees the imminent collapse of everything. Today, having got off to a good start, he slowly drifts towards pessimism.

"Why are times so hard now?" my father asks, and provides the answer himself: "Not because of a shortage of money, not because of the, mm, mm, unstable situation – the main cause is the lack of an ideology. Nowadays that's a pejorative term, but if you live in a state, an ideology is essential. I used to be against the pressure it exerted too, but now I can see that we had only to loosen the screws a little and everything fell apart. Actually, everything seems very simple now. You can do as you please, earn as much as you can, open your own business. Who'd have allowed us to own so many cold frames twenty years ago? They'd have shut us down immediately. And do you remember what was going on in the early 1990s? You could privatise a spanking new Kamaz truck for a crate of vodka, and some factory fleet manager would even be grateful to you for taking it off his hands. For some reason, though, almost all of us behaved like idiots. We made no attempt to get our hands on our rightful slice of the pie. And the reason we didn't is because an average Russian has been trained to be inside the collective, trained to be ashamed of grabbing property. By the way, I heard on the radio one time that speculation is an entirely scientific, economic concept, and nothing to be ashamed of at all."

Here, in this dark, godforsaken little cabin, his analytical monologue seems absurd, and yet in the immediate surroundings there are another two hundred similar dark, snow-covered little houses, each of them waiting to have their electricity restored, and in them people periodically discuss politics and economics, and in each one you can be sure that somebody is grumbling about something. And beyond the village there are forests and fields for forty kilometres, and beyond them the district centre of Minusinsk, and then more forests and fields, mountains, villages, towns and people living in them who are also trying to reason, and remember the past, and analyse the situation.

"All right then, Father," Mum says gently. "Why go on about that now?"

"But it's very upsetting." He grunts irritably and scrapes his fork on the plate. "We don't want to live this way. Russians are probably the most useless traders in the world. Take Mum and me. What an effort it took before we could stand behind a counter. We're embarrassed to sell other people's goods: if we had to trade, then at least we wanted to sell our own produce, food we'd grown ourselves. So many people go into trade only because they're forced into it by extreme poverty. And what about the customers? You meet all kinds, but in the main they're quite respectable, not badly dressed, they look educated – but their eyes! Their eyes are the eyes of beggars. They come and size up your cucumbers or your radishes as if they were licking them with their eyes. They look and then they wander off."

I'm tempted to interrupt my father, to suggest a last glass of vodka before we go to bed, but restrain myself and try to be patient, recognising that they don't have that many opportunities to talk without being in a rush to go somewhere else. It isn't that often they have a listener. My father and mother have no friends here yet, just neighbours, people they know.

"We need to do something, otherwise we'll go completely..." My father pours what remains of the vodka into the glasses. "After all, it's we, our generation who brought this about. We kept hankering after renovation, and now we've got it, smack between the eyes, and when we're old. They come, suck all the money out of us, and then disappear abroad or retire. They're completely unafraid! But... Leonid Andreyev, by the way, has a very good story about this. Let's drink up and I'll tell you. Ouch! That's good stuff, worthy of the meat. Anyway, it's a tale about a governor. In his way he's a fine, honest man, but he's guilty of a crime. Not even a crime, if you look at it from the point of view of the interests of the state. Well anyway, on his orders soldiers opened fire on a workers' demonstration, women and children were killed. After that the whole town knows, and indeed the governor himself is quite sure, that he'll soon be punished, executed. He's expecting it. He refuses to take a bodyguard, or to be transferred to a new job in a different province. He understands that there's no hiding from the judgement, and in due course he's killed. A man with a revolver comes up, shoots him and disappears. So then. I'm telling you this because there should be a power, which punishes crimes. No matter what interests of the state they claim are being served. Perhaps then those people would think twice before they treated the people so shamelessly."

I am reminded of the speechifying of Pavlik, Lyokha, and Seryoga the Anarchist. I forget myself and grin. My father notices and sighs in confusion. My grin has upset him. He gets up slowly and heavily, kisses Mother on the cheek, and goes over to the stove for a cigarette.

With each new heavy gust, the windowpanes rattle threateningly and seem even to bend in slightly. Something is flapping on the roof, gradually being wrecked. It's almost dark in the room, and outside the snow whirls and dances. You can't see even the birch tree, barely ten yards away.

It's uncomfortably cool in the cabin. The wind is blowing the warmth out of it, and the wood in the stove is reluctant to burn. My father grumbles, "The pressure has completely fallen away. There's no draught in the chimney."

My eyes hurt and are watering from trying to read. I can't sleep any more.

Mum has put cushions under her back and head and is lying on the sofa. I can hear her heavy, noisy breathing. From time to time she is racked by a dry, hacking cough. When she has cleared her throat and spat a gobbet of mucus into a slop-pail, she sprays her throat with an aerosol and carries on coughing, but more gently and quietly now. Wheezing painfully, she breathes air in and out, until the next attack.

I look through my cassettes stored in the box from our cassette recorder, which was stolen a few days after we moved here. There are twenty-eight of them, and I recognise each one instantly. I know by heart what's recorded on them. Twenty-four have recordings of songs by my favourite groups. Actually, to call them favourites is not strong enough. These are groups I can't live without. If it were not for these songs I'd probably be quite a different person. They helped me. "Aquarium", the first album of "Kino", "Zoo", Bashlachev, Yanka, "Survival Guide", and another seven 90-minute tapes of "Civil Defence". The hissing, roaring, buzzing squall of instruments rolled up in a ball, and above them the breathless voice of the leader of the Siberian underground, Yegor Letov, who sounds as if he's expecting to be shot after each sentence.

> *There are only two ways out for honest guys:*
> *Grab a rifle and kill everyone around;*
> *Or kill yourself, yourself, yourself, yourself,*
> *If you take this world seriously at all.*

Until recently I did take this world seriously, but now it seems to me ever more often that it's simply a string of meaningless days, and whether you flounder about or not, the end result will be exactly the same.

Not having a cassette player or any opportunity to listen to them, I took first one then another to the hostel and loaded them into Lyokha's player. He'd put up with it for around one minute before pressing stop. Okay, so he likes different kind of music. I understand. Each to his own poison. Often I sing the lines of songs that mean a lot to me under my breath, as if I'm taking some life-giving pills.

And here are the four cassettes with my albums or, more precisely, with the albums of my group, "DIN". Each has photographs of our angry faces, which look comical precisely because of that half-childish anger. Sasha A.O., Ron Tkachev, Yuri Zhundo, and me: "Extreme singer Sen".

Here we are aged between twenty and twenty-two. Every evening for almost a year and a half we assembled in an empty garage built of concrete slabs and played. I yelled hoarsely into an ordinary microphone:

> *Makhno's horsemen, sabres unsheathed,*
> *Facing machine guns and pulling death's teeth.*
> *We're alive now and singing our songs now,*
> *Anarchy's boys making anarchy's noise.*
>
> *Anarchy lives and it's going to win,*
> *And that's the whole reason for making this din.*
> *Systems and states are all just a bad smell.*
> *Presidents, parliaments, fuck off to hell!*

There are more than a hundred songs on those four cassettes, and each of them carries memories, attempts to express our attitude to life. On each song I've strained my larynx, and the lads bloodied their fingers on the strings of their guitars. We used to stride out of rehearsals lit up, as if the stings of the outside, adult world could no longer hurt us. And why not? When we took up our guitars and plugged the microphones into the amplifier, our DIN dealt a real blow to the monstrousness all around us, the mendacious veneer of respectability. When we were invited to the republic's song festival, the noise we made in the Theatre of Music and Drama! We even rated a piece in the official government newspaper *Tyva Respublika* about "young rebels". Only, soon after that my parents and I moved here. I've heard that Sasha A.O. is a journalist now and writes a crime column, Ron is the indispensable computer graphics geek for Tuva TV, and Yuri finished his polytechnic and is now a postgraduate student. It seems, as they say, that these young people have found their way in life, but for some reason, I haven't yet. Or perhaps I have, and just don't want to admit it.

The wall is buffeted by a particularly violent gust of wind, like some enormous paw banging on the logs. Up on the roof something snaps loudly and falls off.

"Lord, what on earth was that?" I hear Mum sigh despairingly. "What sort of November are we having this year... just one snowstorm after another."

My father soothes her: "Never mind, it's better now than in April. Our vegetable garden is in the hollow and the strawberries will be well covered by snow. In the spring we can look forward to a good harvest. By the way, Roman," I hear him raising himself, "I chose five books I don't need for making flowerpots. Look and see whether perhaps there are any you want to keep."

I sweep the cassettes back into their box.

"I'm going to make a thousand small paper pots over the winter," my father goes on, initiating me into his plans. "We'll plant according to the Dutch system of growing everything from seedlings. I'll turn the summer kitchen into a nursery, make a large window, put in stands. You only make real money on early produce. You can work it out for yourself, a bunch of radishes in mid-May costs at least six roubles, but by early June that's down to two. Cucumbers in June are twenty roubles a kilo but you'll be lucky to get three roubles for them in July. If you can beat the competition by a couple of weeks, you can make an appreciable amount." With each sentence my father becomes more and more enthused, his voice louder and more excited. "We have plenty of crates. We'll put seedlings in flowerpots in them, and then transplant them to the borders and try to move everything forward that extra couple of weeks."

I nod agreement, not wanting to argue, although there are serious grounds for doubt. In the first place, transplanting radish seedlings from crates into borders is a lot of hard work. You need seven or eight large radishes to make up a bunch. Suppose you sell it for five roubles, how many bunches are you going to need before you make a serious profit? And in the second place, there's a difference in the climate between Minusinsk and our village. It's usually several degrees colder here, and no matter what you try, you're not going to beat the specialist horticulturalists in Minusinsk. In any case, if radishes get their roots damaged, they're more likely to shoot, and then you won't be able to sell them to anyone even in March.

"Let's give it a try," I say. "Only, you know, I'm working six days a week..."

"Never mind," my father refuses to lose heart. "We'll manage somehow. I have another bright idea, my friend. I've invented a contraption called a vertical bed. I explained the principle to Mother, and she thinks it's good. Let me show you."

He takes a pen and a sheet of paper, sits down in our only armchair, and begins sketching and explaining: "You weave a lattice of wire and willow branches, or you can use thin pine twigs. It'll be a little over a metre high. You form it into a pipe, and put polythene at the bottom to retain moisture. You also line the inside with polythene, pack it with earth and compost, and put sawdust in the middle. You can use a bucket with no bottom for that, so the soil doesn't get too mixed up with the sawdust. Then we can plant cucumbers, or tomatoes, or peppers in the sides, whatever we please. We make a kind of framework of withies on the top, and we can tie the cucumbers in to that. Get the idea? It should be far more effective than simply growing them in a border or cold frame. You save space, and the earth in a pipe like that should hold the heat. On all counts, a vertical border should be a great improvement. What do you think?" My father invites me to share in his pleasure at the invention, and I again nod and smile, a bit worried that my smile may come out as a sceptical smirk.

"In the spring I'm planning to set up ten of them or so. Five, say, in the greenhouse, and five in a sunny spot. We really do need to find some way out of this mess." My father gets up and goes out to the kitchen. I hear him say to Mum, "What do you think, Mother, do you think we can dig ourselves out of it?"

"I hope so." I hear more weariness and even suppressed annoyance in her voice than hope and, as if in confirmation, she has another of her coughing fits.

My father's optimism and enthusiasm vanish, and the wrinkles on his face become deeper. He seems to grow smaller. He stands there for a moment, looks at the clock, and crumples the paper with the diagram of the vertical border.

"Ah, well," he sighs, "It's nearly noon. I need to go and feed the animals. The wind doesn't look like dying down, but after all they're living creatures too."

15

I've brought the curtains, which once hung in my room in our Kyzyl apartment, to the hostel. Heavy, golden-green, they shielded me reliably from the roar of traffic in the street, from the eyes in the windows of the neighbouring apartment block, from the intrusive sun, and the fearful darkness of night.

Now I hang these curtains in the window of my hostel habitation. I kick the old net rags, stained by dirt and cigarette smoke, under Lyokha's bed.

In Elektra I buy the spare part I need and in half-an-hour have the cassette recorder working again. To Grebenshchikov's transrational songs I wash the floor and dust our humble furniture. Without a second thought I throw out all kinds of junk, torn plastic bags, tins and bottles which have accumulated in the cupboard. I use a mop handle found in the washroom to remove garlands of dust from the corners.

I open the quarter-light and, while the room is being aired, go off for a shower. I wash my body painstakingly, pleasurably, and scrape the stubble off my face. When I'm dry, I go to the nearest hairdresser's, and get a crew cut for sixteen roubles.

I'm okay for money. My parents gave me three hundred, which will keep me going for a long time if I don't drink. All the more so because, just before the 'flu closed the theatre, I was issued twenty food vouchers which are intact and untouched and tucked away under the cover of my passport. I have plenty of food. Life is good.

It's a long, long time since I've been in such a great mood. I feel as if I've had a new battery inserted in me and can now do anything. If I just make a bit of an effort, apply a bit more energy and determination, I can accomplish marvels. All obstacles will fall before me. For the first time in ages I'm free and strong, and not being held back either by my moronic roommate (who isn't here just now), or by a lack of money, or a debilitating hangover. I have several days of freedom ahead of me. Perhaps I should go and look for a decent job. As Pavlik's "mum", Ksyukha, rightly said, nothing ventured nothing gained. I need to do something, to seek. Not as stupidly, of course, as those pathetic would-be robbers, but you can't allow the grass to grow under your feet either.

Perhaps I should walk through the Trade Centre and ask the lads there whether anybody needs an assistant, someone to help with delivery or whatever. I might be in luck. Or I might get the group together again, give Sholin a good sharp shake: he was a good drummer. I could sing. Not my old anarchist propaganda, of course, but write some songs more in the spirit of pop, like "Agatha Christie" or "Spleen". There's a live music disco in Abakan with groups, and a music program on local TV. Okay, perhaps that's going too far. I doubt I can shake Sholin up now, and I don't suppose I'm going to write any new songs.

Perhaps I should try to get a job in the Abakan theatre. The pay is better there, and although they pay in Katanov tokens, I've heard they do at least pay it almost on time. I could train some more, become a lighting engineer and, if in luck, even get taken on as an actor. They're having problems with young guys there...

I fry some meat. A whole frying pan full, with onions. You need to eat properly if you want to live an active life. I open a one-litre can of vine tomatoes which Mum gave me in case I celebrate my birthday here. There's still a couple of weeks before that, but who knows what the future holds? In any case, what does your calendar birthday matter? It's just a formality, a number on a sheet of paper. No, I'm having the real celebration right now. I am twenty-five today. Behind me is a quarter century of childish games, mistakes, timidly preparing for adulthood. It's time finally to seriously get my arse in gear.

I take my time, relishing the food. For once I'm actually eating a meal, not just snacking to accompany vodka. How agreeable! The taste of the food is not spoilt by the vapours of the vodka, not masked by its burning sensation. My attention is focused on the food, not on the drink.

The atmosphere in the room detracts from the effect a bit. It is squalid, there's no two ways about it. The wallpaper is so old it's become colourless; in places it's come unstuck at the joins and is curling. It should be replaced. I saw some delicate pink wallpaper today in the hardware shop, with light blue flowers. The colouring was really quite good.

Something always happens to obstruct, destroy, nullify whatever you've achieved with immense effort. I had been resurrected, had roused myself from an endless half-sleep, half-delirium. I seemed to have overcome my own downfall, to have cleaned out the rot. I was certain all the crap had been left behind. Alas, inside your head you can dream and make resolutions to your heart's content; you can sew wings on to yourself and believe you can fly; but there's the outside world to reckon with. You have only to stick your head above the parapet and everything will be made entirely clear. It will strike you such a blow, just to make sure you don't get too carried away.

There's the tiled box of the old kitchen, and five steps further along the corridor there's the washroom with a sink and water where you can wash dishes. Why does this damned defunct kitchen have to come first and not the washroom? I never used to wonder about that. I used to anticipate a warm feeling, almost happiness from this dull, run-down box which looks for all the world like the sluicing room in a mortuary. Whenever I saw that girl with the golden auburn hair sitting on the windowsill, I would freeze and wait for half an hour like an idiot, thinking that at any moment she was going to turn her sweet face, and smile, and beckon me to come to her. I would go over, put my arms around her, breathe in the smell of her hair, and two hearts tormented by loneliness would become one. The happiness I had been waiting for so long would arrive.

Today I didn't need her, her face, her hair, her smile. All that was long since over. I'd moved on, much further on, found my way forward without her. Today I was just taking some dirty dishes to wash, but looked over nevertheless, mechanically. It's difficult to stop doing something you've been doing almost every day. My neck turned of its own accord, and I saw her.

She was standing with her face to the window, her hands clenched and pressing down on the windowsill. She was looking into the darkness beyond the window, but now she was wearing no earphones. It was quiet. Her hair seemed to have become dull, but perhaps that was an effect of the dim light bulb. It was less golden, and seemed to have grown very quickly. It had come to just below her shoulders, but now reached down to her waist. She had grown taller and was almost the same size as me; and not as thin as I had imagined. But I knew it was her. It was just that I hadn't seen her for a long time and my imagination had altered her slightly. For better or worse, who cares? She was still the only one who would help me, and whom I could help. I would make her tear her eyes away from the window, take her back to my newly clean room. I would never lose her again.

Her back trembled as she sensed my thoughts. Now she would turn round, at last...

"What are you looking at?" It's a dry, harsh voice, not her voice. She would have a completely different voice.

Of course it's not her. This woman is around thirty-five, with a flabby face the colour of a tomato and dark, wrinkled bags under pale eyes which seem to lack pupils.

"Forgive me," I mumble in confusion. "I was just..."

"Do you know her? Marina?"

"Sorry?"

The woman twitches, and again I see her back, and the back of her head, and her fists pressing down on the window-sill.

"Marina?" I start guessing and growing bolder. "The girl who was always sitting here?"

Something interesting and terrible is about to be revealed to me. I await the answer more eagerly than I had waited to meet the girl's eyes.

"So you did know her?" Again that dry scratchy voice, like sandpaper.

"Yes. I live down the corridor. Why?"

I'm holding the plates with both hands, and hear swelling up from the woman's breast and rushing to break out a long suppressed fit of sobbing.

We are in her room, which is identical in size to my own but has far more comfortable furniture. It's almost like an apartment. You can tell at once that it's occupied by women.

There are lots of pretty knick-knacks, a smell of perfume and lotions, and the walls are seamlessly covered in photographs cut from magazines: pop-stars, actors, models. Everywhere there are fluffy toy animals, and dolls, but these do not create a sense of untidiness. Much of the space is taken up by a bulky, and evidently antique, three-leaved mirror. One of the mirrors is missing and its dark-brown plywood backing is covered in pictures instead.

It's impossible not to look round the room, there are so many nice little things here, made to be admired, but whenever I take my eyes off Olga Borisovna's face, which is distorted with grief, (she is the mother of the girl from the windowsill), and start exploring the walls, the furniture, feeling the teddy bears and toy mice with my eyes, admiring the vases and the lace, I unintentionally stop listening to her. I pull myself together and make an effort to concentrate on the woman's trembling lips.

"We're completely alone here. What were we expecting? Oh, there it was hopeless... Here at least we're not starving."

We are sitting facing each other across the table. On an oilcloth with appealing cream flowers is a bottle of Bulgarian wine, two crystal glasses, and a piece of paper folded in four. Olga Borisovna is propping up her head with her left hand, staring at the oilcloth, and in her right hand is an unlit cigarette.

"They say it's better in Kazakhstan now. Things have quietened down. They've made Tselinograd the capital. Our apartment is probably worth a huge amount of money. But, no... it was so hard there for us, unbearable..."

An icy draught from the partly opened quarter-light runs over the floor and out into the corridor. It's cold enough to make you ill.

"We lived... Marina and I lived there well. Yes, we did. We got on well together. People say a mother and her daughter are invariably rivals, and all sorts of other nonsense, but she and I were always friends. I had her when I was eighteen, still just a young girl myself. I can remember myself, when I was her age... But what am I... I don't know what I'm saying."

Olga Borisovna has beautiful hands, narrow and smooth. Her fingers are long and slender and supple; her nails are cut short, yet seem oval and elongated. It's only the bluish veins that make her hands seem alive, since otherwise they would appear to be moulded from some kind of unusual pink-tinted clay. Her hands are mesmerising. I could admire them endlessly.

"Only, you see, quite recently something between us has broken. After all, how much can you expect her to put up with? Anybody's patience would snap, and she's just at that age. She started staying out half the night, partying somewhere. It was the same with her schooling, there was no way of getting her to do her homework. If I tried talking to her she just grunted, and shrugged. I understand everything, I realise it's my fault. But what could I do? What? The girl didn't even have her own room or anything... and the future didn't bear thinking about. And... in Tselinograd, you know, we lived quite, quite differently. She grew up in completely different circumstances. Do you see? We had a three-room apartment, friends, all nice intelligent people. She went to three interest groups. How she could draw! She stopped all that, just dropped everything. And anyway, how can you study anything seriously here?"

Every sentence is costing Olga Borisovna an immense effort. She's holding back the tears, which make her speak in a jerky, almost official, deliberately unemotional tone. I can't see why she's telling me all this, why she's complaining to me of all people, another hostel inmate from a once well-off family. Or is that why she chose me, because she recognised a companion in misfortune? Most likely it's all completely random. I stopped at that damned kitchen, so I get a dollop of her misery to share.

"My husband died six years ago. He was a senior lieutenant in the military police. They gave him a medal posthumously. He was shot by a deserter he was arresting. There was a feature about it in *Red Star*. They stopped paying his pension almost immediately. Our orchestra was disbanded – I played in the Philharmonic, the violin. And... and how were we to live? My parents had died: I was a late child for them. We never had time when we were young, we were too busy conquering the virgin lands, living in railway trucks. And now look what there is for us. We just have to flee for our lives."

Her sobs have almost overcome her. She emits some ugly, guttural sounds, drinks some wine, pauses briefly, and then continues: "We decided we had no choice. In 1994, in the spring. Those aborigines were flooding in just then from the south like the Mongol invasion. They practically had a war with the Cossacks. People were constantly being beaten up, there were constant arrests, demonstrations demanding secession. Many people just abandoned their apartments and left with two suitcases. Before they left they smashed everything they could: the toilets, the baths, so nothing should be left for those... There was no money, and anyway, you simply couldn't get food. In Karaganda they were reduced to eating dogs. What choice did we have? I ask you."

The soft, warm little elephants and kittens and hippopotamuses of every conceivable colour smile their happy smiles. Their bead eyes radiate unending happiness. They are full of joy and feel completely at home on the sofa, the tables, the pillows. They ask for nothing more.

"We left, we made our minds up. Marina and I went to my husband's parents. They live in Bogotol, not far from Achinsk. Do you know it?"

I nod, holding her oppressive, feverish look for a moment before quickly looking away. I don't need that look. Her eyes will suck out of me everything I've been collecting these last few days, drop by drop and grain by grain. I can feel it in me, and I need it for myself. What can you call it? Strength? Confidence? No, that's not it. It's just a kind of feeling that everything could work out right. A kind of optimism. If I lose it, if I give this feeling away, I'll fall again, I'll be sucked back into the swamp. And this woman is flooding me, flushing it out of me with her words.

"We wrote to them. On paper they said, of course, do come. I rented a container and we managed to sell the apartment for one million three hundred old roubles, just kopeks really. They were gone in an instant. We arrived in Bogotol and lived there for just over two years. Only it wasn't living! We were in complete despair. I hadn't seen them since my husband's funeral and couldn't believe people could become so degraded. The old man got drunk every day and his wife wouldn't let him into the room. He was out in the corridor, urinating right there. There was a constant stench, some filthy rags. So many of our things were stolen, all my rings, my earrings. The old woman sold pies at the station. She baked them at home and ran along the platforms hawking them. She made me do it too: 'You're a clean girl, not some freak. People prefer to buy from someone like you.' What could I say? I went and did it, of course. And I registered as unemployed, and went to the migration office, but they told me straight away: 'Don't get your hopes up, we have around eight thousand people like you, almost half as much again as our normal population.' There was no work... Marina..."

At the mention of her daughter's name Olga Borisovna gives a loud, shuddering sob, but immediately silences herself with another gulp of wine.

"Marina became somehow... turned in on herself. She lay for whole days on the sofa, reading all the time. I used to have to force her to go to school. I began to despair myself. It was a dreadful, dreadful town. The people... it was full of ex-convicts, there was such poverty, no work of any kind. And I started having such dreadful thoughts. I'd be lying there at night, and there was just one thing in my head: Why go on? What future is there? Why should I go on suffering? I was thirty years old, and already on the rubbish tip. Nobody was the least bit interested in me. Marina was the only thing that kept me going. How would she get on without me? But now... where has she gone? Where should I look for her?" Unable to bear it any longer, she finally bursts out sobbing, choking and snivelling. She hides her face in the sleeve of her fluffy jumper.

I venture to take the slip of paper from the table, bring it closer to my eyes, and read, "Mum, I've left. I have money. Forgive me, don't worry. Marina."

"I'm alone... It's all over... I'm completely alone, do you see? Oh, but how could you ... what it is to be left alone?" Again the short, abortive sighing and sobbing which hurts your ears. "Nobody needs me... nobody! They look at me, they look at me like that... for them I'm just... Not a single person has talked to me like a human being. Of course they haven't. Why would they? People told me in Bogotol how wonderful it was in Minusinsk. Such a great place, everything's marvellous, so stable. Just then I heard that the art college here needed someone to teach sight-reading. I came over on my own first and found somewhere to live, then I brought Marina, some of our things. But here, what did I find here? This is what I found!" Olga Borisovna gives a strangulated cry from deep in her throat, hiding her face behind her hand and spreading out her long fingers.

I pour her more wine, and some for myself, and say,

"Perhaps they'll find her. Have you told the police?"

But instead of a polite response I hear a cold, sepulchral voice from behind her hand say, "Go away!"

"What?" I say, surprised. "Why?"

"Go away. Just go away, please. I've told you everything. That's all there is. Lord, she's been away six days already and I'm still alive, sitting here drinking wine!" She throws up her hands and knocks the glass over. A rust-coloured puddle spreads over the oilcloth. "I have to run somewhere, I have to find her!"

"Calm down," I blurt out, saying the first thing that comes into my head. "She'll come back. I tried to run away from home when I was a child too. I faffed around for a couple of days and then went back. I went back and said sorry."

"That's enough! She..." Olga Borisovna jumps up and starts pacing back and forth in the room, clutching her head in her hands. "She'll... no, she won't... she... I know her. She's made her mind up... She won't come back. Don't you understand? She'll never come back!"

I really have landed in a pile of shit. Up till now the day had been going really well. Now I'll have to spend half the night fussing over somebody I don't know or need. I'll have to listen to all kinds of stuff and try to calm her down.

"No, why do you say that. Don't say that," I urge her in a kindly voice. "Everything will turn out right. At her age it's only natural. She needs to find her own way, to understand herself. I know from my own experience..."

"For Christ's sake, just shut up and go away now! That's enough."

Goodness, the way she looks at me, almost with hatred. Is she trying to make me a scapegoat? I bet ten days ago this madam was still proud and self-satisfied and spent ages every morning rubbing cream on her face in front of her mirrors and manicuring her elegant fingers and snarling at her daughter, forcing her out of the room in the evenings so she could cosy up to some clarinet-player from her art college. That's why her daughter went first to the old kitchen and then to the Trade Centre. And now she's gone, mumsy is distracted with grief.

She's right. What the hell am I doing here? Why should I be wasting my time getting my brain clogged with other people's problems? I'm planning to do masses of things tomorrow and am going to need my strength.

"Suit yourself," I sigh. "It's your problem."

I feel, nevertheless, that I really ought to say something kind, a few strong, heartfelt words. She didn't have to drag me in here, after all. She was the first to speak in the kitchen, she was the one who took the initiative, and now she's waiting. I should take a step forward, put my arms round her. I suppose I wouldn't kick her out of bed.

We stand and look each other straight in the eyes. We are nearly the same height so it wouldn't be difficult if it were not for her sole desire for me to leave that I read in her eyes. If the corner of her lips were to tremble, if her gaze were barely perceptibly to change, I'd put my arms round her and press her to me. The words, uniquely appropriate, would immediately come to me. I'm ready to persuade myself and her that our meeting was not by any means random, and that her daughter, sitting on the windowsill, was preparing a time and a place for us to meet.

"Well?" she asks, barely moving her lips. "Are you going to stand there much longer?"

"You mean...?" And I step boldly towards her.

A violent, intrusive banging on the door wakes me. Somebody is battering incessantly, like a maniac. It sounds as though, if I don't open it immediately, they're going to break it down. Even Sanya when he came home pissed as a newt didn't make a racket like this.

I jump up and turn the key to the left. It's just as well I went to bed with my clothes on or I'd feel a right idiot in my underpants. All the more so since it is the police at the door. Before me is an ageing, stocky sergeant, and behind him two men not in uniform who, however, as is immediately evident, are in charge. The rear of the procession entering my room is brought up by a withered old woman I often see on our floor, and a corporal in a grey-blue donkey jacket.

The room immediately seems crowded and unfamiliar. I feel I'm in an unknown place to which I've been brought against my will. Without shoes on my feet I feel small and defenceless.

"This one?" one of the plainclothes asks the old woman. He's wearing a long coat of fake leather with the collar raised.

She nods vigorously and replies nastily:

"That's him, that's him. I know him. He was there, and there was a noise. He's always hanging around in the corridor, drunk, smoking."

"I see. Thank you."

The corporal promptly moves the old woman out into the corridor and stands in the doorway like a sentry. The top dog, in the coat, looks round the room and, without appearing to be talking to me, barks, "Passport!"

Oh shit, here we go again.

"What's up?" I attempt resistance.

"Passport, I said!"

I squeeze my way through to the wardrobe. The corporal tenses, itching to land me one in the solar plexus, so it's best not to annoy him. I take my passport out of my jacket and hand it to the character in the coat.

"Right, then. Place of employment?"

"Scene-shif..." No, it's better to be official: "Stagehand, at the theatre."

"Place of residence?"

"Well, here..."

"Your passport says Zakholmovo Village, Minusinsk District. What are we to make of that?" He focuses a fixed, sheep-like stare at me. "Well then?"

"Well, you see," I mumble. "My parents live there, but I work here."

"Right, right. We'll let it pass. That's not what we're interested in right now. What we're interested in, young fellow, is something else." He shoves my passport into his coat pocket and asks in a clipped manner, "When did you last see Citizen Trushanina?"

"Who?"

"Listen, stagehand, I don't like it when people pretend to be stupider than they are. Get it? I can take you right now down to the police station and there we don't ask questions twice." The thug in the coat is obviously trying to imitate some film hero, and under different circumstances I'd smile appreciatively at his comic artistry, but with his unwelcome attention currently focused on me this doesn't seem a good idea.

I stand surrounded by four large, warmly dressed, all-powerful men and really do not have much of a clue what is going on. One thing, however, is clear: I do need to say something, and quick.

"Have you remembered?" the second plainclothes asks wearily. He's younger than the first one, evidently junior in rank, and less abrasive.

"No point denying it?" the old woman pipes up from behind the back of the corporal. "You were there with her last night, I'm a witness!"

"With Olga Borisovna?"

"Of course."

I turn to the fake leather coat.

"Forgive me, I simply don't know her surname."

"Time?" he continues his questioning.

"Around seven o'clock, more or less."

"Right, fine." He turns to the second cop and says, "Take him there. Let him have a look."

"Right."

They take me along the corridor. Obviously something serious has happened, but the question is, what has it got to do with me? Okay, I did decide to put my arms round her, and she pulled back and started screaming. I blurted, "Forgive me" and left. Then I went to bed. Is that exactly what happened? Well, of course it is. I was sober. The two hundred grams of zero-degrees Bulgarian wine didn't have any effect at all. Yes, I left quietly and went to bed. So? Actually, they've got every right to go for my throat. It's just what I deserve for sticking my nose into other people's crap. Yesterday had been going so well, but I had to go and try to be sociable with another human being. And now, like an idiot, I'm getting my deserts.

My mind fills up with stuff I've heard, read about, seen on television of innocent people being accused of murder, robbery, rape, being beaten to death in police stations and preliminary detention cells for not confessing. Welcome to my new life, what a great birthday present! I have truly been reborn. But anyway, what right do these goons have to take me off somewhere, confiscate my passport, and boss me about? I wonder what to do, where to turn for protection. The clatter of their boots transmutes into the angry shouting in a whodunnit: "I demand to see my lawyer! I have the right to make a phone call!"

Opposite the door to Olga Borisovna's room there is a stretcher and a bundle of black polythene. Two men in a blue rubberised uniform are sitting on their heels smoking. I would very much like to smoke, if only a couple of drags.

The one in the coat goes into the room and orders the others, "Wait here for now."

The old woman, as if someone had stuck a pin in her, starts telling the second policeman, "I saw this man coming out of her room, and that's a fact. I'd gone to bed and then I heard shouting and people stamping about, it was really... Well, I just opened my door a bit..."

"You can tell me all about it in a minute, aunty," the second one stops her. "Save your energy. We'll just find somewhere to sit and you can describe everything to me in detail, and I'll note it down. Perhaps we can go into your room?"

"Well, and why not. It's clean in there. I live on my own. And you can have a cup of tea."

The boss man returns, takes me by the elbow, and suggests in an unpleasantly playful tone, "Right, let's take a look at what you've been up to here."

A room, which so recently was warm and cosy, seems now to have been turned upside down. Order has become chaos, even though everything seems to be more or less in place. But it has all been fingered, inspected, and breathed over by outsiders, of whom there are seven. Doctors, policemen, forensic specialists wearing suits, ties, and gloves. They're muttering to each other but I can't make out what they are saying. They're measuring things. The wine glass and bottle have a brown layer over them. There is a metal suitcase beside them, and a fat young man in glasses is leaning over it.

Olga Borisovna is lying almost in the middle of the room next to a little table. I hadn't even noticed her in all this crowd. She's lying face down and there's a small bloodstain by her head. I've never seen a dead person before not in a coffin, but I'm not frightened. At present I'm more scared of the living.

"I'm finished, Igor Yurievich," the bespectacled young man says cheerfully to the goon in the fake leather coat.

"Take this clown's dabs while you're at it," he says and gives me a shove in the back. I go over to the table.

"No problem." The man readily picks out of his little suitcase a wad of cotton wool and a vial of black liquid. "Hold out your hand. Left one first."

The chief is talking to the doctors but too quietly for me to hear what they're saying. My ears are pounding, as if there's a storm in them.

Having smeared my fingertips with an inky fluid, the young man in glasses presses them hard into the paper while turning them. God Almighty, I'm watching some moronic thriller, even though I'm in it. That doesn't seem possible, but I really do feel none of this has anything to do with me. It's probably a defence mechanism. If you really thought about what's happening it could drive you crazy. Imagine: a woman you were talking to just a few hours ago, looking into her eyes, seeing her lips tremble, admiring her beautiful hands, a woman you were trying to calm, to put your arms around, is lying on the floor. Her skin has an odd whitish, almost grey tinge, and there's a small dark puddle next to her head. I mustn't think about this. I mustn't think! I'm just an observer. Nothing can happen to me. I'll just watch, and listen, and get a bit upset, and then I'll go back to bed.

She is packed into a black sack. The uniformed policemen

turn the body over with obvious distaste and reluctance. The dead woman doesn't care. She no longer has a will, she's prepared to put up with anything. And yet just a short time ago, just a very short time ago she was sobbing her heart out, she was talking, moving, looking at me with hope or with hatred. Why did I leave her? I shouldn't just have left her. Now I'll have to answer for that. And my parents – who's going to tell them? What's going to happen? What a mess. What a mess!

"Right, Senchin, tell us what happened."

I'm sitting on the same chair as I was then, and the second plainclothesman is in Olga Borisovna's place. He has a pile of papers and a folder in front of him. The main one, parodying the commissar in a Soviet film, is pacing up and down the room smoking.

"Tell you what?" I say, trying to collect my thoughts.

"Everything, boy, everything. In your situation it's best to tell us everything."

I give a long sigh and prepare to begin.

"What are you sighing for, you cunt!" the first one barks, materialising instantly in front of me. "Are you trying to play the pansy boy? You'll have plenty of time for that where you're going!"

"Right," the second one interjects. "Why don't you tell us where and at what time you met the murdered woman?"

They say 'the murdered woman' seemingly without implication, but I notice they are both peeling their eyes, watching for my reaction. Trying not to shake, I say in what I believe to be a calm and steady voice, "At about eight in the evening I went to wash the dishes. She was standing in the kitchen. Well, it isn't a kitchen any more now, so..."

"And what happened then?"

"She asked whether I knew her daughter and I said I did."

"Her daughter, incidentally, as you may know, is a minor!" the goon in the coat tosses in.

I look at him. He has a smug grin on his face, as if I've blurted out something incriminating.

"Right, go on," the second one orders, noting something down.

"She..."

"Who?"

"Well, Olga Borisovna... she invited me back to her room. She was complaining that she was completely alone."

At great length, in great detail I repeat the tale she told me about her involuntary emigration and her late husband's parents. The main one carries on pacing up and down while the second sometimes notes things down and sometimes just listens, tapping his pen on the table.

In the end he hands me a sheet of paper: "Check and sign the statement."

I have difficulty deciphering his terrible handwriting but force myself to make sense of it. Not to read it could be a disaster. They may simply have inserted something that would make me seem guilty. I reach the last sentence: "I was awakened in my room number 408 by police officers accompanied by witness E.S Okulova." "What kind of witness is she supposed to be?!" I feel like demanding indignantly.

"Well, have you checked it?"

"Yes. That all seems accurate."

"Now write here: 'I have read the above, which is a true record of my words', and sign."

I do as I'm told.

Both of them go over to the window and talk quietly for ten minutes or so. I make a point of not looking in their direction, busying myself with getting the black dye off my fingers, but I'm eavesdropping more intently than ever before in my life. I catch fragments of sentences:

"... but the door was locked and bolted."

"... the fingerprints will show..."

"... the belongings, the belongings..."

The second one seems to be on my side but the moron in the coat is standing on his head to find some trivial detail to show that I'm a killer. He gets so worked up he blurts out audibly, "Well, that's all very neat: she has a fainting fit or something of the kind, falls down, hits her head in a way that kills her outright. No, someone else had to be involved, I'm telling you!"

The second whispers something in reply while I carry on mechanically rubbing my sweaty, shaking hands. Good-looking singers and models smile down on me from the wall.

"Okey, then, you're free for now," Number One announces slowly and reluctantly. "Sign to say you'll remain at this address and go back to bed."

The second one puts a typed form in front of me and indicates where and what to write.

"Can I go to see my parents?" I ask. "Forty kilometres from here, in Zakholmovo?"

"No!" the first one barks. "Until the case is closed you're to stay here and go to work only. Give the exact addresses! Don't forget that if we can't find you within a three-day period we'll issue a nation-wide search warrant. I hope you know what happens when someone is arrested on one of those."

"It'll only be a week," the second one consoles me. "They'll carry out forensic tests, prove that death was from natural causes, and then you're welcome to travel to Paris if you like."

"Unless they don't..."

16

It's the first working day back at the theatre after the 'flu break. Vadim, Andrei, Igor and I are hanging out in our bolthole. I'm just coming to the end of the tale of how I almost got done for murder.

"I came back to my room, and everything had been gone through. Not obviously, of course. They hadn't turned it upside down, but it was plain they'd been nosing about thoroughly enough. They'd even checked the meat between the window glazing frames. To make matters worse, I forgot to get my passport back from that moron in the coat. I spent a whole day running round the cop shops and just managed to find it."

"Yes, you really landed in it," Vadim sighs. "They could easily have banged you up."

Andrei is gleeful. "Look at us. We're all marked men now. We all have criminal charges hanging over us!"

"What do you mean all of us? Igor is clean, so far."

"Well, he's mixed up in it too, as a victim."

"Mm, yes. Lyalin is certainly making life difficult for us."

"What a freak."

My story did not cause as much of a stir as I'd expected, kicking around these last few days on my own, not knowing who to share it with, expecting that at any moment some special operations unit would burst in and drag me off to the slammer. When I finally had the opportunity to at least partly dissolve my fear in a story about it, sharing it with people who are close to me, they really weren't that bothered. Perhaps it's not surprising. Their problems are no less pressing than mine.

Now they've forgotten about me completely, at least Vadim and Andrei have. They're chatting together about their own worries. "I hear Lyalin is still in hospital," Andrei reports anxiously. "He doesn't want to withdraw his complaint."

Our team leader dismisses this: "They're making it up! He's been slobbing around at home for ages. They're just winding us up to make us sweat. I had a heart-to-heart with Semukhin."

"How did it go?"

"Total shit. 'Everybody's against you.' That's what he said. 'They want you out of here.'"

"The scumbags!" After a moment's reflection, however, Andrei comes up with an unexpected simile: "I suppose you can understand it. They're like wasps. Lay a finger on one of them and immediately the whole swarm retaliates. To look at them from the outside, you'd think they were all at each other's throats."

"And how!" Vadim suddenly turns to Igor. "And you, not a word about leaving. Understand? This all blew up because of you, you little prick. We might've killed him when we were that drunk."

"Without a second thought!" Andrei confirms.

Igor guiltily purses his lips.

"Yes, of course, guys. I'm with you all the way."

It's hot and stuffy in our bolthole. There's no doubt we'd be better off sitting on our favourite sofa in the greenroom, but that's not an option. We're now Public Enemy No. 1 of the acting fraternity. Even the women have hatred in their eyes when they look at us. You can see from Victor Arkadievich's expression that he's coming to a managerial decision about Vadim, Andrei and Lyokha (I hope he's remembering I was not among Lyalin's attackers) and, from the guesswork and rumours in circulation, the decision is not going their way. This might not in fact be entirely bad news. If they get fired, new guys will have to be taken on, and they might decide to make me the team leader. I'd feel better about myself then, and my pay would even go up a bit.

Just after five, as we had finished setting up the scenery, Dima turned up. We didn't recognise him at first. He had changed markedly in less than a month. From a stocky, impudent regular guy he'd become a haggard, stooping, peevish little geezer.

"How are you, guys?" His greeting really is in the form of a question, and he starts proffering us a dark hand covered in scratches. "The woman at security didn't want to let me in."

"That's ridiculous," Vadim responds disapprovingly. "How's life treating you?"

"Yes, well, not that great..."

We descend into the bolthole and Dima produces a bottle of Minus from his pocket.

"Let's celebrate with a tiny hundred grams. I just looked in for half an hour. Oh dear, I'm missing you. Let's drink to all of us, eh?"

Andrei's eyes light up immediately, but Vadim frowns. He doesn't approve of drinking during working hours.

"Between five of us we won't notice it, Vadim," I reassure him. "If it's a problem, we can finish it off after the performance."

"Well, fuck you all, let's have it!"

Igor declines to drink and, choked by the cigarette smoke, leaves the bolthole. In turn, we gulp down our ration from the one and only tumbler. Andrei, the first to imbibe, is transfigured and starts recounting, "Here, Dimentius, so much has happened that my head is ready to explode! In a word, we celebrated Tanya Tarosheva's birthday, good and proper, with plenty to drink, and everything seemed to be fine, and we were just going to get into the bus when our young friend, the one who just went out... he's replaced you, by the way..."

Having let them tell the story of how Lyalin got beaten up and the consequences of their queer-bashing, I try to contribute my mite with the tale of how I was practically framed for murder, but Dima soon interrupts with an envious sigh. "I see you're all living the high life. You haven't clocked the cashier yet then?"

"We called that off," the team leader breaks in and pours more vodka into the tumbler. "We're in enough shit as it is without that. Later, perhaps..."

"It's not so bad. At least you taught that shirt-lifter a lesson. As for me, well..." Dima again sighs bitterly. "Nothing to boast about. It was a bad mistake leaving here."

"What?" I say. "Isn't it a laugh a minute at the cemetery with the stiffs?"

"It's not the stiffs that are the problem."

"Go on, tell us!"

Dima gulps the vodka, breathes into the sleeve of his tatty shorty coat, waits for the others to finish drinking and then, punctuating the flow of words with sighs and scratching of his head, paints a picture for us of his new life. "There are four men in our team and the foreman, Leonid Georgich. We work every day. We can take one or two days off but, oh dear, officially it's counted as sick leave and you don't get any money for that. As a rule we get three graves a day ordered. They tell me it's easier in the summer, but right now, hell... for the first half metre the soil is frozen as hard as bone. You can burn tyres to thaw it, but where are we to get enough of them? We scour the highways looking for them. On top of that, those old geezers from the veterans' home are breaking our backs. They're falling off the perch one after the other. We bury them in rows, put the coffins side by side, in a kind of trench. We don't get a rouble for burying them, and even from ordinary funerals you only get a bottle of vodka between the five of us and a towel each. I've got so many of these towels now I could set up a stall. One time we did bury a rich guy. We each got a hundred, they gave us five bottles of Stolichnaya and some sliced sausage to go with it... But God knows, we really slave at it. You can see, my hands are all blisters from the adze."

Dima shows us his mangled maulers and hides them away, squeezing them between his knees. "As for getting paid, I haven't seen a rouble yet. If at least they'd give us vouchers to exchange for goods. I ring here every day: they're supposed to settle up for my final pay packet. Today they finally did give me part of it."

"What? They paid you?" Vadim jumps up, so interested that he drops his fag.

"Six hundred and forty roubles. They still owe me almost a thousand. I'd like to buy some fur boots. I work all day out in the bitter cold."

Our team leader, no longer listening and without a word of explanation, vanishes through the door.

"Where has he gone?" Andrei asks in bafflement.

I have an inkling but hesitate to get my hopes up, let alone suggest out loud that Vadim ran to find out about our pay. I grab the Minus and suggest, "Down the hatch?"

We finish off the bottle, leaving some in the tumbler for Vadim. We hide the empty bottle under the sofa.

"One time they told me to nail down the lid of a coffin," Dima is continuing. "I got a nail, took up the hammer and – just couldn't bring myself to do it. My hand wouldn't obey me. The girl in the coffin was so beautiful, I was staring at her the whole time they were taking their farewells."

I hear him without the least interest. My heart is in my mouth as I await the return of our team leader.

The cashier is understandably cross: "Why do you all have to turn up just two minutes before closing time..."

Igor already has his stash and is smiling happily. We shake him, "How much?" "I got three hundred, but I think you get more."

Vadim, signing the ledger, breaks out in an unrestrained guffaw. A wad of banknotes is lowered into his outstretched hand, with small change on top.

"Well? Well?" Andrei hassles him "Three hundred? Five hundred?"

Vadim clutches the money in his fist and moves aside. Andrei sticks his head in the cashier's window.

"Take your head out!" comes her irritated voice.

He jerks backwards, hits his head on the plywood, and further alienates the all-powerful dispenser of money. She almost shrieks, "Now look at you! You're breaking everything! Look at you!"

"Sorry," our burly giant replies, avidly taking in all that is going on in the little room stuffed with cash, and quite certainly thinking what a good idea it would be to smash his way in there.

Vadim meanwhile has checked his wages, and exclaims in satisfaction, "Five hundred and eighty-five, fallen from the skies!"

"What do you mean fallen from the skies," I say. "We sweated good and hard for that."

Andrei gets his pay and promptly starts checking it.

"You can do that to one side," I say and try to push him out of the way. "You're blocking the window."

The dumb giant doesn't react, merely tensing his muscles and turning into a rock. Only his fingers move as they rifle through the bank notes, and his lips whisper, "twenty, thirty, forty..."

"Senchin!" I shout over his shoulder to the cashier. "Senchin, also a stagehand!"

Getting paid is not merely cause for celebration, it is a major event which immediately gives meaning to your life and work, and enables you to see a kind of light in the distance. You get paid so infrequently, so rarely do you hold such a quantity of money in your hand, that you feel quite at sea.

Money changes us instantly. We become tense and uncommunicative. We now have something to lose, and we are very keen not to lose it.

We tuck our pay away in our pockets, richer by over five hundred roubles, and sit in that stuffy, claustrophobic little bolthole looking like chilled sparrows, saying nothing. I can sense that we'd all like to drink, to eat something nice, but it's so difficult to pull those beloved wages out in the presence of others, to throw two or three tens into the kitty and say: "Let's get hammered!" When those two or three tens are all the money you have in the world, it's somehow much easier.

"Mm, yes," Dima grunts and fidgets on his chair, wanting to say something, unable to bring himself to say it, but hoping to encourage us (and it's clear enough what he wants us to do) by his grunting.

He gets no support, and a few minutes later stands up. "I'll be off, then. I need a good night's sleep. We've got two graves to dig tomorrow."

Vadim overcomes his fear of thinning his thick wallet and manages to suggest, "What, perhaps we should get jolted? Celebrate the occasion?" His suggestion falls on deaf ears. Andrei mutters something about a new sweater, while Dima hastily says goodbye and leaves.

I'm afraid of getting drunk. I picture an entirely plausible course the evening might take. I knock back a bottle and a half (when you really have cause for rejoicing you can knock back that amount almost without noticing). In a state of exaltation I march home at two in the morning, bawling a song, importuning any girls I see, and spend the rest of the night in the sobering-up station. In the morning all I have is a hangover, a fine to pay, and bitter memories of my pay which has vanished into the waters of the Lethe. It's better to play it cool.

"Oh well, if it's no, then it's no." Vadim accepts our refusal with covert satisfaction. "There'll be time enough. The Lord has many days." In order to move on from thoughts of drink he starts cursing and swearing. "For Christ's sake, we nearly missed out on our money. Not one of those turds so much as raised an eyebrow to let us know we were being paid. But we'll get them, the shits!"

I'm travelling from the theatre, not in Uncle Gena's rattly old bus but in a sleek, luxurious, fast foreign saloon car. Japanese, I think, because it's got the steering wheel on the wrong side. Just for kicks, I flagged one and it stopped. I offered the driver twenty and am now enjoying the thrill.

I sprawl in the front seat, smoking a Bond, looking ahead. The black asphalt, the black sky, and to either side the poverty-stricken, snow-covered log cabins and crooked fences. The so-called private sector. The foreign car bears me to the new part of town, to the place where I can find that long-awaited joy.

The cars coming towards us flash by, dazzling me and the driver with the brilliance of their headlamps. It's a scary but agreeable sensation, feeling those seconds of danger and vulnerability when, half a metre away from you, a metal cage whistles by, and you see only white emptiness. It's past. The cage is already behind you, retreating further and further into the distance, and you feel an unforgettable sense of relief and are ready to shout and jump for joy. No, shouting and jumping are not the done thing. I'll just take a good, hard drag on my expensive cigarette.

Already another car is in front of us, the white dots of its headlamps coming closer, becoming clearer, and again those few seconds of anticipation followed by emptiness.

The cassette player is on, and from its loudspeakers comes a purring, thin little voice, flirtatious and breathless:

> *Her boyfriend is far away*
> *somewhere in the sun,*
> *supping the juice of other girls,*
> *singing them songs.*
> *Not very nice, perhaps,*
> *But probably rather fun.*

"Who's that?" I ask.

The driver is happy to explain. "There's a new group called Mummy Troll. I bought their cassette and now I can't stop playing it."

"They've certainly got something," I say, nodding and listening to the tinny voice coming from the player. The driver goes on, by now just annoying me by stopping me from listening to the song, "They say drug addicts find some kind of universal meaning, but I like it just as it is. It's a bit like some of that extra-terrestrial stuff. In a minute there's a song about dolphins. It's a really good one!"

The Trade Centre is full of life, as usual. It really is the heart of the city, pulsating with people, music, lights, cars driving up and driving off. Perhaps it's only my imagination, but with every day the Trade Centre seems to grow stronger, and to draw the city to itself more firmly. This enormous heart beats ever more powerfully. Even last summer it seemed less frenetic and less in-your-face than now, on a frosty evening in late November. They are practically queuing at the kiosks, and the cafйs and mini-markets are packed with customers. There're even traders at many of the market stalls, which used to be almost deserted after six or seven in the evening.

Perhaps today is a holiday? But no, it's a perfectly ordinary Thursday. Perhaps every day and night is like this now and I've simply been trying not to notice in order not to whet my appetite. Tonight, however, I am as good as any of them.

I drive up to the Baltika bar in the white foreign saloon and the driver brakes. Handing over the money, I tell him I'll be sure to get the Mummy Troll cassette; the driver gives me a companionable smile and nods.

Thanks to those five hundred and fifty roubles, the events of the past week have drifted far, far away. They've faded and been all but forgotten. Olga Borisovna and her daughter, my undertaking not to leave, the problems faced by my parents and the theatre, and all the others... To hell with the lot of them! How much shit can you be expected to take?

I stroll into the bar in a lordly manner. I try to look indolent and well-fed, but my lips form themselves into a smile. It's a long time since that last happened. The most I usually manage is a smirk or a snigger.

Thin, bluish lighting, a dozen small tables, guys and girls at them. The smoke from aromatic cigarettes makes my head swim. When you first come in from outside it feels airless, but that soon passes. There's a large television over the bar counter with a video of a song in a foreign language: an extremely cool convertible is cruising along the highway. At the wheel is an attractive, far-out blonde in a T-shirt and fashionably torn shorts. She doesn't give a damn about anything. She's burning along down the wrong side of the road and singing. Cars swerve to avoid hitting her, fly into the ditch, overturn, but the blonde doesn't twitch an eyebrow. She closes her eyes and puts her feet on the steering wheel. I'd love to know what she's singing. The words must be very meaningful. The accelerator is jammed down to the floor by a rock. It's clear the girl is not going to stop, that this is her last ride, and that she's one hundred percent wild.

Still watching the video, I go over to the bar and toss down a fifty.

"A bottle of Baltika No. 9."

"In a glass?" the barman enquires courteously.

"That would be good."

The beer is poured out of the bottle into a tall, delicate glass bearing the "Baltika" logo. There are logos everywhere. Baltika owns the bar.

Sipping the potent beer, waiting as the barman counts out the change, I add, as if it were an afterthought, "Oh yes, and a packet of bacon-flavoured crisps."

"Lace? Estrella? Russian Gold?"

"Estrella is fine."

To tell the truth, I've dreamed of being in a bar like this for the past thousand years. Just like this. The music sounds perfect. It's awkward looking up to see the screen, so instead of watching the videos I look over the bottles on the glass shelves in front of me.

There are dozens of different wines, vodkas, whiskies, beers, and liqueurs. Tequila, gin and tonic, Fanta, Mirinda, Cola... Until now I've hardly had a chance to try anything from this fabulous range. So many things have been invented and I, like a relic from the Stone Age, drink cheap vodka, smoke Prima, and listen to pathetic songs from my broken down cassette recorder. It has all passed me by, and it's nobody's fault but my own.

I light up. I put the pack in front of me on a counter made of plastic but looking like marble. Today I'm smoking Bond, so don't need to feel embarrassed. The barman immediately puts a clean ashtray down next to my cigarettes, but I'm in no hurry to knock the ash off. I observe it hanging on the end of the cigarette like a fragile, grey wand. They say that if you can smoke a cigarette down to the filter without dropping the ash or saying a single word, any wish you make will come true.

I've divided my pay in two, stashing three hundred and fifty roubles away in my inside jacket pocket next to my passport, and putting the rest in my jeans pocket for tonight's celebration. I'm not going to have too much to drink – only beer, and maybe some low-alcohol wine. Real wine. I've read so many books and watched so many films where people savour their Bordeaux, or their Chardonnay, roll their eyes and moan in ecstasy. All I know is the sweet burning of "No. 33" or "No. 777" so-called port wine, and the acid taste of Sauvignon and Monastery Hut. These tipples don't tempt you to savour the taste. You just want to gulp a couple of bottles down and wait for the result.

Looking like a man out on the town, I saunter along the row of kiosks checking out the goods and the people and remembering to hold myself erect and be debonair. I've pushed back my black rabbit fur hat and taken a look at myself in the window of a closed shop. I reckon I look pretty cool. The jacket sits perfectly, the shoulders are broad, and my hips are narrow; the jeans are just what is currently fashionable. Everything is entirely fine and there's no reason to get in a sweat. Even the weather is doing its bit: it's warm, but not warm enough to make the snow melt. It's just the right temperature for winter, like in the mountains, warm but with the snow crunching underfoot.

The people around me are mainly young, and there are a lot of girls who are very easy on the eye. Many are not with men. Yes, for some reason there aren't many men. Here's one girl strolling up and down the pavement. She's about my height and wearing a short white jacket. Beneath the jacket I can see the narrow band of a leather skirt and her legs sheathed in warm woollen tights. Her dark hair is fanned out over the white jacket. There's something Asiatic about her face. She's either a Khakass or a half-caste. Most likely she's waiting for her boyfriend. They've got a date. Any minute now her guy will run up, put his arms round her, and off they'll go to the Surf nightclub or the Young Ones disco.

I stop about ten paces away from her, light a cigarette, and pretend that I too am waiting, for my girlfriend. I discreetly run my eye over the girl in the white jacket and decide she is just my type: strong, supple, and just a bit predatory. That little slapper from the windowsill doesn't bear comparison. This girl is already the only one in the entire world that I want, and I'm ready this time to love.

Her boyfriend still hasn't shown up, and none of these dozens of people walking along briskly or lazily sauntering by seem even to notice her. As if she's not there, so seductive, so provocatively dressed. It's amazing. Or was this meant to be? Destiny itself is giving me another chance to seize my share of happiness. Fate is turning other men's eyes away from this exceptionally beautiful girl in order to give her to me.

Mm, so why am I still standing here? Again. Like a complete cretin.

"Hello!" I give her a big smile, at the same time trying not to show my bad teeth too much.

"Hello." Her reply is slightly suspicious and reserved.

"Great atmosphere this evening, just like a holiday. Don't you think?" I do my best to strike up a conversation. "I couldn't just hang out at home. Are you waiting for somebody?"

"Not really..."

"Perhaps we could go to a bar. We could sit and have a beer together." I again give a friendly smile. "Would you like that?"

"I don't drink beer. I don't like bitter stuff."

"What do you like? This evening, and for such a sweet girl, I'll run to anything!"

I'm probably saying all the wrong things in quite the wrong way, but my awkwardness is redeemed by my sincerity. I'm sure my eyes are glowing with love. No one could resist such a gaze. Yes, it's impossible to refuse me. The few seconds during which I await her reply seem like an eternity. I gaze into her eyes. They have a slight slant which makes them seem to be laughing at my clumsiness. I sense the warm smoothness of her fresh young cheeks, the tenderness of her full lips. One more moment and I won't be able to contain myself. I'll just go right ahead and put my arms round her, and nobody will ever tear her away from me.

"Well," she finally says in a flirtatious and pensive way, "I do like gin and tonic, or Isabella wine..."

I take her arm and say: "That's fine, that's splendid."

The spacious warm saloon of a Moskvich-41. The car is speeding along deserted, sleeping Michurin Street. The balding, elderly driver is in a hurry to drop us off at the address he's been given. I'd be only too happy if he were to lose his way and take ages to get us there.

The girl and I are in the back seat, with a plastic bag on my knee containing a bottle of good vodka, three cans of gin and tonic, a smoked chicken, some apples, and some olives.

"Is it much further?" Zhanna asks. At last an unusual name. I'm tired of meeting nothing but Lenas, Marinas, and Olgas.

"Not at all," the driver says. "You could walk it in ten minutes from here, but it's less direct if you're driving."

The last thing I need is to walk it. I need speed, warmth, the semi-darkness of the saloon. Every moment in here is bringing me closer to the girl. I sense I have permission to touch her. I run my fingers over her leg. Beneath the thick woollen tights I feel her knee, slide my hand higher, spread my fingers and hold the softness of her thigh. She moves my hand away, but not hastily, not roughly, just as if to say, "Wait. It's not time for that yet. When we arrive, then..." Her fingers brush my hand and she gives a little squeeze as if to say, "Soon, soon".

We sat in the Baltika bar for almost half an hour, hardly speaking. We looked at each other and listened to the music; Zhanna was drinking gin and tonic and I was drinking beer. Then I suggested I might buy something nice to eat and we could go back to my place. She agreed amazingly easily, and now we're on our way. I try not to think about her reaction when the Moskvich stops in front of the furniture factory hostel. I have a fair idea, but try not to picture it. That's why I want to put off the fateful moment, to drive for a long, long time, to touch this girl, to breathe the same air as her, to feel her next to me, and know she's willing to come back with me.

I take her hand, our fingers obediently clasp. I quietly murmur the song I heard in the other car:

> *Release beneath my skin*
> *A school of dolphins,*
> *Swim together with them*
> *Far away forever.*

"Do us a favour!" Zhanna interrupts with unexpected vehemence. "Those aren't the right words."

"Sorry. I haven't learnt them yet. It's a new album."

"Have you got it?"

"Alas..."

"Pity."

That short word almost ends my hopes of a pleasant night. Everything is about to graunch to a halt.

"In here, if I'm not mistaken." The driver turns off Michurin Street into the black abyss of the courtyards, and then his headlamps light up a U-shaped five-storey apartment block, with the usual group of people hanging around outside on the porch. I fumble in my pocket for the fare.

The car does a semi-circle round the courtyard and stops

five metres or so from the entrance. I hand the money to the driver, open the door, rustling the plastic bag, and get out. I hold out my hand to the girl, but she stays put.

"We've arrived, Zhanna." I bend over and look into the car. I meet her startled gaze, which looks about to turn nasty.

"Is this a hostel?"

"Er, yes..." I suddenly feel weary, sleepy, and fed up. The bag of food is heavy in my hand. I just want to get back to my room as quickly as possible and go to bed, but something tells me I shouldn't give up that easily. I try to entice her out of the car.

"Zhanna, please... we need to talk. I have a good room, a cassette recorder..."

The driver fixes his eyes on the windscreen and waits patiently.

"Zhanna," I call piteously, but by now without hope.

"Goodbye," she says in a flat, offended voice. The slamming of the car door serves as an emphatic full stop.

The car moves unwillingly off and drives away. I watch it go, the red tail lights above the rear bumper getting smaller and fainter. The wheels scrunch in a slurry of snow and gravel and I see a wall. The car has disappeared behind it. Zhanna is no more. I'm alone again.

I wander towards the hostel, to the porch with all the Vietnamese, or Chinese, and the girls. A bottle of port wine is being passed round. I squeeze between them, trying not to look at anybody or bump into them.

"You've started living it up, Rom!" I hear a familiar voice. "Driving around in taxis."

It's Lena. A stocky, slitty-eyed little man with an enormous dog-fur hat on his head has his arm round her waist.

"Yup," I reply. "I'm in the money for the next couple of days."

Lena's escort gives me a mean look, as if warning off a rival, and I make myself scarce in the entrance.

Music is coming from my room. Underworld songs. The door is partly open, and I push it and go in.

"You've finally turned up, you bastard!" Lyokha is sitting at the table. He's had a haircut and shaved. He's looking younger and grinning from ear to ear. "Crawl back in, you sad moron! What gutter you've been lying in?"

Something breaks inside me and I feel empty. I can think of nothing to say. I carefully put the plastic bag on the bed. There's a litre bottle of Ferain on the table, a tin of Chinese stewed beef, and a loaf broken into lumps.

"Come on, sit down. Let's get pissed!" Lyokha says, sticking a filter cigarette in his gob.

I sit down and watch him pouring vodka into two glasses, almost to the top.

"Where did you get all this from?"

He gestures hospitably. "Drink up and be damned!" He crashes his glass against mine and proclaims his toast: "Cheers!"

"But, for heaven's sake..."

"Aren't you pleased?" Lyokha's half-drunken pleasure threatens to change to offence.

"Of course I am," I hasten to reassure him. "Of course I am." I take two large gulps of vodka and choke on it.

"Have something to eat, you moron, quick! Look, there's tinned stew, bread."

In order to counter his expansiveness, I produce my own riches out of the plastic bag. I throw a pack of Bond on the table, but Lyokha blossoms even more.

"Not bad! The feast of a lifetime! Perhaps we should invite Lena?"

"You go," I snigger. "She's out on the porch with the slitty-eyed fraternity."

"Oh, the bitch. She's found her level."

We drink some more and, not stinting ourselves, snack on the chicken. Lyokha starts telling me what he's been up to.

"I had a good trip and, most importantly, gained a vital insight. Yes. You have to keep your head above water, Rom, you know? Now we'll start living. I've got a little money. I said a fond farewell to my parents. They could see for themselves there was nothing I could do there. They'd be glad to get out themselves, only where could they go now?" Lyokha picks up the bottle and the vodka again gurgles into the glasses. "I met such a sweetie on the train! And from Minusinsk! She gave me her address. I'll go and see her tomorrow, take her out somewhere. How much does entry to Surf cost, do you know?"

"Fifty, I think." I shrug.

"That's a bit pricey. Never mind, we'll see. Cheers!"

We drink.

"We mustn't, Rom, let them grind us down, that's what I realised. In times like these that's the height of idiocy! Pavlik is a cretin, but he understood that. You haven't expropriated the chief cashier yet? Good. That's a dumb approach. We need to think big. The things people are doing all around us, Rom, the money they're making! While we're on our knees. No, I've woken up, I've seen what we have to do. I've finally understood! I'll get to the top just to spite the lot of them! Rom, we're going to hit the big time!" He fills up the glasses again.

I feel like asking, "Where are you in such a hurry to get to?" But instead take the glass and obediently raise it to my lips. I just want to pig out and crash out and knock today on the head.

"Over there everybody's coining it in non-ferrous metals. That's the way to go. Wire, spare parts, all sorts of handles they take to collection points. Children, the homeless, grafters. Nobody seems to have picked up on that here yet. I've had a word with some people, they're prepared to come in on it and help us open collection points. We'll really pull in the readies, you know, like managers of a branch of that business. How about it, want to join in?"

"We could try," I mumble, giving in to a vodka-induced heaviness suddenly overcoming me.

"Well, put it there, Rom. We'll make so much money nobody will believe it! Think how much bronze and copper there is in Victory Park. You just have to be a bit clever. Tomorrow I'll go and collect my things from the wife. She's got my coat, my trousers, my shirts. I couldn't be arsed before. I looked like a pathetic deadbeat. No, you have to use your brains! What's new at the theatre? Lyalin still alive, is he, the sicko? He got off lightly. But what about you?" Lyokha narrows his eyes and looks me over appraisingly. "Nattily dressed, all cleaned up, with your gin and tonics. A real gentleman, you've become. You haven't got your leg over that floozy of yours from the windowsill yet? Oh you sad git! You mustn't let them grind you down. In times like these you can't afford to let them grind you down!"

■ ■ ■ ■ ■ ■ ■ ■